LEGACY OF FLAME AND ASH

A HANNAH'S HEIRLOOM STORY

ROSIE CHAPEL

Legacy of Flame and Ash
A Hannah's Heirloom Story

Rosie Chapel

First printing: 2021
ISBN: 978-0-6451985-0-8 (ebook)
ISBN: 978-0-6451985-1-5 (paperback)

Ulfire Pty. Ltd.
P.O. Box 1481
South Perth
WA 6951
Australia

www.rosiechapel.com

Cover Design: Rosie Chapel
Images Courtesy: Deposit Photos (Artists: AlexsDriver, FairytaleDesign, PAPASTUDIO, YAYImages).
Designed in Canva.

❀ Created with Vellum

This book is for Jackie, who has badgered me to write Marcus' story since she read The Pomegranate Tree.

You could say our friendship, which stemmed from a shared passion for Ancient Rome, was also born of flame and ash...

ACKNOWLEDGMENTS

To Janet, Melanie, and Jackie — heartfelt thanks for your generous and, no doubt, long-suffering support, especially during the final editing and proofreading process of this novel. Your help has been invaluable, and I am endlessly grateful.

To Kirsten — thank you for your beautiful artwork in designing the ring used as a major scene separator in the book. I am in awe of your talent.

To Graham from Fading Street Publishing Services — thank you for editing this manuscript. I am truly appreciative.

To my husband – thank you for believing in me.

AUTHOR'S NOTE

Italian Terms

There are a few Italian expletives used in this novel, the meanings of which I believe can be inferred by context - however, just in case...

Testa di cazzo - D$ckhead
Segaiolo - Wanker
Cazzo - F*ck
Merda - Sh$t
Porca miseria - Dammit
Figlio di puttana! - Son of a b$tch
Li mortacci tua - Your dishonoured dead ancestors (this is very rarely used, but I felt it suited the context)

The Underworld

Taratarus - where the damned are tormented for eternity.
Aecus, Rhadamanthys, and Minos - In Greek mythology, the three judges of the dead.

English-ism

Lay-by - I know this can cause confusion. In this book, a lay-by is a pull-in just off the road, usually wide enough to park at least three or four vehicles. Typically, areas of cleared ground which have been adopted as temporary parking spots.

PROLOGUE

HERCULANEUM - AD 79

The earth trembled under his feet. Involuntarily, Titus Salvius Aelianus glanced up at the sombre sky. The constant rumble of thunder was almost unnerving. Summer storms were not uncommon, but this one felt different.

If prone to fancy, he might postulate the gods were having a heated argument. One which was about to burst out of the heavens and into the human realm.

A practical man, Salvius pushed aside such nonsense and concentrated on the discussion. The four around the table had been negotiating a trade deal for the better part of two days and Salvius was bored. It should not be this complicated. *Did they want his wool or not?*

Out of habit, he twisted the chunky, onyx seal-stone ring on the third finger of his right hand. An instinctive gesture, which never failed to have a calming effect.

"Come, my friends, the sun is above us, surely we can put this to rest and enjoy a meal together in the knowledge we have settled the deal," he suggested, jerking his head towards the thermopolium along the bustling street. The aroma of hot soup and warm bread wafted on the breeze, making more than one stomach growl.

"I concur..." Anneius Corvinus, a merchant from Ostia, broke off what he was about to say, changing it to, "...my but that soup smells delicious. We can conclude after we have eaten."

"Are we not already in agreement?" Salvius rejoined. He looked each of the other three in the eye.

"I do believe we are," Tuccius Dorsuo observed. He reached out to pluck a hunk of wool from the small bale on the table, rubbing it between his fingers, feeling the texture and the oils.

"Salvius has not raised his prices for two years and I believe the quality is improving with each consignment. If we are not careful, he will realise he has made an error and double his percentage," he ribbed, waggling his bushy brows.

The fourth member of their group, Gabinus Musca dipped his head in quiet approval. Somewhat taciturn, Gabinus was the steadying influence on his friends when they went out gambling or drinking. An astute businessman, it was a rare day indeed when someone out-thought him.

"Then we are done. Time to rel—" Tuccius was interrupted when the rumbling intensified, and, as one, all four swivelled to face the mountain.

While they were standing, mouths hanging open in shock, an enormous cloud of dense black smoke billowed from the lofty peak. Incredibly, it climbed higher and higher, the sky darkened and the ground beneath them undulated. The noise was deafening. All around them, people began running every which way, screaming about the wrath of the gods.

"I think perhaps lunch can wait," Anneius shouted over the clamour. He flashed a grin, and his three friends reciprocated good-humouredly. Anneius was always one for the understatement.

"What in Hades *is* that?" Tuccius quizzed. "Do you suppose it is a threat to the city?"

The others shrugged.

"No idea. It *is* a peculiar sort of tempest." Gabinus studied the sky. Lightning was visible, white streaks throughout the clouds, and the roar continued unabated. "I have witnessed some terrible storms. This one beats them all. I *do* recall mention of mountains which explode and rain fire."

He turned to face the others. "What do you think? Ought we to take cover, or maybe even evacuate?"

"The mountain is miles away. What harm could come to us here?" Salvius remarked. "It is just a bad storm. If it rains, I daresay we are safer in town than on the road. Landslides are common in inclement weather."

He waved a hand towards the chaotic crowd milling about like headless chickens. "These people seem incapable of behaving rationally. Wrath of the gods... more likely a result of over-imbibing yesterday." Referring to the festival of Vulcan held the previous day, although, when he thought about it, it was quite apt. A celebration to honour the god of fire and forges, culminating in an erupting mountain.

A notion he deemed worthy of mention to his friends, adding to their amusement. "Exploding mountains? Undoubtedly a fable, although there are merchants who tell of strong winds which, in certain conditions, whip high into the sky in a wild frenzy, and the weather has been unnatural of late. It is probably our vantage point which gave us the illusion the top of the mountain blew off."

Salvius' explanation sounded feasible and, while they watched, the wind did indeed appear to be blowing the immense cloud in the opposite direction. Visibly, all four men relaxed and strolled along the street to the thermopolium.

The crowd began to disperse, and peace was restored. Placing their order, the friends settled down to a meal of hot soup accompanied by a plate of fresh flat bread drizzled with olive oil, and a goblet of mulsum — the popular honeyed wine.

With the assistance of several more goblets of mulsum along with generous servings of candied fruit and *spira* — the sweet pastries seldom seen in a street eating house and therefore a treat — lunch stretched out for a goodly portion of the afternoon.

The storm did not subside, neither did the heavy clouds diminish. The sky over Herculaneum remained gloomy. When Tuccius, Gabinus and Anneius took their leave as the day began to wane, a light covering of ash had fallen over the town and there was a foul odour on the air. The mood among the friends had gone from cheerful to solemn.

"Do not tarry, Salvius," Tuccius implored. "You have many days travel ahead and if the wind changes, the roads can become impassable. Moreover, if this ash is anything to go by, the storm has ignited a fire in the forest. The wood will be tinder dry after the hot summer we have suffered. Fire or flood will not be easy to bypass."

"I will leave at first light," Salvius pledged. "To depart at night is too hazardous."

Anneius frowned and nodded towards the mountain. "Looking at that, I would take the risk. Tuccius is correct. You could be stuck."

"Thank you for your concern, my friends. If it will allay your anxiety, I shall do as you ask. First, I need a snooze. Good food and better conversation has left me drowsy."

The others guffawed, knowing Salvius' penchant for a post-prandial nap.

Goodbyes were said and promises to meet again soon, made. The friends wended their slightly unsteady way to their respective homes — Anneius was staying with Tuccius who happened to be his brother-in-law — or, in Salvius' case, a room above one of the shops.

It would be the last time they saw each other.

Salvius awoke with a start. Momentarily disorientated, he squinted into the blackness, trying to remember where he was. Then it flooded back... Herculaneum. He sprang out of bed and pushed open the shutters. Overhead, the sky was inky; the moon was obscured, and the sprinkling of stars seemed veiled.

His eyes were drawn to Vesuvius. A strange glow hung over the peak. It must be the fire Tuccius had mentioned earlier, now burning out of control. He glanced down to see the amount of ash blanketing the town had increased considerably. The tales about rivers of fire pouring down mountains and engulfing everything in their path, pestered the edges of his mind.

Salvius closed his eyes, silently admonishing himself for sleeping the evening away. He pondered his options. Did he wait until first light or leave immediately? Another glance at the mountain, and his inner voice compelled him to depart with all haste.

Grabbing the tablet from the table, he scratched a quick message to the landlord, then tossed the last of his belongings into his leather satchel and hurried down the stairs. He was surprised when he all but ran into said landlord, propped against the door jamb, sipping what smelt like calda from a battered goblet, and apparently lost in thought.

"Caeso, my good man. You cannot sleep?" Salvius greeted his host, a man who kept his three rooms for hire spotlessly clean. A luxury few of those offering accommodation could boast.

Caeso turned with a ready smile. "Ah, Salvius." He spotted the satchel, and his tone became one of astonishment. "You are leaving? Why? You still have two days paid. Are my lodgings so lacking in comfort you feel it necessary to vanish in the middle of the night, without a goodbye?"

Salvius grinned. "You know you offer the best rooms in town. No, I think it prudent to set off now. I do not want to be delayed by that fire and this atrocious weather. I presumed you would be asleep and did not wish to disturb you. I left a message." He tipped his head towards the room he had vacated."

"If you seriously want to leave, I think you might be wise to head to the port and try to buy passage on one of the boats instead of taking the road. I have seen an assortment out on the water." Caeso nodded towards the docks.

"There's been a steady stream of people going that way for the past hour or so. All babbling about evacuating the town because of whatever is happening up on that mountain and the possibility of a bad earthquake."

He shook his head, and patted Salvius on the arm. "Take care, my friend, take care. There is a madness afoot. Volcanalia has unhinged them this year." He rolled his eyes, smiled again, and went inside, the door swinging shut behind him.

Salvius mulled over Caeso's advice. Absently twisting the ring on his finger, Salvius concluded to travel by sea might be the sensible option. To get to Ostia would be mere hours by boat, instead of days by road. Decision made, Salvius hoisted his satchel over his shoulder and trudged down the hill towards the docks.

He was amazed at how many people waited on the shoreline. Three men, who Salvius assumed to be in charge, were collecting coin and directing people to various boats lined up along the quay.

He stood in the queue and gazed out over the bay. It was surreal. At any other time, the flaming orange-red of the wildfire on the high slopes of the mountain reflected in the water would be a spectacle to admire. Tonight, all it caused was a gnawing terror to nudge at his senses.

This was more than a summer storm.

By the time Salvius was called forward, an hour later, the moon had deigned to make an appearance. Its ethereal luminescence, in stark contrast with the fire belching from Vesuvius, heightened the eerie atmosphere. Salvius recollected his earlier thoughts. *Was this a battle between the Gods after all?*

He stared at the malevolence spewing from the peak. Thick black smoke, clearly visible despite it being close to midnight, sporadically eclipsed the moon, like the fingers of a sinister foe intent on dragging the pale orb into the conflagration. What, in the light of day, he could ascribe to a vivid imagination, no longer felt like fantasy.

Innocence against evil
Profane versus sacred.
Vulcan conquering Luna.

. . .

Salvius shook his head to dispel the inanity.

A boat, he could see it bobbing on the tide, would be docking shortly. He could board as soon as the captain gave the nod. Relieved, Salvius perched on a convenient mooring post and watched the boat glide towards the wooden jetty.

At almost the same moment as one of the crew looped the rope around the stanchion, there came an horrendous boom. Everyone on the quayside turned to look behind.

Following on its heels, a whooshing sound, and a hot wind billowed along the streets buffeting around the houses, rocking the boats out on the water. The vast black plume which had been hovering over Vesuvius all day appeared to be collapsing.

Salvius blinked, certain his eyes deceived him. "Run," he bellowed and shoved the group standing in front of him towards the sheds. Precious seconds were wasted when panic took hold, but Salvius was a big man and his bulk acted like a moveable wall. He ushered those nearest him into the closest boatshed.

"Quickly," he exhorted. "Get as far to the back as you can, there are many who will need cover."

He was correct, they weren't the only ones. Dozens of people flooded into the vaulted buildings, their terrified mutterings buzzed under the perpetual roar from the mountain reverberating around the bay.

"Will we be safe here?" a young woman with a small child, piped up.

"I do not know." Leaning against the cool stone of the arch, Salvius was not prepared to give anyone false hope. He stared out over the water. Oddly, it seemed to be receding, eliminating what he suspected to be, their only chance of escape.

He rubbed his forehead distractedly. *This was worse than he could have possibly envisaged. Why in Hades did he not follow Tuccius' advice.*

"I have no idea what is happening. That cloud seems dangerous, but what it carries I cannot tell." He shrugged, in uncertainty rather than nonchalance. "We can only pray the Gods will spare us this night."

They huddled together talking, and a spark of courage induced by their shared adversity created an unexpected, albeit brief, bond.

Their hope of escape from this unassuming port town was short-lived.

Within an hour, Herculaneum was swamped by a surge of volcanic gas — so hot it killed all remaining inhabitants, including those sheltering on the shoreline, instantly. This would be followed by wave upon wave of burning debris which, inexorably, buried everything in its path.

Titus Salvius Aelianus who realised, too late, he had persuaded the townsfolk into a tomb not a sanctuary, was saddened. His final moments were spent thinking of his wife and their two children, his elderly parents, and his brother — a soldier.

He whispered a heartfelt apology that his return home was fatally delayed.

. . .

Salvius' last conscious act before the searing heat sucked the life out of him was a hissed curse at the Gods for abandoning him, and those sheltering with him to so horrific a fate.

CHAPTER 1

ERCOLANO - OCTOBER 1995 - MIDNIGHT

The moonless night meant the darkness was almost complete. The soft radiance from the glittering blanket of stars provided enough illumination to reveal the criss-crossing pathways. Two men, clad entirely in black, slipped silently through the ruins, hugging the buildings — shadows had more substance.

Cautiously, yet with haste, they made their way towards the docks. The area of the site where, to date, over three hundred skeletons had been excavated.

By chance, one of the men had overheard a discussion regarding these remains and the riches associated therewith. That there were *any* bodies left at the ruins, not to mention valuable artefacts, was unexpected news. He, along with most who followed the story of Herculaneum, assumed everything had been removed when first uncovered, a decade previously.

It was too good an opportunity to miss. A handful of archaeologists had been assigned to preserve what was there, but more often than not were called upon to work in other areas of the site.

The man knew he and his partner had a tiny window of opportunity. Any excavated artefacts tended to be recorded and transferred to the museum with dispatch. It was essential to act quickly. Get in and 'appropriate' a select few items before the authorities had the chance to document and, probably, remove the finds.

No one would be any the wiser.

Or so they thought.

Approaching the loosely designated 'boat-sheds' or arcades, the duo slowed their pace, moving stealthily so as not to attract the attention of the night watchmen.

They had done their homework. Surveying the site over a few days, monitoring the movements of the guards, noting it was uncommon for them to patrol the surrounds more than once every couple of hours.

Moreover, Herculaneum was not like Pompeii. Access to the site was challenging, and those in charge did not think anyone would be insane enough to break in.

The doors to each of the sheds, were, as expected, secured, which proved no hindrance. In seconds, the first padlock fell to the expertise of the taller of the two. He opened the door wide enough to allow them to squeeze through.

Switching on a torch, covered to dim the beam, he swept it around the space. Nothing. It was empty, save a few weeds. They moved to the second and third — their interiors a repeat of the first.

In the fourth one, the light picked out a cluster of skeletons. Nestled on a bed of straggly grass and slowly disintegrating, the contorted faces of the dead, seemed to reproach the interlopers.

Why disturb us? Why disturb us?

As neither man was blessed with much imagination, the accusation was ignored.

A mistake?

Maybe.

A quick check exposed nothing of value, so the thieves moved on to the next one, a similar result. When they reached the sixth, their luck changed. Although, as with the previous three, the arcade was partially excavated, the subdued ray of the flashlight picked out the glint of what the pair guessed to be gemstones.

Grinning at each other in glee, they crept in further, taking care not to crush any of the skeletons. While unmoved by the possibility of malevolent ghosts loitering in this ancient graveyard, the sound of a bone snapping in the stillness would, undoubtedly, draw unwanted attention from the security guards.

A handful of fine gold chains, dulled from centuries beneath the ash, were liberated from the clenched fingers of their owners. Earrings and rings followed suit.

"That will do," ordered the shorter of the two, already on the threshold, aware the watchmen would be on their rounds.

"Just one more," his partner promised. "This is a beauty."

"Leave it. We have to go. Now."

"Wait, I've almost got it. It is solid and will bring a good price."

"Hurry, you fool." The second man was losing patience.

The reply was a growled expletive.

Simultaneously, there was a loud crack which, in the silence, ricocheted off the massive walls. The two men froze. Seconds ticked by with agonising slowness. There was no sound of running feet or alarmed shouts. Breathing matching sighs of relief, they retraced their steps with celerity, and minutes later were over the fence, dropping soundlessly onto the Via Mare.

Behind them, under the darkened arch of the boat house, one might be forgiven for thinking the dead were *not* at peace. From the skeleton, whose ring had been so brutally seized, rose a faint coil of black vapour, followed by a sibilant hiss.

A trick of the light, of the breeze?

The distant swish of a tyre?

Perhaps.

Seven Hours Later

It was a perfect autumn morning. The air was crisp, and the azure sky cloudless. The scattering of trees seemed wreathed in jewel-like shawls, their leaves already preparing for winter.

As he did every day, Alessandro Rossi paused at Herculaneum's main gate to admire the view across the Bay of Naples, the far horizon sharply defined, heralding a cool day.

He glanced around, his curiosity piqued by a hive of activity at the boathouses, seventy feet below. Puzzled — it was unusual to see so many people this early, the site would not open for another hour — Alessandro peered over the railing.

Their behaviour indicated something was gravely amiss. Rather than speculate, he hurried down the long path, greeting one or two of his friends as he passed. At his hurried query, they shook their heads, indicating they were equally at a loss.

Five minutes' fast walking brought him to the specially constructed boardwalk in front of the boathouses.

"What's going on?" he asked the nearest person, an officer of the local Carabinieri.

"Theft," came the abrupt reply.

"How on earth did they get in?" he wondered out loud. The site was not easily accessed.

The Carabiniere shrugged. "Not much stops those who are determined," he replied. "We think they entered somewhere up by the car park, or possibly came over the fence along the Via Mare."

Alessandro shook his head, dumbfounded at the audacity. "Do we know what was stolen?"

"Various pieces of the jewellery due to be photographed and removed this morning. They must have been disturbed because one of the skeletons is damaged."

Alessandro tsked and shouldered his way through the crowd. The first three sheds, although lacking padlocks were apparently untouched.

When he reached the sixth one — beyond the clicking cameras and the group of people muttering in undertones — he saw Tomas Durante, site director, on his knees. Alongside him, another carabinieri officer. Masked and gloved, the two were examining the field, meticulously checking the skeletons, dictating notes and findings.

"Tomas." Alessandro interrupted their conversation, his tone respectful.

"Ah, Sandro, glove up, we shall need your expertise here." The director barely turned his head, his focus on the artefacts.

Donning a mask, gloves, and booties, Alessandro joined the two men, soon wholly absorbed by the remains.

"How did they know of the existence of *these* artefacts," Alessandro mused, while they worked. "We were careful to insinuate everything had been relocated."

Tomas frowned. "The excavations have been all over the news, here and internationally. We cannot keep anything quiet anymore. To be honest, I am more shocked it's taken this long for the fortune hunters to risk a snatch and grab." He blew a resigned sigh. "We should be thankful we had already moved the most valuable items. I hope the poor souls are forgiving.

Alessandro glanced up at the director's whimsical turn of phrase. "Superstitious, Tomas? I am astonished."

"If your rude awakening, after being buried with your most treasured possessions for two millennia, is to have one of those precious belongings literally torn from your hand, would you forgive? Or would you exact revenge? Many who disturb the dead come to a sticky end." In clear reference to certain Egyptian excavations.

Alessandro, while respectful of the artefacts, was also a realist. "He died a long time ago, Tomas. I daresay he is at rest. Is what we do any different? Anyway, such curses have been debunked."

Tomas grimaced. "We, at least, are reverential in the way we handle any remains, human or animal. These victims were not afforded proper burial rites, their shades may still be wandering the banks of the Styx. All I can say is, pity the thief."

Alessandro could see they were going to have to agree to disagree. "In that case let us ensure we have removed anything which might encourage a repeat performance. Will you be making an announcement?"

"It is being arranged."

The three men hunkered down and by the end of the day, every last object was in the secure preservation room in the

Naples museum.

Arriving home, Alessandro was met at the door by Cristiano, his twelve-year-old son.

"Papa, Papa, we saw the news. Tell me," the child implored before his father had made it across the threshold.

Alessandro chuckled, and rubbed the boy's dark hair.

"May I come indoors first?" He held Cristiano's shoulders and walked him backwards into the house. "Maddalena." He smiled over their son's head at his wife who was coming towards him across the cool atrium.

"Sandro, I expected you to be much later today." She stretched up on tiptoe to kiss him.

He released Cristiano and gave his wife a hug, returning her kiss with interest.

"You guys, ewwwww," Cristiano objected, sticking his finger down his throat.

"One day, you will want this more than anything in the world," Alessandro rejoined, unapologetically.

"Nope, never," contradicted his son, his face the picture of disgust.

"I'll remind you of this moment the day you bring home your wife to meet us." Alessandro grinned.

"Then you'll be waiting a long time. Never mind being all lovey dovey with Mama, tell me about the skeletons," Cristiano wheedled.

Cristiano was fascinated by his father's job. An eminent archaeologist, Alessandro had worked on excavations all over the world and who, if he was going to be away for more than a couple of weeks, took his wife and two sons with him.

Despite his young age, Cristiano had made up his mind to

17

follow in his father's footsteps and read everything he could get his hands on regarding the subject.

All teasing aside, Alessandro was gratified by Cristiano's enthusiasm. His older son, Vincente, had never shown any interest in archaeology or history and, of late, opted to stay with his grandparents instead of accompanying his family to remote ruins.

At seventeen, Vincente was keen on eco-agriculture, and was currently learning all aspects of farm management on the Rossi's extensive property outside Rome. Their differences aside, the two brothers were very close, and Cristiano missed Vincente when he wasn't around.

Taking a seat at the kitchen table, Alessandro explained the theft and the site's response, concluding with Tomas' comment.

"Signor Durante believes a ghost will haunt the thief?" Cristiano's eyes grew wide.

"Who knows." Alessandro opened his palms, in an 'I have no idea' gesture.

"I'd like to see that." Cristiano's mind flew off on different tangents to stories of ghouls and gruesome murders.

"Cris," Maddalena chided.

"Well, they shouldn't steal from the dead," Cristiano retorted. "I am going to stop people from doing it."

"Good for you, son," Alessandro smiled. "Good for you."

CHAPTER 2

ROME - JUNE 2015

In a modest office on the third floor of a quaint old building along a quiet backstreet, Cristiano Rossi steepled his fingers together and studied the man on his screen.

Miles Hathaway, his counterpart in the UK had requested a video call to discuss the possibility of a joint operation to recover some ancient artefacts.

It needed to be covert. Spooking those dealing in stolen treasures sent them further underground, and any thread tracking them down was lost. The shields surrounding their networks, both virtual and physical, were ironclad and so secret, the chances of hearing even the whisper of a sale were infinitesimal.

"Miles, good to see you. What do you know?" Cristiano greeted his friend.

"Afternoon, Cris, and not entirely sure. They change their damn codewords in the messages every time. How they keep up is anyone's guess, and we always seem to be one step behind." Miles shook his head in frustration.

"That said, Todd... you know, my cryptologist..." Miles

didn't wait for Cris' response, "assures me it's definitely three items, and at least one of them is a piece of jewellery. He's still working on the details of the other two. He reckons something about the wording in the ciphers indicates there could be a small mosaic — in its entirety, and the other might be a *pugio*." These were the small daggers Roman soldiers used as a secondary backup weapon to the *gladius* — their broad sword.

"Worth?"

"Todd estimates the piece of jewellery alone could, potentially, bring upwards of ten, even fifteen thousand. More if it can be dated and is known to have come from a specific site."

Cristiano pinched the bridge of his nose. "Plan?"

"We want to infiltrate the network. Set up someone as a buyer. They will need an airtight back-story, something along the lines of a recluse who is wealthier than Croesus. We have been liaising with a couple of historians who we—"

"A couple of *historians*? Miles, what the hell?" Cristiano interjected, feeling his day going to shit. "You can't recruit any old person to assist. This is sensitive and confidential information. How do you know you can trust them?" He slapped his palm against his forehead.

"Keep your shirt on." Miles grinned unrepentantly. "Before you go off at the deep end, have some faith in me, in this department. We have never been compromised. These two are eminently trustworthy and have already discovered a range of artefacts which had come up for sale on the black market.

"They work at a museum along Hadrian's Wall. A totally innocuous place, but they have access to an extensive collection of databases, only available to researchers of antiquity.

"Hannah Vallier has an uncanny knack for tracing the untraceable and Bryony, her admin assistant…" The inflection in Miles' voice suggested admin assistant was the least of the latter's talents. "... is a whiz at hunting down information on the dark web through firewalls even we struggle to breach.

"Plus, I know Hannah's husband, Max. We went to uni together. He's one of the good guys. We wanted him to join our organisation, but he prefers engineering."

Miles' perplexed tone indicated anyone who preferred *engineering* to clandestine investigations was patently bonkers. He leant forward in his eagerness to convince his Italian colleague. "Putting that aside, the only question is whether the person we want to act as the buyer will do it."

"Have you asked him, or is it her?"

"I was awaiting your approval of the scheme before I went ahead."

"Go, make yourself a coffee and let me think," Cristiano said, his brain churning over Miles' proposal.

Miles' grin reappeared and he nodded. "Take your time." He rose from his chair and strolled out of Cristiano's line of sight.

Cristiano's eyes were on the picture of the office filling the screen, but his thoughts had turned inward.

Since his childhood, Cristiano's goal had been to get a job chasing down stolen artefacts. After completing an undergraduate degree in ancient history, he confounded his family by applying to the Military Academy of Modena. Completing the course with flying colours, Cristiano embraced army life.

That was until one summer evening, almost four years ago, when a single conversation with his father's long-time friend, Massimo Caravello — now President of the Council of Ministers, and a man who wielded significant clout — changed everything.

Massimo had levelled his dark gaze at Cristiano. "I am astounded, for someone with such enthusiasm for all things historical you have not considered a different career path. Have you not heard of the Carabinieri Command for the Protection of Cultural Heritage?"

When Cristiano looked blank, Massimo elaborated.

"It is the branch directly responsible for tackling art and antiquities crimes, colloquially known as the Art Squad." He grinned and went on to provide a succinct yet detailed description of the inner workings of the department.

Thus began a serious discussion, and the longer they talked, the more Cristiano knew this was his calling. As soon as he was able, he put in for the transfer. Whether Massimo — who, coincidentally, was then the Minister for Cultural Heritage — had fast-tracked the application, Cristiano never knew, but his request was granted almost immediately.

He had risen to the position of captain, in the main because of his reputation for being meticulous during his investigations, not to mention his tenacity. Cristiano refused to be beaten, uncovering and... or... foiling numerous art heists, with the added benefit of disrupting several global syndicates.

The illegal trade in historical artefacts was prodigious, and the money available to finance the deals — seemingly inexhaustible. Shutting down these organisations was problematic because they merely went to ground and resumed their activities once the dust had settled. To weaken them, even briefly was generally the best they could hope for.

Cooperation between international police forces had tightened the noose around the networks, but it was a constant battle, and neither side would ever concede defeat.

Nor was it a job for the irresolute. Months of painstaking work could be ruined in a split-second.

That said, when one of the teams successfully thwarted a theft or recovered a treasure thought forever lost, the feeling of accomplishment was indescribable.

While Cristiano deliberated over Miles' suggestion, the image of his father arriving home twenty years ago, following a brazen robbery at the ancient Roman site of Herculaneum, teased at his mind. Only twelve years old, he was already passionate about history in all its forms, but it was this incident which had turned it into an obsession.

A handful of the less valuable artefacts stolen that night were eventually retrieved from the clutches of a crooked gold merchant, but most had never been recovered. Not even the hint of a possibility of a maybe. Over fifteen years of fruitless searching had ensued but, recently, the case was declared closed.

Publicly, Tomas Durante and Alessandro Rossi continued to pursue every lead.

In private, both men admitted it was unlikely they would find any of the missing items.

Cristiano wrenched his thoughts back to the present. He refocused on the screen to see Miles had resumed his seat. "Email me the usual documentation. I will need a few hours to get the approval. Who do you want to act as the buyer?"

Miles fist-pumped the air. "You!"

CHAPTER 3

The Airbus A320 taxied down the runway, gathered speed, and rose smoothly into the air. Glancing out of the window, Cristiano spotted the turquoise hexagonal that was Portus — the artificially engineered port of Ancient Rome, and now known as Lago Traiano.

Quickly, his gaze sought and found Ostia Antica, one of his all-time favourite sites. Then they were banking. The plane turned north en route to England, and into his eye line slid the sparkling blue of the Tyrrhenian Sea.

Settling into his seat, Cristiano reflected on how certain events throughout his life — every last one of which was connected to Ancient Rome — had led to this moment. The moment when he was in a position to sanction his department's involvement in a classified operation to infiltrate an international, antiquities trafficking ring.

His mind wandered back to the year the artefacts were stolen from Herculaneum. Three days after the theft, Massimo

Caravello arrived at the Rossi's front door, a small boy in tow.

Alessandro was not in the slightest surprised. "Welcome, welcome. Come in, come in."

"Morning, Sandro. Permit me to introduce my youngest? This is Gian. Gian this is Alessandro Rossi. We met at university, and he was my best man when I married your mama."

"Pleased to meet you, sir." The child shook Alessandro's hand and gave a cheeky grin.

Alessandro responded in kind and ushered his visitors into the kitchen. After asking Maddalena to brew up some coffee, he called for Cristiano, who traipsed down the stairs, a book in his hand.

"Cristiano, you remember Uncle Massimo? This is his son Gian. How about the pair of you go out into the garden?" Alessandro suggested.

"Hello, Uncle Massimo. Hi, Gian," Cristiano greeted the visitors with a sunny smile. "Are you going to talk about the robbery?" He canted an inquisitive head at his father.

"Possibly, but that's none of your business, Cris," his mother remonstrated gently.

"What do you know of it?" Massimo raised a brow at the boy.

"Everything." Cristiano braced his shoulders, importantly. "I'm going to stop people who do that when I grow up."

"I'm going to join the Carabinieri," Gian piped up, stumbling a little over the long word.

"They are *very* cool," agreed Cristiano, making Gian beam in delight.

The two fathers smiled indulgently at their offspring.

"Enthusiastic for one so young," Massimo nodded at Cristiano.

"All things ancient intrigue him," sighed Maddalena. "He'll either be an archaeologist like his father, or a detective."

"Well, if you ever need any advice, don't hesitate to call." Massimo held Cristiano's eager gaze.

"Thank you, sir." Cristiano did a sort of bow, feeling this was the correct response. "Papa, may I take Gian to the site?" The staff always let Cristiano in, knowing he was a responsible and respectful child.

"How about we all walk over there after coffee?" Massimo proposed. "It's a while since I last toured the ruins and would appreciate a look at the crime scene."

When Cristiano looked back, the whole thing seemed so benign. Two friends strolling around an archaeological site, chatting about the robbery. Two children tumbling around the ruins, playing cops and robbers, or hide and seek. The games changed depending on the day, for this was to be the first of many visits.

Even at so young an age, Cristiano divined Massimo's interest in Herculaneum was not solely related to the site's historical importance. Overheard snippets of conversation that first day, led him to believe the minister was engaged in something far more complex than a robbery. Then, he had no idea exactly *who* Massimo Caravello was, or the breadth of his influence.

Over the next few years, Massimo turned up periodically, usually with Gian. The adults had coffee and gossiped about their respective families, while the children played. Then, the men and their sons would head off to Herculaneum.

Leaving the boys to explore the ruins, Massimo and Alessandro — who, without fail, were greeted by Tomas Durante and a handful of Carabinieri — vanished into one of the offices. An hour or so later, they would reappear, their

demeanour testament as to whether their discussions had
been satisfactory.

Regardless of how much Cristiano pestered his father,
Alessandro refused to be drawn on the reason for Massimo's
visits or the subsequent meetings. An astute child, Cristiano
found this confidentiality acted as a spur — determined
there would come a day when he would be the one
convening such meetings.

Cristiano's friendship with Gian strengthened, and
continued even after Cristiano went to Modena. Whenever
an opportunity presented itself, he and Gian had caught up.
Of late, that was less frequent, but both accepted it as
inevitable, given their choice of careers.

Absently sipping the hot coffee poured by the steward, Cristiano coaxed his mind back to his current investigation.
Opening his briefcase, he withdrew a slender folder.

All it contained were the background checks on, and
photographs of, Hannah Vallier and Bryony Emerson. He
had perused them briefly the day Miles sent them through,
but now he took the time to scrutinise them thoroughly.

Married to an engineer, Hannah Vallier, on the face of it,
was a typical working wife and mother. She lived with her
husband and their young twins in a converted cottage not far
from the museum where Hannah worked. The couple had
been part of archaeological excavations at Masada, and
Pompeii, and had moved into the cottage after their marriage
five years ago.

Cristiano studied the photograph of Hannah, an odd wisp
of recognition rippling through him. He disregarded it. He
had never met the woman in question; doubtless she
reminded him of someone else.

He set her information aside and transferred his attention to the file on Bryony Emerson. The attached photo depicted a young woman, whose auburn hair was styled in, what Cristiano guessed would be described as a pixie-cut. Tawny eyes fixed him with a shrewd gaze which was a tad unnerving.

Twenty-four years old, Bryony grew up in a tiny village in Northumberland, not far from Hadrian's Wall, went to boarding school, and then onto university. She held a double degree in IT and art history, and a Masters in IT. An unusual combination, but one which had, unquestionably, served her well, bearing in mind her aptitude for unearthing valuable data buried deep within the darkest recesses of the internet.

There was little else. She was an only child, her parents were both dead, and it appeared she had no personal life, leaving Cristiano mildly nonplussed at the negligible detail.

Lunch followed by a brief nap, and Cristiano heard the pilot announce they were on final approach to Heathrow. Two hours later, he was buckling himself into his seat for the flight to Newcastle. For so short a hop, he was content to read the paper without the usual disruptions.

It seemed the plane had barely reached altitude when it began descending. Staring out of the window, Cristiano got his first look at the north east of England.

They were flying over green fields which seemed to go on forever, interspersed here and there with hamlets and criss-crossed by a spiderweb of roads. In the far distance he spotted an irregular greyness, indicative of a city — Newcastle he presumed.

The plane turned and swung in a massive arc, going out over the coast before lining up with the runway. Within moments they were on the tarmac and taxiing to the gate.

He had arrived.

CHAPTER 4

Wearily, Cristiano strode into the arrivals hall at Newcastle airport. The trip from Rome to the north of England had taken the better part of a day, and he was looking forward to a hot shower and a cold beer.

"Captain Rossi."

He turned at the sound of his name, to see one of the women whose photograph was in his briefcase, hurrying towards him. That same prickle of awareness teased at his memory. He ignored it.

"Captain Rossi? It is you, *sì*?" she repeated.

"Mrs Vallier?" Cristiano was rewarded with a warm smile.

"Yes..." as though something perplexing had struck her, the woman paused to study him, briefly, then shook her head. "Oh, I do beg your pardon, that was terribly rude of me. Have we met before?" Her nose scrunched in puzzlement.

"No, of that I am certain. I would not forget so charming a lady." Cristiano bowed slightly, his Italian accent giving his words a poetic cadence.

"Only you remind me of someone, maybe..." she trailed off. "Never mind. Returning to your question. Yes, I am she, and please, call me Hannah. Mrs Vallier makes me sound as though I'm in my dotage."

Her smile was infectious and Cris, who was inclined to be reserved, found himself reciprocating.

"Thank you for meeting me, and I will gladly call you Hannah, if you return the favour and call me Cris."

"It will be my pleasure. I know you were expecting to lodge at a B and B. Bed and Breakfast," she clarified, catching his bemused expression, "but Max and I felt it would be too impersonal and possibly a little difficult, initially. We should like you to stay with us. If you don't think that is inappropriate."

She hesitated, a slight flush washing up her cheeks. "Oh, maybe you being undercover as it were, might make that awkward. Perhaps you prefer your own space—"

Seeing Hannah was about to retract her offer, Cris was quick to reassure. "Hannah, do not panic. I am grateful for your hospitality and would enjoy very much staying with you. Yes, I appreciate my own space, but not in a country with which I am unfamiliar. It can be lonely."

"That's what we thought. Excellent, I am so pleased."

The relief on her face was almost comical. Cris bit his lip to stifle his amusement. "It is agreed then. When we are closer to retrieving the artefacts, it might be prudent for me to move to a hotel or a, what did you call it, B and B?" At Hannah's nod, he continued. "To keep everyone involved safe. A bridge we can cross if we find it necessary."

"Good plan, but I hope it doesn't come to that. You must be exhausted. To say it's only about five hours flight as the crow flies, the journey from Rome takes forever." She grinned and steered him out into the sunshine.

"I should tell you, our home can be chaotic. We have

three-year-old twins who are imps, and a dog of question-able heritage who thinks she rules the house. To be fair, she kinda does, but is so cute she gets away with it. She is very well-behaved though." Suddenly realising her invite was sounding less welcoming by the second.

Cris could no longer control his mirth and burst out laughing. "Hannah. Stop. Honestly, I am used to chaos. My brother and his family sound similar to yours, only they live on a farm with an assortment of crazy animals running amok. I would choose pandemonium over silence, any day of the week."

By this time, they had reached Hannah's car, a slightly battered yet solid-looking SUV.

"This is Romi." She nodded at the vehicle.

Cris looked at her askance.

"A play on the word Rome, my favourite thing… and you can't call a car Rome. That sounds ridiculous, as does Remus or Romulus and the number plate didn't offer any hints. A friend suggested Romi, and it stuck." She shrugged noncha-lantly, leaving Cris to surmise that life in the Vallier house-hold bordered on the eccentric.

The journey to the Valliers' cottage passed quickly. Their conversation concentrated on Hadrian's Wall and its surrounds, with Cris making a mental note to visit as many of the ruins as possible while in this part of the world.

"Here we are." Hannah's voice drew his attention to a large, white-washed cottage nestled at the bottom of a gentle rise. The car crunched along the gravel drive and stopped in front of a sizeable garage. She shifted in the seat to look Cris in the eye.

"Before we go in, I should tell you my husband knows the real reason you are here. I do not keep secrets from Max;

that was part of the deal when I agreed to undertake these investigations. He is privy to all manner of highly confidential information, unrelated to ancient artefacts. Rest assured he can be trusted."

"I understand, and Miles already briefed me on your Max."

"Oh…" Hannah, who had expected some kind of argument, paused, "…so we're cool."

"We're cool," Cris affirmed.

Climbing out, he stretched and, inhaling a lung full of the cool fresh air, did a slow full circle. The view was breathtaking — almost uninterrupted countryside as far as the eye could see. "How lucky you are. What a beautiful place."

"Thank you, we're rather partial." Hannah, accepting the topic was closed, beamed.

A chorus of voices could be heard from somewhere to their left.

"Mama," a high-pitched shriek.

"Hannah, you made good time," spoken in a much lower register.

Cris saw a tall man of comparable age with him striding down the path from the door, a little girl clinging to his hand and jumping. The man was lifting the child with each stride, making her scream with glee.

"Mama look, I'm flying," she chortled.

Behind them came another child, a boy, hurtling towards them, a dog on his heels, yelling, "Wait for me."

Hannah grinned in delight, saying in undertones to Cris, "Welcome to our home. Don't say I didn't warn you." Turning to the man she continued, "Max, this is Cris Rossi, Cris, this is Max Vallier, and the small fry are Claudia, Luc, and Aggie." She pointed each one out, while Max opened the gate. Aggie — the excited mutt — wound herself around and around Cris' legs.

"Crumbs, sorry, Cris. Clearly, you are an exalted guest. Aggie is usually very stand-offish with new people," Hannah apologised. "Aggie, come away, you horror."

Cris watched his unorthodox greeting unfold, a wide smile creasing his face. "Please, do not fret. To be accepted by the family dog is an honour." He crouched down to pat Aggie, who wagged her tail, her tongue lolling out of a smiling mouth. "Aggie?" he questioned.

"Short for Agrippina," Max explained and put out his hand. "Good to meet you, Cris. Come on in and take a load off." He motioned toward the house. The two men shook hands and Max, ignoring Cris' protests, collected his suitcase and wheeled it up the path.

"Thank you for being kind enough to open your home to me. I am looking forward to getting to know you and your family." Cris followed Max into an airy kitchen.

Surprised, he gazed around. He had seen photographs of English cottages; most consisted of several small rooms. Here, spanning almost the full length of the structure was one charming kitchen-living area. The latter was delineated by open framework, original to the house, if Cris wasn't mistaken, maintaining the illusion of two rooms while allowing in light from the numerous windows. High ceilings and minimal furniture added to the feeling of space.

Noting Cris' astonishment, Max explained they had wanted to create a modern living area without losing the traditional exterior.

"It was a pretty radical change, but provides the flexibility we need, especially now the kids are growing up. The more rooms you have, the more places they can wreak havoc." Max chuckled.

"I think it is perfect," Cris replied, earning a slew of brownie points from his hosts.

"I'll show you to your room," Hannah offered. "Then we

can relax with a beer or glass of wine. You've had a long day. Tomorrow is soon enough to start worrying about the artefact."

She led the way upstairs and along the hall to a well-appointed guest suite; two rooms joined by an arch. "I hope this is suitable. The bathroom is next door and it's all yours. The kids still use ours."

Walking into the sun-drenched bedroom, Cris was possessed with the oddest notion he had come home. The mellow palate of colours was reminiscent of the Italian countryside, lemon and cream with hints of warm orange and the odd splash of turquoise. Fine linen curtains billowed in the breeze which brought with it the delicate scent of blossoms.

"Your towels are already in the bathroom. There's a sort of ante-room here," Hannah pointed through the archway, "with a desk, a television, a phone, and a variety of sockets for charging stuff up or whatever."

"This is well organised. A not so simple guest room," Cris commented before he could stop himself. "Forgive me..."

"No need to apologise. Occasionally, we have visitors who require more than a place to sleep. Adapting this area into a study of sorts, seemed a good idea." Hannah didn't elaborate, but Cris was reminded of Miles' comments regarding how often Hannah had worked with them on investigations.

"This is the bathroom, nothing complicated." Hannah opened the door into a gleaming bathroom. Stark white tiles alleviated by accents of lilac, repeated in the towels and curtains. "The shower runs from the mains, better water pressure that way, and only one set of taps to worry about." She grinned, and once again, Cris was taken with how comfortable he was around her. An unusual sensation. He tended to take a while to warm to people, he had just met.

"Thank you. I am sure, I shall manage."

"Ok, I'll leave you to settle in. We'll be in the garden." One last smile and Hannah disappeared down the stairs. The sounds of a family having fun wafted up through the open windows.

Cris nodded slowly. *This was going to be very interesting.*

CHAPTER 5

The evening passed pleasantly. When Cris joined the Valliers in the garden, he was pressed into a beer, while the twins had their meal. With minimal argument, Hannah managed to chivvy them off for a bath and bed, leaving her husband to barbecue a selection of meat. The aroma set Cris' stomach rumbling, to Max's amusement.

The back door swung open to reveal Hannah carrying a tray of crockery and a medley of salads. "Nearly ready?" she asked Max who nodded. "Good, I'm famished.

"As is our guest." Max grinned.

"Oh, goodness, Cris, I never thought. All that travelling, you must be half-starved. I should have put out some nibbles," Hannah wailed.

"I am fine and what, may I ask, are nibbles?" Cris sought to mollify and divert.

"Hmmm… like your antipasti, only here we usually just have chips and dips." Spotting Cris' confusion, Hannah chuckled. "Crisps and crackers with an assortment of thick sauces to dip them in, such as hummus," she clarified. "I picked that phrase up from an Aussie friend and it stuck. Too late now. Oh well, it's a good job you're hungry, I seem to have prepared a mountain of food."

Hannah arranged the plates and cutlery around the large wooden table, and shortly thereafter they were eating.

Conversation flowed between the trio, and it wasn't long before they moved from the mundane to the serious.

"I know I said the artefacts could wait until tomorrow, but I am too excited. What can you tell us?" Hannah asked.

"What do you already know?" Cris countered.

"We know there are at least three items, and that one of them is almost certainly a piece of jewellery."

Max, who had been listening attentively to their discussion, interposed, "Will they try to sell all three at the same time?"

"We doubt it, but it's possible. Too risky to bundle them together and they can get more money if they sell them individually."

"Bryony has been keeping a close eye on the usual underground sites. So far, the auction is only a hint of a rumour but there have been umpteen bites, already. I am endlessly appalled at how many people think it's okay to buy what are indisputably stolen artefacts. Why else would they be on the black market?" Hannah's voice rang with contempt.

"Collectors of such things are unscrupulous by nature. They know international governments are clamping down on trade in any kind of historical relic, be they manuscripts, mosaics, sunken treasure, whatever. The rarer the piece, the more they want it, and don't care how it came to be available." Cris shrugged.

"We are only uncovering the tip of the iceberg, but every sale we intercept, every seller we arrest, every site we dismantle is a win for us and a loss for them. If nothing else, they do not have the luxury of becoming complacent, and it sends the message that we will never stop hunting them down." The vehemence in Cris' voice left his listeners in no doubt as to his commitment to his job.

The discussion went back and forth. Ideas were tossed about regarding how to trap the seller, but until they had more details, there was little point fleshing any of them out.

"Best to wait 'til you talk to Bryony tomorrow," Hannah suggested. "Do you think you'll have time to visit any of the forts along the Wall, while you're here?" She changed the subject.

"I hope so. It the first time I have had the opportunity to visit anywhere in England, outside London, and I am eager to explore," Cris replied.

"Well, you have a great guide in Hannah," Max remarked. "She knows this area like the back of her hand."

Cris saw an odd look pass between them. Unable to interpret it, he pushed it to the corner of his mind to mull over later, then all but forgot about it when Hannah asked whether he wanted a hot drink.

The next day dawned bright and sunny and, once breakfast was out of the way, Hannah asked Cris whether he fancied walking to the museum where she worked and where he would be based.

"We've got plenty of time. It only takes half an hour or so and kinda sets you up for the day."

"I should enjoy that," Cris affirmed.

"Yay." Hannah smiled and went to finish getting ready.

Waving goodbye to Max and the twins, they set off.

"Max works from home most of the time and is happy to look after the kids. There's a little crèche at the museum for when he has to go into Newcastle. It works well," Hannah explained.

"You are nicely set up here, I think," Cris rejoined.

"We really are, I could not imagine living anywhere else. I have an affinity with this place, which came as a surprise, given I grew up in and spent most of my life in one town or another. Big cities I hate with vehemence, except Rome. Rome is something else completely."

She paused.

Cris had the impression Hannah was about to continue but she switched to another topic of conversation. He didn't push her. If she wanted to tell him, she would. They were virtual strangers after all.

They chatted while they walked, sharing snippets of each other's lives.

"I expect you have a dossier on Bryony and me," Hannah said when they were almost at the museum. She grinned at Cris' dumbfounded expression. "What, you think Miles would allow me to be part of anything connected to a department as important as the Art Squad without doing his due diligence? You can stop pretending you don't know my favourite food, and where we go on holiday, and how much online shoe-shopping I indulge in."

"Forgive me. I am not used to working on a case of such importance with a... errrm... civilian and had no mind to cause offence."

"No worries," she waved her hand, airily, "but, since you know all about me and by extension my family and doubtless Bryony, I'm going to make it my business to ferret out every last piece of juicy information about you while you're here."

Hannah wagged her finger at him, and Cris stared, unsure

quite how to respond. Then she winked and he realised she was joking… well, he hoped she was.

"I will do my utmost to satisfy your curiosity." He bowed, being deliberately formal.

"Awesome! Here we are." Hannah pointed to an innocuous looking wooden gate in a stone wall, adding, "Employees' entrance."

Hannah introduced Cris to her colleagues as a visiting historian, who was on secondment from London. The casual way they greeted him suggested Hannah had already laid the foundations of his visit.

"Thank you," he murmured as they headed upstairs to her office. "I dislike prevarication."

"I decided it was more plausible than you showing up out the blue. We often get people coming for brief sojourns, and no one questions it. Seemed the easiest explanation. Here we are." She unlocked a door, opening it into a spacious room, its picture window overlooking the remains of the Roman fort of Magnis.

"The original footprint of Magnis, or Carvoran as it became known, is bigger than Vindolanda. Something like three acres, I believe." Hannah stood at the window and gave Cris a brief overview of the ruins.

"Most of it is under the grass now. Probably set up as a temporary marching camp, when Agrippa was moving into Caledonia, decades before the Wall was even a figment of Hadrian's imagination. Eventually, it became permanent and was added to. An aerial survey exposed traces of a vicus as well as other buildings, maybe workshops, or storage facilities.

"Today you can see what's left of a mile castle, some parts of the Wall itself, and the vallum. The few artefacts which were unearthed are in the museum. It stood at the junction of two major trade routes which gave it the perfect position. It was an incredible fort…"

Hannah's gaze was fixed on a spot beyond the window.

If Cris didn't know better he'd guess she was seeing a whole other scene. Forts and soldiers. It would require little effort to conjure them up here. There was a wildness, an untamed beauty about the landscape that leant itself to fantasy, immediately discounting his sentiment as ridiculous. *Fantasy indeed.*

Hannah shook herself and turned to face him, an apologetic smile curving her lips. "Sorry, I am prone to getting caught up in the past. This is why I love history. Bryony should be here shortly, let's make ourselves a coffee and then we can get down to business."

Bryony Emerson parked in her usual spot and waited until the song she was listening to, finished. The Flower Duet from Delibes' Lakmé, sung by All Angels was one of her favourites and she *always* had to listen through to the end. Her head full of soaring voices, she grabbed her bag and laptop.

Alighting from her recently acquired pride and joy — a pearlescent, emerald-green Vauxhall Astra — she hit the lock button on the remote, and sauntered around to the administration entrance at the rear of the museum.

Calling a 'hello' to those of the staff she spotted, Bryony made her way to the office she shared with Hannah. She still had to pinch herself, she had this job. When she finished her Masters, to land a position where that qualification *and* her double degree in Art History and IT, would be required was beyond her wildest expectations.

When Bryony spotted the advert for an assistant in the

archives at the Roman Army Museum, she had jumped at it. That was almost two years ago, and she never regretted applying for the position.

Databases and research were like food to Bryony. The knottier the obstacle, the happier she was. Her talent in this field was acknowledged and within two months of starting the job, she was promoted, becoming Hannah's sort of second in command.

The two worked well together, each bringing a different set of skills to the table, and quickly became great friends. The job was interesting enough when they were doing conventional research into ancient artefacts, but one day, Bryony uncovered something unexpected.

In the course of hunting down some source evidence, she came upon a strange link. It led to a website purporting to offer replica artefacts. One she could not access. Exasperated, but resigned, she made a note intending to go back to it and resumed her search. She had almost forgotten about it, but a couple of days later she caught a news article detailing the theft of a rare, Ancient Roman mosaic.

The report niggled, motivating her to mention it and the website to Hannah, who gave her the green light to follow her instincts. Hours of trolling through the internet came up a blank, so she dug deeper.

Cognisant with the labyrinthine composition of those areas of cyberspace invisible to normal search engines, Bryony used her talents to find a 'back door' into the website.

What she found shocked her.

It appeared to be a site for the unauthorised trade of artefacts. Relics of the ancient world, illuminated manuscripts from the medieval period, artworks from the Renaissance to the modern era, and everything in between. If you wanted something specific it could be procured... for a price... a colossal price.

Careful not to leave a single digital footprint, Bryony scoured the pages, making notes and, where she deemed it necessary, taking photos — with her phone rather than screenshots.

Hannah, recognising the significance of Bryony's findings, contacted the relevant authorities. The next day, they received a visit from Commander Miles Hathaway, UK section chief of the so-called Art Squad. Following hours of interviews, the signing of numerous papers and the swearing of oaths, Hannah and Bryony became special consultants to the covert department.

Between them, they had unearthed a significant number of illegal sites and helped in the recovery of artefacts, many believed lost forever. Some stolen prior to anyone being aware of their discovery.

CHAPTER 6

This new case captivated Bryony. Once a week, she tiptoed through the dark web, in search of suspicious trading sites. To find one auctioning artefacts as opposed to outright sales was unusual, although not unheard of, because having a number of people bidding for an item left the 'hosts' vulnerable.

Ordinarily, activity on these sites was kept to a minimum to avoid leaving a trail and was the reason Bryony found it. Someone had been careless.

Once the minor players had been whittled out from the serious buyers, the auction proper was held at a prearranged venue. Not on the web. A private function in a remote area and only used once. Abandoned buildings in the middle of nowhere were the preferred choice. When the auction was complete, the organisers vanished, leaving no sign they had ever been there.

During a routine scan, Bryony had come across a sequence of scarcely discernible breadcrumbs, whose digital footprint tugged at something in her mind. Careful not to alert anyone to her presence, she scouted out the site briefly, before backing out. Discussing it with Hannah, they informed Miles who had his cryptographers work on it.

That was three weeks ago. This operation warranted something different. Someone had to infiltrate the circle of buyers. Miles and Bryony had already set the wheels in motion. Cleverly worded messages left on sites, traders were known to frequent, had resulted in a few bites. It required a delicate touch. Too eager and it might alert the smugglers. Not eager enough and they wouldn't get a response.

Bryony had worked out there would be three separate auctions. Once the first item was sold, the site would be moved to another unidentifiable corner of the internet. Buyers would be contacted via a string of untraceable emails, the final one containing a list of detailed instructions on how to access the new site.

It was an interminable process but, for the sellers, it was worth it. They hoped their convoluted systems were enough to foil anyone other than the most persistent; a select few clientele who wanted to keep their identities hidden.

Now, all Bryony had to do was get the sellers to take the bait.

Entering the office, Bryony was brought up short when she saw the tall stranger whose presence seemed to dominate the room. She knew he had arrived. Hannah texted her the previous evening, but this man was not at all what she expected. Hannah had informed her his name was Cristiano Rossi, he was Italian, and worked for the Carabinieri Command for the Protection of Cultural Heritage.

Bryony hadn't seen a photo of him and visualised someone more… stocky, swarthy… okay… gangster-like. The overly dramatic image in her head made her want to giggle. The man was supposed to fit in with unscrupulous dealers. This guy looked like a god, a movie star. She canted her head. He seemed familiar. Probably reminded her of someone on the telly.

"Bryony," Hannah's voice broke into her thoughts as she made the introductions. "This is Captain Cristiano Rossi, our lead for the operation. Cris, Bryony Emerson."

"It is lovely to meet you, Ms Emerson," Cris gave a slight bow, "and please, call me Cris."

"Likewise," Bryony replied, "and I am happy to, on the proviso you call me Bryony." She stretched out her hand, and they sealed their greeting.

When their palms met, Bryony had the uncanny sensation that this moment was pre-ordained. Absurd though this was she did not dismiss it but, unwilling to seem affected, tucked it away to be revisited later when she was alone. Smiling, she said she was going to make a coffee, and did anyone else want one?

In his turn, Cris was afflicted by a corresponding awareness. The Bryony who walked into the office looked quite different from the picture in his file. Currently, her auburn hair, not as short, was threaded through with an array of colours: turquoise, purple, pink, and green. He had to admit, the choppy cut suited her, as did the colours.

She was wearing a black T-shirt, under a stunning brocade waistcoat, knee-length tailored shorts, black tights, and chunky boots — Doc Martens if he wasn't mistaken. Her style was… eclectic was the best word he could come up with, but she carried it to perfection.

The instant their skin touched, a flurry of images flittered through his head, so quickly he couldn't hold onto a single one. Ignoring them, he turned his attention to the computer screen flickering to life and, when Bryony came in with her coffee, the three started their day.

Bryony explained her findings in detail, after which Cris gave a summary of what she might not have already been apprised. Now all three were as up to date as possible and began to plan their strategy. Bryony had been dropping minute morsels of information regarding this new buyer. Someone with unlimited resources, someone who had done more than his fair share of shady deals. Someone of whom the authorities were vaguely aware but could not track down.

The back story Bryony had established was infallible. From birth, through his schooling, to his business, and all the people associated therewith, down to friends, their spouses and even children.

Named Enzo Sculleri, the bogus buyer was a reclusive multi-millionaire, who owned a legion of secluded properties across the world. Bryony had included the occasional newspaper snippet about legitimate purchases such as artworks, sold for astronomical sums. The buyers were anonymous, but Bryony had created the illusion Enzo Sculleri was behind them.

Now they had to wait and see whether he would be accepted into the first level of the auction.

Given they could not do any more with the auction until Cris received an invitation, Hannah asked whether he would be interested in a walk around the museum and the adjacent remains of Carvoran. Cris accepted with alacrity and the trio spent a fun couple of hours immersed in all things ancient.

Cris divulged a little about his childhood. How he accompanied his father to archaeological digs, and that he had virtually lived in Herculaneum when his father worked there.

"Ruins, whatever the era have always fascinated me, but I think my love of history was cemented at the time of the robbery."

"What robbery?" Bryony queried.

"When I was twelve, there was a theft from the skeletons in the so-called boat-sheds at Herculaneum. The majority of the treasures, and bodies for that matter, had been removed, but a number remained. Today, access to Herculaneum out of opening hours is difficult, then it was almost impregnable, but thieves broke in one night and stole miscellaneous artefacts. One of the skeletons was damaged in the process and I remember Papa saying the supervisor on site reckoned the looters were cursed."

"Seems an unusual type of statement for a scientist," Hannah said.

"Tomas Durante is an unusual man. He believes while it is important to excavate, conserve, and protect ancient relics, it is also wise to be respectful. If that was not feasible to achieve, whatever you had unearthed ought to be left where it lay."

"I happen to agree." Hannah nodded. "Some things should not be disturbed." An odd expression descended over her features and, once again, she seemed to be seeing a whole other scene.

In that moment, Cris made a decision. If he was afforded the opportunity to get to know Hannah better, he would ask what secrets she was concealing.

. . .

They exited the museum through the staff door at the rear of the building and seconds later were overlooking Carvoran. Hannah pointed out the vallum and the remains of a watch tower and described how the fort was laid out in antiquity.

To an indifferent bystander, Hannah sounded like she had swallowed a journal article, or studied the geophysical survey, but a nuance in her tone mesmerised Cris.

Something about Hannah's account suggested she knew the fort and its inhabitants, intimately. An impossibility. He was starting to think there was a whole lot more to Mrs Hannah Vallier, than met the eye.

Hannah caught his quizzical gaze. "There I go again, sorry, as I said, this was an exceptional fort. I think in the main because of its position and that it underwent several phases before it became the stone fort whose ruins we are standing on today. That they recognised the necessity to transform it from a temporary marching camp to a more permanent structure astounds me. Then, if I'm honest, most of what the Romans achieved astounds me."

She stopped speaking and a faint frown furrowed her forehead.

"I hope you get chance to see some of the other forts along the Wall while you're here," Bryony piped up, diverting Cris' attention from Hannah.

"As do I," he replied. "It is my first visit to this part of the UK, and I am excited to see Hadrian's Wall. He was my second favourite emperor," he added with a conspiratorial smile.

"Who was your favourite?"

"Trajan."

"Oh wow, he's mine too. Although I do have a soft spot for Domitian."

"*Domitian?*" Cris' eyebrows shot under his hairline.

"Yeah, yeah, I know, he was cruel man, but he did so

much good which is usually overlooked." Bryony contended, and the two began to banter back and forth about emperors and their contributions or lack thereof.

By the end of the day, Cris felt as though he had known Hannah and Bryony for years, not hours. Conversation, while lively, was also relaxed, their common interests meaning they were never at a loss for topics.

CHAPTER 7

B ryony monitored her carefully scattered trail, without leaving her own footprints. She knew when anyone checked Enzo Sculleri's details and the more they dug the more she was persuaded they had taken the bait. If they judged the fictitious Enzo's interest spurious, they would not be trying to verify his information.

Two weeks after Bryony had created Cris' alter ego, Enzo Sculleri received an invitation to the first stage of the auction. Reading between the lines, Bryony surmised the item, as Todd had indicated, was a piece of ancient jewellery. probably Roman, maybe Greek. Not much to go on, but it was better than nothing.

"So now what?" Cris asked. The three were studying the email intently as if the answer was somehow magically embedded therein.

"Now, we wait for a judicious period before we respond," Bryony explained. "Nothing happens quickly and, from what I can tell, any prospective bidder who sends an immediate reply is rejected outright as are those who delay too long. It's a fine balance."

She shrugged. "Miles is also analysing the usual communications in case I've missed anything. He mentioned one of their guys might be coming up this way as extra support. I'll reply in a day or so, then we'll see what happens."

With nothing to do but wait, Hannah proposed a tour of the vicinity. "I think we need a break from all this, and it's a lovely day. What do you say?" she asked.

The other two agreed instantly.

"How about Birdoswald?" Bryony suggested. "You haven't taken Cris there yet, right?"

"No, not yet and that's perfect. Close by and they have a great cafe."

Bryony chuckled, and even Cris grinned at this. Despite their brief acquaintance, Hannah's penchant for coffee had become well known.

Determined Cris did not leave Northumberland without having seen as many Roman monuments as they could fit in, Hannah and Max — twins in tow — had taken him to Vindolanda and Chesters the previous weekend.

This coming weekend, Bryony had offered to show him Housesteads, and Coria — the Roman Fort adjacent to Corbridge, if they had the time. That covered the major centres, anything else was a bonus.

Birdoswald was only five minutes down the road and, on a Wednesday afternoon in term-time, quiet.

Cris paid, refusing any reimbursement. "No, this is my... I think you say, treat," he smiled.

While they meandered through the little museum, chatting about the artefacts on display, Hannah explained that the fort was originally known as Banna which means horn in Celtic.

"Apparently named because of its geographical position. It sits on a craggy spur overlooking a bend in the River Irthing. I'll show you when we go outside. The view is spectacular. Perhaps one of the best from a fort, although the one from Housesteads gives this one a run for its money."

She was about to continue then hesitated.

"Please," Cris coaxed.

"You'll regret it," Bryony warned jokingly, earning a childish gesticulation from Hannah.

"Okay, you asked for it. Initially, Banna was a turf and timber fort before eventually being rebuilt in stone and was occupied from about 112AD until at least the mid-fifth century. There are pockets of evidence suggesting a continued presence throughout the middle ages. In the fifteen hundreds, a fortified farmhouse was built, which was renovated and extended during the Victorian era. It's the best place to see the original turf wall."

Well into her stride, Hannah elaborated. "This fort had six gates, all of which are visible except the north gate, and had all the usual buildings, including a *basilica exercitatoria* or exercise hall. This is another first for a Roman fort. The experts hypothesise it was probably in response to the awful weather we can get here, especially in the winter, which would prevent regular outdoor training.

"Even more noteworthy is the enduring impact of a specific military unit. The *cohors Prima Aelia Dacorum* or the 1st Cohort of Dacians were stationed here during the third and fourth centuries. The loyalty of these soldiers, once the sworn enemy of Rome, is attested to in the form of ancient graffiti."

Hannah paused for breath and rolled her eyes at the

tolerant grins wreathing the faces of her two listeners. "Oh lordy, I'm so sorry. You know I can't help myself." She raised her palms penitently.

"You ought to get a job as a tour guide, Hannah." Cris quipped.

"Nah, I don't like people enough." She replied, drily. "Come on, let's go outside. The actual ruins are amazing."

The trio took their time exploring the ruins before venturing beyond to admire the view over the valley. Cris conceded it *was* utterly spectacular.

Throughout the afternoon, Hannah was not overly surprised to notice how often Cris' eyes sought out Bryony and vice versa, when they thought the other wasn't looking. During the previous fortnight, the spark of attraction kindling between her friend and her visitor had become apparent to Hannah, even if the two in question hadn't registered it yet.

It both warmed and perturbed her. Bryony led a relatively solitary existence; a romance would do her the world of good, and Cris seemed to be a stand-up guy. The downside being, he had to return to Italy soon, and Hannah hoped he wasn't going to leave behind a broken heart.

She gave herself a mental shake. It was none of her business. They were adults and knew what they were getting into. She set it to one side and refocused on the current discussion.

By the time they returned to the office, the working day was almost over.

"No point starting anything now." Hannah tidied her desk and closed down her computer. "Let's take an early one. Fancy joining us for dinner, Bryony?"

Hannah's tone was innocent, prompting Bryony to narrow her gaze. Her friend's face gave nothing away, but Bryony knew that note. That said, a meal with the Valliers was guaranteed to be fun and she only had a microwave option at home.

"Thanks, that'd be great, if you're sure."

"'Course I'm sure, meet you there."

The evening disappeared in lively conversation, great food, and perhaps a glass of wine too many, except Bryony who had to drive home. When Bryony stood to leave, Cris was seized by an emotion akin to melancholy.

She said her goodbyes, and there was an awkward pause as their eyes locked for seconds longer than necessary, oblivious of the knowing glance Hannah and Max exchanged.

All of a sudden, Cris wanted her to stay, even if all they did was talk, unaware the object of so unexpected a sentiment shared his impulse.

Later when the house was quiet, Cris propped himself against the open window of his bedroom and stared at the clear night sky. Millions of stars pierced the endless ebony. The moon, a pale sliver, highlighted the landscape flowing out as far as the eye could see.

Cris breathed in the balmy air, a curious notion of familiarity tiptoeing through his subconscious. Shaking it off, he turned his back on the view and prepared for bed.

Magnis - AD 91

"Hannah."

A deep voice arrested the steps of a petite young woman hurrying across a large quadrangle.

"Marcus, is there something you need?" The aforementioned Hannah smiled at the tall dark-haired man striding towards her, swerving slightly so he fell into step alongside.

"I wonder…" An uncharacteristic flush warmed his cheeks.

"What is it, Marcus." Hannah came to a standstill to study him. His face was etched with fatigue. "Aelia keeping you up at night?" she hazarded, sympathetically. Two months ago, Senna — Marcus' wife — had given birth to their third child. An undisturbed sleep was a forgotten pleasure.

Marcus grinned. "No, the imp managed almost five hours last night. Senna was so worried, I had to stop her from poking the babe." His smile slipped and he ran a hand through his neatly cropped hair. "This is more… by the Gods, I never thought I would ask this…"

"Marcus, surely nothing is so bad you cannot tell me. Please." Hannah pressed her hand on his forearm.

"Might we go somewhere where we can talk without being overheard?" Marcus asked diffidently.

"Of course. Our quarters will be quiet at this time of day. Come." Hannah, puzzled by his demeanour, changed direction, and the pair strolled to the residence, chatting about mundanities. Asking Annant, the overseer, whether he might organise some refreshments, Hannah led the way to the triclinium, where they made themselves comfortable.

Refreshments served, their conversation dwindled while they sipped the sweet tea Mabina, their cook, brewed.

"Now, what is so bothersome?" Hannah broached after a few moments of quiet.

Marcus looked down at his beaker, swirling the liquid around as he gathered his thoughts.

"Of late, I have been troubled by strange dreams. Something by which I am seldom afflicted. They do not vary. A man and two young women wearing unrecognisable attire seem to be here, at Magnis. Although there is no sign of the fort itself, the landscape around them is this landscape." He spread his free hand in an encompassing sweep.

"The man reminds me of someone, yet..." Marcus paused. "I know, I know, it is just a dream, but they recur with uncommon regularity. With your... errr... connection, I wondered..." he trailed off, loath to express what he feared might be happening.

Hannah Valerius was an unusual woman. A Roman citizen of Hebrew heritage, she had met Marcus and his commanding officer, Maxentius who was now her husband, on Masada over two decades previously, following a Zealot ambush.

Since then, the three had travelled halfway around the Roman world and survived many dangers. Marcus had become as a brother to Hannah — their bond unbreakable.

He knew all about Hannah's mysterious link to a woman who lived centuries in the future, but it unnerved him and was a subject he avoided unless he had no alternative. Once Hannah had explained their connection, he had chosen not to think about it.

The concept was too hard to wrap his head around. He

accepted it and moved on. That said, this other woman, also called Hannah, had saved them from certain death by sharing her knowledge.

"Why do you think I might be able to help?" Hannah pried gently.

"One of the women… she reminds me of you."

Marcus' words startled Hannah. She was constantly aware of her other self, but never anticipated her merging with anyone else. If indeed, she had.

"Please recount your dreams in detail. Leave nothing out."

"They started about two weeks ago. The man is very tall, dark haired, and his skin tone is similar to mine. The complexions of the women are lighter. The one who bears a resemblance to you, is of average height, but her hair is not as dark. The other is more your stature, her hair is much shorter than that of the first lady, with streaks of bright colours through it. She also seems familiar, but…" he frowned.

Summoning up the figures, now lodged his memory, he tried to describe them.

"Their attire is… unconventional. On his legs, the man wears something comparable with braccae, but long, to his ankles. His tunic is short, only waist-length, and seemingly tucked into the braccae. Very odd. The clothing of the women… I cannot explain, it is outlandish, but I confess the garments look comfortable."

"Might you be able to sketch them?" Hannah asked. Marcus had some skill with a stylus and regularly drew pictures for their children.

He considered her question. "Possibly."

"Wait here." Hannah hurried to Maxentius' private office within the residence. Locating a couple of scrolls, a reed pen, and an inkstand, she retraced her steps and set them on the low table between the chairs. "Take your time. I will leave you to it and come back shortly. It is difficult to concentrate when someone is at your shoulder." She twinkled.

Marcus smiled his appreciation, and applied himself to the task, hardly aware of Hannah's retreating footsteps.

Hannah used this opportunity to walk over to the principia, where she found Maxentius buried in reports.

"Hello, my love, what brings you here in the middle of the afternoon?" He stood and came around the desk to kiss his wife. Hannah explained Marcus' dilemma. Maxentius rubbed his chin. "He *has* been a mite distracted. I presumed it was Aelia keeping him awake."

"That was my first question. Although she is part of the problem, the greater concern is the content of his dreams. Why Marcus and not me?" she mused. "I hope his sketches will shed more light on this. We have been blessed with peace for years. I do not wish to face the prospect of unrest."

"There is nothing to indicate any issues in the vicinity," Maxentius reassured. "Bearach and Iden..." two of the local headmen who, along with their tribes, were great friends with the Roman garrison, "...keep me abreast of any potential for dissension. We are in accord, and I believe they favour concord over strife. Have you heard anything from...?" He signalled with his hand.

"Not for some time. Our link is unwavering, but on the periphery of our minds. Only the other day, we melded. She was here, in the fort, or at least on the grass where this fort used to stand, telling someone about Magnis." A thought nudged. "I wonder..." She tapped her lip. "Goodness..."

She dashed off, leaving Maxentius grinning.

Her goodbye floated back to him as she vanished through the door.

Shaking his head, he turned back to his desk, sighing at the pile of work confronting him. Minutes later, he was engrossed, his wife's interruption put aside for now.

CHAPTER 8

"Marcus." Hannah slid into the triclinium with little regard for decorum.

Marcus lifted his head.

"Have you finished? The drawings?" She was puffing a little from her headlong dash.

"Almost." Absently, he pushed a scroll of papyrus along the table, concentrating on the third and last sketch.

Hannah picked up the sheet and studied the illustrations of the two women. Marcus was correct, the taller one *did* resemble her. The etching depicted her future self; someone Marcus had never seen and thus, his perception was untainted by prior contact.

The only person to have seen the other Hannah was Maxentius. It had happened twice, once in Rome and once right here at Magnis, but that was years ago. Hannah had a hazy understanding that time in their individual worlds moved at a different pace. Ten years in one life could be significantly more, or less, in the alternate.

The tenuous link — a fine thread binding them was the best description either Hannah could come up with — meant each was aware of momentous events. Content and safe in their own lives, neither had felt the need to connect for some time.

Hannah scrutinised the second figure, unable to prevent a grin at the quaint attire. She never failed to find the clothing of the future bizarre, but it looked very freeing. The face nagged at her... a fleeting recognition, gone before she could pin it down. She was not overly concerned. If it was important, it would come to her.

She waited with rapidly evaporating patience as Marcus put the final touches to the third portrait. Her eyes were drawn to the likeness he was creating.

"There." He had barely lifted the reed pen before Hannah snatched it off the table. He gave a muffled laugh; her lack of self-restraint was notorious.

Hannah held up the papyrus, her gaze swinging between it and Marcus.

"What?" he demanded, noticing the look on her face.

"This man, I have seen him before. I also see him here, today."

"You are speaking in riddles, Hannah. How can you see him here?" Marcus expostulated.

"This man." She waved the sheet. "I too have seen him, although he is not confined to my dreams. I saw him mere days past, right here, feet from where we are sitting."

Knowing a little of what Hannah experienced, Marcus blanched slightly. In his heart of hearts, he perceived there was more to his night-time visions than happenstance but held onto the hope it was nothing more sinister than an overwrought imagination brought on by broken sleep.

He croaked something unintelligible.

"Marcus, this woman may favour me," Hannah jabbed a finger at the first etching, "but this man," she paused for dramatic effect, "could be you."

Marcus barked a sceptical laugh. "You are mistaken," he argued. "How is that possible?"

"Come with me." Hannah grasped his hand and led him to her sleeping chamber. Balanced on the largest wooden cupboard was a polished reflecting dish. "Look," she instructed.

Marcus faced the mirror, while she held up the papyrus.

"Look at yourself, then look at the drawing. You could be brothers." She pointed between the two.

Marcus stared, nonplussed. Hannah was not incorrect. The depiction bore an uncanny resemblance to his reflection. He shook his head trying to dispel the buzzing which was increasing with every passing minute.

"What does this mean?" His question was naught but a whisper.

"I do not know," Hannah replied, unsatisfactorily. "Perhaps I am about to learn something." She shrugged.

"Can you not…"

"No, I cannot manifest her out of thin air," Hannah grinned, "but when I need her, she comes."

"I profess to feeling unsettled. While we have reaped the benefits of your… gift, I find it disconcerting. I have never told Senna, but what if this is something which may affect her. What do I do?"

"For a start, there is no point getting ahead of yourself. This might be nothing. Permit me a little time and hopefully I will be able to allay your alarm."

Marcus looked as though he was about to say something. Hannah took his hand. "Do you trust me, Marcus?"

"With my life," he replied, reiterating his response to the question Hannah had asked several times since that fateful day when they met on an isolated citadel in the middle of the Judean desert.

"Leave it with me."

They returned to their respective tasks. Marcus, although moderately discomposed, saw no point in dwelling on their conversation and stored it away.

Northumberland - July 2015

Bryony estimated four days to be a suitable period. She had observed the comings and goings on the auction site, already aware of who had been rejected and the amount of their bids.

Even had Miles not informed them of the value of the artefact, Hannah and she were not naive. They both knew the worth of relics, stolen or not and, since Bryony was playing with a fictitious budget, she had no qualms about placing a significant bid.

Again, it was a case of hurry up and wait. Never one to look a gift horse in the mouth, Hannah cajoled their visitor into doing some archiving. It was not particularly exciting but, as Hannah pointed out, there was always the possibility of an 'ah ha' moment.

Cris took little persuading, and the next few days flew by.

The weekend was taken up with more exploring. Cris had been riveted by Vindolanda and Chesters, but nothing prepared him for Housesteads. Bryony was lucky enough to snag a parking spot and, once all required fees were paid, they set off.

Prior to leaving Hannah's, Bryony had advised Cris to wear sturdy shoes or boots because there was a ten-minute walk from car park to the fort.

Assuming it would be comparable with the gentle stroll from the ruins of Vindolanda down to the cafe, Cris was astounded when he spotted the fort perched atop an escarpment which, Bryony informed him, was called Whin Sill. Its strategic location offered a commanding view across the landscape and would please any self-respecting *legatus*.

"No chance of sneaking up on *this* garrison," he muttered to Bryony as they tramped to the bottom of the dip and up the slope at the other side towards the ruins.

"And I pity any who tried." She smirked.

Dodging the odd sheep, they followed the path, which took them almost to the museum before veering to the right, entering the fort through what in antiquity had been the south gate.

"Constructed within a decade of AD122, this fort, which the Romans called *Vercovicium* or 'the place of effective fighters', is the most complete example, and one of the largest in the UK, as well as being one of the best known from the whole of the Roman Empire." Bryony paraphrased the flyer.

"It was garrisoned, in the main, by a cohort of Tungrian soldiers until the end of the fourth century. Besides the well-preserved building within the walls, excavations also revealed there was an adjacent *vicus*."

Cris' mock-pained expression made her giggle.

"No more, I promise. Just giving you an overview. Much more fun simply to explore." Without thinking, Bryony clasped his hand and led him through the ruins to the north wall.

"I reckon it's better to start here and work our way around the ruins back to the entrance. Also, it's slightly downhill and therefore easier." She grinned impishly.

They leant against the lichen covered stones. Bryony pointed out that this north rampart formed part of the main wall and was skirted by the Hadrian's Wall path — a popular walking trail. Beyond where they stood, the ground dropped away steeply, highlighting the fort's advantageous position.

Dutifully admiring the untamed wilderness, Cris was more interested in the ruins themselves. The distinctive layout, repeated in every fort throughout the empire was clearly visible, its footprint unmistakeable.

Cris trod the site like a seasoned archaeologist, identifying specific buildings without the aid of the signs, stunned by how much had survived the usual stripping such places tended to suffer in the hunt for building materials.

Workshops, granaries, the principia, and the praetorium. The hospital, the barracks, and the latrines. Something he could not help but point out.

"The amount and quality of preservation is staggering. Is there a reason, do you know?" he asked Bryony while they stood in the middle of the granary.

"I think probably, it was partly to do with its occupation by the Border Reivers, and partly because it was too hard to lug... sorry carry," she amended at Cris' puzzled frown, "the stones to where they were building houses."

"Border Reivers?" Cris probed.

"From the thirteenth to the seventieth centuries, raiders plundered either side of this border region with equal vigour. Their loyalty shifted to support whoever suited their cause, some even becoming mercenary soldiers. This was one of their strongholds," she explained.

"While I have no doubt they were a scary bunch and merciless, in the same way as history has treated highwaymen and Robin Hood, they have been romanticised. Their daring deeds retold in folk tales, elevating them to legendary status, even immortalised in works by Scott and Wordsworth. Another claim to fame, Neil Armstrong was a descendant."

She gave a wicked smirk. "I too am descended from a reiver family.

"Now, why does that not surprise me?" Cris teased. As they turned to leave the granary, a cloud drifted across the sun, plunging them into shadow. For a split second, he could have sworn Bryony's face was overlapped by another's, familiar yet unknown.

He blinked, and blinked again, but it was gone. He disregarded it; being caught up in history was messing with his head.

While meandering through the ruins, between serious debate about sections of the site, their conversation quite naturally, began to circle their respective childhoods — thankfully happy — school, university, and career paths.

Cris knew everything there was to know about Bryony Emerson, right down to her bank account pin numbers. Now, he yearned to discover the person behind the soulless data in his file.

"Do you mind me asking a personal question?" Bryony quizzed while they explored.

"That depends how personal." Cris feigned a grimace.

"How is it you speak English so well?"

"Ahhh… that would be telling," he stalled.

Bryony elbowed him. "Well duh, kinda the point," she parried.

"Okay, I give in. I learnt English at school, it is taught as our second language. Also, I have visited London many times with my job, and must confess to a weakness for your English police dramas. It is amazing how much you pick up, specifically frequently used phrases and slang, if you watch them often enough."

They spent a few minutes arguing about which TV series was the best, before moving onto other topics, to find they had a lot in common. A love of classical arias and similar tastes in modern music. Coffee was life. A passion for history in all its forms. To while away hours in museums or art galleries or exploring monuments was the perfect day out. They were in agreement that the best way to relax was with a mug of coffee — or glass of wine — and a good book or a movie.

It was early afternoon before Bryony was satisfied Cris had seen everything, including the museum.

"I would enjoy doing some of the Wall walk," Cris said as they made their way back to the car park, weaving through the throng of people. A popular site at any time of the year, on so glorious a day, it was full to bursting. The air rang with cheerful voices. "Goodness, it's like Rome. I did not expect it to attract so many visitors."

Bryony wagged a finger. "Just because we are a long way north of London and off the beaten track and just because this isn't Rome, Pompeii, or Herculaneum, doesn't mean it's neglected by tourists."

Cris put up his palms. "I had no mind to cause affront," he placated. "Forgive me?" he pleaded engagingly.

"Only because you are also a visitor," she scolded breezily. "Come on, it's way past lunchtime, and I think we'd better leave Coria for another day. Not enough time to appreciate it now. I was thinking Hexham. It's only about twenty minutes and there's some great eateries."

"Sounds perfect," Cris agreed with a grin.

As they approached the historic market town, Bryony had a brainwave. "Instead of finding a cafe, how about we grab a sandwich and some drinks and eat picnic style in Sele Park? It's a lovely spot." she proposed.

Cris was only too pleased to fall in with her suggestion, preferring the outdoors. Bryony was a charming companion, and she seemed genuinely delighted to play tour guide.

They found a peaceful corner under a sprawling beech tree away from the crowds. Bryony had brought a small blanket, which she kept in the boot for this exact purpose. Making themselves comfortable, they munched their sandwiches, gossiping about this and that.

The combination of the morning's explorations in the fresh air, full stomachs, and the sun's warmth took their toll. Before long, both had dozed off in the dappled shade.

CHAPTER 9

C ris woke first and lay on his back, staring up through the canopy of leaves dancing in the breeze. He shifted onto his side which, coincidentally, allowed him to contemplate Bryony in repose.

He recalled the mental image he had created prior to meeting her, the corners of his mouth tilting in a slight smile. She was quite different from what he had envisioned.

It would be easy to assume from her quirky attire and spiky hair that Bryony was a bit of a hellion. Cris had no doubt she could be when riled, but her demeanour was one of reserve. This was in contrast with her wicked sense of humour — Hannah and she dead-panned some of the most ribald stories he had ever heard, then collapsed into gales of laughter — but she was also polite and respectful.

Not to mention, she was one of the most beautiful women he had ever seen — and he was from Italy. Her svelte figure, elfin features, and mischievous smile had been drifting through his dreams almost every night since the day they met.

He couldn't fathom it. He was not one for brief affairs of

the heart… or body. That's not to say he hadn't dated, but relationships of any kind did not fit with his life, his career, so he avoided them.

Now, unexpectedly, he had met someone who gave him pause. Made him examine his future. Made him wish he was staying longer. To surrender to the impulse to unwrap the real Ms Emerson — an enchanting proposition.

He shook his head. *Don't be ridiculous,* he admonished internally, *you have no time for romance, or a fling or whatever.* As he thought this, Bryony's nose crinkled; ridiculously cute and begging to be kissed.

He was administering a mental kick up the butt, at the precise moment Bryony opened her eyes. They were the most unusual colour. He had thought they were tawny, but in the sunlight, amber came to mind, and currently held him transfixed. He felt himself lean closer. His head screamed at him to stop this foolishness, while his heart drowned it out.

Bryony didn't move, although she offered a shy smile.

With a gentle finger, he traced her jawline.

"My apologies," he murmured, "but I have the most urgent desire to kiss you."

Her eyes widened, the amber darkening to chestnut and he swore they sparkled. She ran the tip of her tongue over her lips, causing Cris to swallow a groan.

"Would you have any objection?" he pressed quietly.

Mutely, she shook her head.

He angled his body until their faces were inches apart. Tentatively, he grazed his mouth against hers. That tingle, the one he had discerned when first they shook hands, commenced a slow glissade along his spine. The same pictures darted though his mind, to vanish as he was ensnared by the heady sensation of kissing Bryony.

Bryony had been dreaming of a handsome Italian Cara-biniere. A man who had, of late and somewhat annoyingly, taken root in her head. A man who, if she had to make a list of essential attributes for her perfect date, matched every single one of her criteria and then some.

He was polite, respectful, witty, intelligent, and cultured. He loved history, books, and coffee... the benchmark by which any prospective love-interest was gauged. That he was devastatingly handsome, an added and *very* charismatic perk.

A man whose sojourn here in Northumberland would be over almost before it had begun.

Following one or two disastrous and, mercifully, short-lived romances, Bryony had given up on the whole dating game. She refused to be dictated to or ruled in any way, shape, or form when it came to matters of the heart.

It would require a special person to meet her exacting standards, and she was pretty certain such a paragon did not exist. Her work consumed her days, and she was not prepared to waste her precious free time with someone who wanted a replica of themselves.

Then she met Cris. Without knowing anything about him, she wanted him to take care of her, cosset her, protect her, possess her — *dear lord, did she want him to possess her.*

When she woke and their eyes met, her heart did an odd flip. His dark gaze entranced her, and she found herself unable to speak. He asked whether he might kiss her... *he actually asked her permission,* which she could not have denied any more than she could fly to the moon.

The instant their lips touched, a flood of impressions flashed through her mind. A tall dark-eyed man, wearing clothing she identified as belonging to a soldier of ancient Rome. Three small children — one a baby. The man seemed to be looking right at her, his face so full of love, she swore her heart missed a beat. He reached out to take her hand.

The kiss deepened and the images fled. Even though this was new and heart-stoppingly thrilling, there was an underlying sweetness, a familiarity, as though they had been kissing like this for a lifetime.

Bryony never wanted it to end.

Neither did Cris, but he remembered they were in a public park and, with great reluctance, lifted his head. He studied Bryony through glassy eyes. *Was it even remotely possible to fall in love that fast, in the time it takes to kiss someone?*

"Bryony..." he brushed his lips to her nose and then to her forehead, "...you are, without a doubt, the most kissable woman I have ever encountered." A tinge of red crept up his cheeks at the admission.

Bryony levered herself up on her elbows to look at him, a puckish smile forming at his words. "Goodness, that's a compliment coming from a drop dead gorgeous Italian hunk." Mortified, she clapped one hand over her mouth. *Dammit she had said that out loud.*

"Drop dead gorgeous? Hunk? Hmmm... I approve." Cris grinned, twisting a spike of pink hair around his finger.

"Sorry, I didn't... it's... I only meant... oh, crap." Bryony gave up, there was really nothing she could say to excuse or justify her remark.

"No need to apologise, it is very flattering." Unable to stop himself, he recaptured her lips. His hand dropped from her hair, to caress the soft shell of her ear, her skin cool under the warmth of his fingers.

He felt her arms come around him, anchoring him to her. Their bodies aligned and, as a completely different appetite flared, the couple became insensible to their surrounds.

. . .

A derisive hoot brought them back to earth.

"I think it is time we moved on," Cris said begrudgingly, his disgruntled expression, pulling a snort from Bryony. "Not a good idea to continue kissing you. I might not be able to stop." He raked a hand, which was not quite steady, through his hair.

"Did you hear me complaining?" she quizzed lightly.

"No, but…" he let that hang.

"I know." Bryony concurred with wink, making Cris smile.

Standing, each ensured the other looked presentable and, while Bryony folded the blanket, Cris gathered up the remnants of their picnic. As if it was the most natural thing in the world, Cris took Bryony's hand, and they strolled back to the car park resuming their casual conversation.

Clipping in her seatbelt, Bryony checked her watch, amazed to note it was almost three o'clock.

"Wow, time really does fly when you're having fun. Errr…" unwilling to monopolise his day — he was a guest of Hannah's, after all — she faltered. "I should probably be getting you home," she suggested, praying he might want to spend the evening with her.

Cris did not reply immediately. She glanced across to the passenger side, to see him engrossed in his phone, his fingers flying over the screen. He was sending a text, or maybe an email. *Really?* Considering his words scant moments ago, it seemed an odd, and unexpectedly thoughtless reaction.

Trying to quash her irritation — with herself for being sucked in by his Italian charm, and him for oozing Italian charm — she shuffled in her seat.

It was only a kiss. She didn't own him. They hardly knew each other. Yeah, so he had a silver tongue, so what. What if he had a girlfriend? Oh no, what if he was married?

Inexplicably, Bryony felt the burn of tears. *This was why she didn't date. Grrrr.*

Shaking her head, she turned on the ignition, ground the gears, and gunned the engine, shooting out of the parking space faster than was prudent. Fortunately, without hitting anything,

"Whoa, Bryony. What's the rush?" Cris' startled question pierced her indignation, and she eased off the accelerator.

"Don't want you to be late home," she bit out curtly, zooming out of the town with more haste than care.

"I thought we…"

"Nope…" she cut him off.

"Bryony, please will you pull over?"

"No," she growled.

"Per favore, cara,"

Wait… did he call her 'dear'?

"Bryony… sweetheart…"

She could hear his concern. Spotting a suitable lay-by, she veered into it and slammed on the brakes. The car came to a juddering halt. Gripping the steering wheel, Bryony leant her head against its cool, faux-leather and gulped, once… twice… three times. *God, she was an idiot.*

"Please will you tell me what that was about?" His lilting accent wrapped around her, soothing.

She could fall in love with him for his voice… *love… don't be ridiculous, what you feel is purely physical, a hormonal response, nothing else.* Oh dear, reproached her heart, *of course you love him. You have loved him across millennia.*

This brought her up sharp. *Millennia? Now she **was** losing the plot.* Becoming aware of Cris' hand on her leg, Bryony's whimsical speculations were cast aside, overtaken by the delectable frisson spiralling out along her veins at even so gentle a touch.

When Cris felt the Astra jolt out of the car park, he looked up in shock, expecting to plough into another parked car or oncoming vehicle. One glance at Bryony's face told him a storm was brewing. He frowned, scouring his brain to figure out what on earth had happened in the last ten seconds to cause it.

Unwilling to perish in a fiery car crash, he was relieved when his coaxing resulted in her coming to an abrupt halt at the side of the road on the outskirts of Hexham. Bryony laid her head on the steering wheel, and his heart cracked. She looked... crushed, defeated.

He reached to squeeze her thigh lightly. "Bryony, what's wrong?"

"Nothing!"

He burst out laughing. She was bristling all over, like an angry fire-sprite. *Fire-sprite...* a memory flickered and was gone before he could grasp its significance.

"Don't you dare laugh at me." She scowled at him. "You bloody Italians are all alike, with your god-like looks and your body-melting accents. You said... and I believed... then..." She dived out of the car and marched up and down the tarmac, waving her hands erratically, ranting about her stupidity and goodness knew what else.

Cris bit his lip. She was a miniature virago. Anyone would think she was of Italian heritage with that temper. He *knew* she would be magnificent when provoked. Taking his time, he climbed out of the car and walked towards her. *She thought he had god-like looks and a body melting accent...* he smirked, inordinately elated, and just a little bit... smug.

"Don't you come near me," she hissed.

"Or what?"

"I'll kick your cute butt."

Mirth rumbled through him, and ignoring her directive, he closed the gap between them. Catching one of her flailing arms, he hauled her against him, moulded her flush to his body and kissed her... hard.

Bryony's squeak when Cris yanked her to his muscular frame became a moan under his searing onslaught. She wriggled in a vain attempt to break away, which only made him tighten his hold.

Dazedly, she tried to coerce her body to do as her brain instructed, to no avail. She was putty in his hands. So, she gave up and sank into his kiss, blithely ignoring the voice in her head issuing dire consequences for her lack of sense.

After what felt like hours, but was less than two minutes, Cris lifted his head, but did not relinquish his hold. He ran a light finger under her chin, tilting it upwards gently, compelling eye contact. She lowered her eyelids, unaware how provocative was the sweep of dark lashes against glowing cheeks.

"Bryony, look at me," he beseeched.

With a huff, she did as he bade, her extraordinary eyes cloudy with passion and uncertainty.

"Are you going to tell me?" he asked.

She wriggled again. This time, he released her, and she moved to stand a few feet away, twisting her hands together.

Cris could almost see the argument going on in her head. The silence lengthened until he thought she was going to ignore his plea.

At a loss but determined not to push her or fluster her

any further, he propped himself on the bonnet of the car, folded his arms, and waited.

"You kissed me, said all those lovely things, and I thought, I hoped, you might want to... but you couldn't wait to get back on your phone, desperate to text some sultry beauty no doubt." She flipped her hand in an 'I don't give a toss' gesture.

"If you were that bored, why didn't you say so? Why did you bother? Pity for the pathetic, single, English woman?"

Bryony knew her accusation to be unfounded, but the pinching in her chest made her want to lash out. It was that or cry, and she hated women who used tears to manipulate. *He was her colleague. How in the hell was she going to be able to work with him after this little outburst of petulance?*

"Never mind, forget it. Let's go. I'll have you at Hannah's in ten minutes."

CHAPTER 10

S wallowing his amusement at her mini tantrum, Cris intercepted her as she stalked to the driver's side of the car.

"If you had let me speak, I was about to tell you I was texting Hannah to ask whether she minded me staying out for the evening. I don't have a key and didn't want them to wait up for me. I was hoping to take you out to dinner. I *still* want to take you out to diner, in spite of your attempt to catapult me across the Styx," he joked.

The wind went out of Bryony's sails. Her shoulders slumped and her face dropped. *Oh great, way to jump to conclusions, Bryony. Now she was the bad guy... awesome.*

"Yes... well..." She could feel her face burning.

"Bryony, I do not kiss women for fun... even though it is fun... or to satisfy an urge. I am not the playboy you seem to think I am and before you ask, because I know you're going to, I am not married, neither am I in any kind of relationship. My work takes me away from my home constantly, and it is less complicated to remain unattached."

"So, why…?"

He placed a finger on her lips stemming the tide.

"I do not know." He gave a quintessential Italian shrug. "You are always in my head. Your smile, your eyes, your body-melting accent." He twinkled, pleased when Bryony's frown relaxed a little.

"All I know is, I believe we share more than the common interests we talked about today. Something is happening between us, as beguiling as it is baffling. I know I am only here for a short time. Yes, it is selfish of me to want to explore where these feelings might lead. Yes, it might be better to pretend it never happened, to forget today but, if am to be honest, I do not think I have the strength."

Slack-jawed, Bryony listened. Nobody had ever spoken to her with such… poetry before. The sincerity in his tone matched the truth in his eyes. The tightness in her chest evaporated, and her heart thudded. Without pausing to question her motives, she grasped his forearms and lifted up on tiptoe to kiss him.

"Forgive me," she apologised. "I am not very good at this. I saw you texting, and it dawned on me how little we know about each other," she said, unaware of the dossier, Cris had on her.

"We are professionals, work colleagues, and we have crossed the line or, at the very least, blurred it. I never thought to check whether you have a wife or a girlfriend waiting for you, reducing me to a casual fling, never mind that I abhor cheating. Dating and me are mutually incompatible," she gave a rueful smile.

"I decided ages ago, I would rather be alone than become nothing more than an extension of my significant other."

She was about to add something else but thought better of it. It was not the right time to admit she would renounce every one of her high ideals in a heartbeat if he loved her. It might never be the right time.

"I do not think we are so very different," Cris mused, gathering her in his arms, relishing the sensation of her snuggling against him. "Instead of trying to define or dissect these emotions, might we embrace them, and see where the days take us?"

"I think that sounds absolutely perfect," Bryony replied gruffly.

They stood together. Resting his chin on the top of Bryony's colourful hair, realisation smacked Cris full in the face.

He was in love with Bryony Emerson...

...and he had neither the will nor the desire to protest.

Their momentary discord dismissed, they enjoyed a wonderful evening. Despite Cris' suggestion that he take her out for dinner, Bryony, diffidently, offered a counter proposal. Takeaway and eat at her place.

"If you like Chinese, of course. We can open a bottle of wine, it's more relaxing, cheaper, and we don't have to be on our best behaviour," she had said, noticing a fleeting disappointment chase across Cris' face. She interlaced their fingers and pressed her lips to his knuckles.

"That's not to say I don't want to be wined and dined, I most certainly do but, after today, I think a quiet evening together without waiters and other customers, and noise might be more beneficial." She held his gaze, trusting he followed her reasoning.

Cris, who loved Chinese food, was not averse. It had been a busy day, and it was much more comfortable to unwind in Bryony's cosy cottage than at an upscale restaurant. Wine and conversation flowed, and it was after midnight when Cris called a taxi. He declined Bryony's offer of the couch so politely, it seemed he was doing her a favour by leaving.

Bryony would never know how hard Cris fought the temptation to stay. To carry her up the narrow cottage staircase and lose himself in her, but it was too soon... much too soon.

He kissed her until they were both breathless and a little unsteady, waved goodbye, and got into the taxi. Glancing over his shoulder, Cris saw Bryony standing on the kerb, arms hugged around her waist watching him drive away.

Settling back in the seat, he mulled over the day. Bryony had revealed more by her actions than her words, although her 'body-melting accent' accusation made his lips twitch. He empathised with her reticence. To risk your heart on the possibility of a maybe, made harder when one of you had a whole life in another country, was nothing short of absurd.

Which only served to make him want it more.

The next day, the Valliers, Cris and Bryony spent the day at Kielder Water. The largest man-made lake in Northern Europe — as Bryony took pains to boast — was about an hour's drive from Hannah's, and a favourite haunt.

It gave the twins the opportunity to run their legs off, and Aggie, who had been permitted to accompany them, romped around with canine glee. It was an uproarious excursion and they tumbled home, tired but happy, with Cris declaring he *had* to go back and hike some of the trails before he left for Rome.

Monday morning saw Bryony at the office long before the others. Her policy was not to get sucked into anything work-related during the weekends and it had been a challenge not to check her emails over the last couple of days.

She all but yelled her excitement when she spotted a brief response from the auction organisers popping up in her in-box via a ghost server.

She had to wait a full half an hour before she could tell her co-conspirators, who turned up at a far more sensible time.

"Hannah, Cris, we've been approved." She jigged up and down on her chair, to the humour of the other two.

"Excellent." Hannah peered over Bryony's shoulder to read the missive.

Thank you for your generous bid, which permits you to attend the auction.
An invitation will be sent within 48 hour and requires an immediate response.
Failure to do so, automatically renders your bid null and void.

"We'd best keep a close eye on the emails," Cris interjected.

His fingers brushed Bryony's nape. It was quite the most delicious feeling. She forced herself to concentrate and typed in a brusque: *Received and understood.*

She sat back in the chair and twiddled her thumbs. She

hated this part, it always reminded her of sitting in the waiting room at the dentist, knowing you needed a filling, or worse, a root canal.

"I need a distraction," she mumbled, "but first, coffee. Anyone else?" she asked and, after receiving answering nods, went to the adjacent room. Not much bigger than a broom cupboard, Hannah had persuaded management to turn it into a kitchenette.

An espresso machine, kettle, and sundry mugs stood on a purpose-built bench top, under which was a bar fridge, and a cupboard containing sugar, biscuits, coffee mate, washing-up liquid, sponges, and tea-towels. On the opposite wall was a tiny sink, complete with draining board.

Bijou was the politest description for this cubbyhole, but Hannah and Bryony were very appreciative. It saved them, and the two other staff members who had use of it, walking to the other end of the building every time they wanted a coffee... which was frequently.

Brewing the coffee, Bryony tried to calm the fluttering in her stomach. She couldn't decide whether it was because of the auction — which was like balancing on the edge of a knife — or whether it was working in proximity with Cris.

The previous day had been great fun. Cris was gratifyingly attentive: holding her hand, dropping the odd kiss on her cheek or hair, and generally behaving in the manner of a gentleman from a bygone era.

The transformation in their relationship must have been blindingly obvious to Hannah and Max, who never so much as mentioned it.

Bryony had watched him interact with Luc and Claudia, hoping she had managed to mask the stunned awareness she wanted to see him mess about like that with their children.

How precipitous can you get? she had reprimanded herself. *Lordy, the man would vanish in a puff of smoke if he knew what you were planning for him. Wishful thinking.* With fierce determination, she had pushed aside her fanciful thoughts and got on with enjoying the day.

That had lasted until she was in bed listening to the sounds of the night through her open window. *Did they have any chance of a future together?* It would be a long-distance relationship. *Could she hack it?*

Her forehead had puckered in thought. Yes, of course, she could hack it, but she didn't want to. What was the point of being with someone if you were never actually with them? Then her musings became jumbled as slumber claimed her.

She had dreamt of the man wearing the strange clothing, and again the tug of recognition. *Was he depicted in one of her art or history books? An artist's portrayal taken from a bust or statue, or perhaps a fresco?* Even asleep, she scoured her brain to identify their faces. She felt she knew him, belonged with him, simultaneously rejecting it as nonsense.

With a sigh, she carried the tray next door, handed out the drinks, and the three began their day proper. There were always websites, information sheets, and flyers which required checking or updating.

The archivists were routinely called upon to research source evidence for any number of reasons, not solely connected to the sites along the Wall.

Periodically, the artefacts in this and a handful of other

museums were rotated, meaning those returning to storage had to be recorded, and packed correctly.

Additionally, it was not uncommon for the various academic institutions to borrow items to supplement their courses, which required equally careful processing.

When Hannah and Bryony were not on the hunt for stolen relics, their primary responsibility was cataloguing artefacts, and research. Hannah, in particular, relished tracking minuscule, abstract, or obscure snippets of information to their origin.

The atmosphere in the room was tranquil as each became absorbed in their respective tasks.

Engrossed in translating a partial and badly degraded inscription, Cris did not hear Bryony ask whether he wanted a sandwich from the little café. She repeated the question, and her amused voice penetrated his concentration.

He lifted his head, his mind miles away in place and centuries in the past. "I beg your pardon, Senna that would be lovely. Chicken salad if they have it."

"Senna?" Bryony's face reflected her puzzlement.

Cris stared, his focus returning to the present moment. Registering his mistake, he was quick to apologise.

"Please forgive me, Bryony, how impolite. I have no idea where that name came from. Perhaps it was in one of the data bases I've been checking." He smiled absently.

"You are as bad as Hannah," Bryony chided, with a grin.

"You need talk," Hannah retorted. "When you get fixated on something, a bomb could go off next to you and you wouldn't notice."

"True enough," she acceded and headed off to get lunch.

CHAPTER 11

H annah's spirited response meant neither Cris nor Bryony noticed her cheeks had lost some of their colour, and her eyes were shadowed. *Why had Cris mentioned Senna? Is a word with my other self in order? Is something about to happen?*

She reckoned about a decade had passed in her ancient world since the last time her connection with them was more substantial than dreams. That would make it AD91, near as dammit.

The historical record for the time period spanning AD84 to the reign of Hadrian was sparse to non-existent. Certainly, nothing to indicate there was any cause for concern. While conceivable a major disaster had somehow gone undocumented, it was unlikely.

Hannah knew Maxentius had been persuaded to extend his term as legatus at Magnis, and that Marcus would assume control upon his commander's official retirement. She knew Marcus and Senna had three children... the third born only recently. Ephraim was now a soldier, his legion based in Hispania.

She was aware, even though their unions were not officially recognised, Liora had married Julius, and Petronius had wed a woman from one of the local tribes. Unusually, both couples, along with a handful of others, lived within the fort.

Unwilling to have his older daughter reside in the gradually expanding vicus beyond the palisade, Maxentius had instructed that two of the barracks be remodelled to create married quarters. It suited everyone, most notably, Liora's parents.

Claudia was learning everything she could about medicine and healing, under the conscientious tutelage of her mother and Atius — the medicus. At ten and one, Luc — his father's replica in every regard — was a typical rambunctious boy, applying himself to his studies and his friendships with equal gusto.

Hannah leant back in her chair and brooded over the possibility she might be needed. Not the best time to be 'vanishing' from her current life. A husband and two children were her priority now, not her other world. Never mind she had an important guest staying. She swallowed a sigh. She would never deny a plea if issued.

Nothing she could do about it right at this minute.

At that moment, Bryony returned bearing lunch, an effective, if short-lived, diversion.

Knuckling down to her work, Hannah managed to shelve her anxiety until she got home.

In the privacy of their bedroom, Hannah told Max what had happened in the office. Her husband studied her face, reading trepidation in the startling green of her eyes.

"What does this mean? For us?" He enfolded her in his arms.

"As yet, nothing. I have had no pull to go to them since... you know..." she did not need to finish her sentence.

"Dreams?"

"I have them, but they are more like regular updates, snippets of their lives, there does not seem to be anything remotely disturbing. You know as well as I do, there is a dearth of evidence for the era. I am sure if some huge catastrophe had occurred, there would be *some* source material. They weren't illiterate or bad record keepers, as the Vindolanda tablets attest." She shrugged. "I am at a loss. I am hoping if I reach out, Hannah will enlighten me."

Max smiled and kissed his wife with intoxicating deliberation. "Until then, I have a way to distract you."

"Hmmm... you do?" Hannah's pert reply was countered by the wicked gleam in her eyes.

"Minx, yes I do."

And he did.

The anticipated email materialised. The office was quiet. Hannah and Bryony were buried in cataloguing, while Cris was wearing a groove in the path outside, talking to Miles.

It was not that Cris didn't trust Hannah and Bryony, but he had no idea why Miles had rung. It was better for everyone to keep their conversations confidential... for now.

"Hannah, it's here." Bryony beamed her elation across the table.

"Goodness, twenty-four hours. That was quick. What are the details."

Making sure all the firewalls and protective shields on her computer were activated, Bryony clicked on the icon.

The screen went black. The two women held their breath.

A tiny silver dot appeared. Slowly, an intricate yet delicate design reminiscent of a fractal, began to uncoil from the centre. They watched without speaking. When it had half-filled the screen, the vignette vanished, to be replaced by the depiction of an ancient manuscript, bound by gold ribbon.

The scroll unfurled and, as though someone was reversing the effects of invisible ink, words appeared in elegant copperplate. Reminded of a certain map in a popular book, Hannah joked.

"How very…"

"…Harry Potter," Bryony finished for her.

Fans of both books and movies, they exchanged a grin, then read the instructions.

The Auction
Date: Saturday 18th July
Time: Arrive by 6:30pm for a 7pm start.
Venue: Hardington Manor, Cumbria.
RSVP: Without Delay

The 18th was a week on Saturday, which gave them plenty of time to ensure everything was in place. They did a search for Hardington Manor. By a stroke of luck, it was about an hour's drive from the museum.

The minimal collection of photographs online showed what appeared to be an abandoned, seventeenth century mansion, crumbling under decades of neglect. Hidden from the road by a dense barrier of trees, it stood far enough off the beaten track to deter the inquisitive.

"Perfect place to host an event of this nature." Bryony tapped her chin.

"We need to arrange a car for Cris. I don't want anything to be traceable to one of us. It might be an idea for him to hire it from the airport. That way, if anyone feels the need to check his movements it would fit the scenario that he's recently arrived from overseas."

"Good plan. I'm accepting this invite as requested. The sender will know it's been opened." Bryony hit the appropriate arrow and dashed off a suitable reply.

Once they heard the ping of the email leaving the outbox, the two women watched to see whether they would receive an acknowledgement.

Nothing, nothing, nothing... then... as Bryony was about to close out mail, they got their receipt. With less flourish, but repeating the silver swirl, a modest *thank you* appeared.

"It's done. Wow, this one feels more... I dunno... dicey isn't quite right... unpredictable maybe?" Bryony couldn't put her finger on what was different about this auction.

"I know what you mean," Hannah agreed. "Maybe it's because we know the buyer. Up 'til now they've been anonymous. People organised by Miles. People we had no contact with, never mind, met. I'll go find Cris. See if I can have a quick word with Miles."

She left the office in search of their Italian guest.

Hannah found Cris on one of the benches near the car park. He was winding up his call and she asked to speak with Miles if Cris didn't mind.

"Not at all." He gave her his phone, with a "later Miles."

He made to leave, allowing her to talk in private, but she

waved at him to stay. "You may as well wait and listen, that way I don't need to repeat myself," she said.

Cris grinned and resumed his seat.

"Miles," she greeted. "We're in." She caught Cris' eye and nodded. "We received the invitation and Bryony has replied." She mentioned their plan to hire a car and buy a pay-as-you-go phone.

"Great idea, Hannah." Miles agreed to her proposal without question. "I'll have one of my guys create a passenger manifesto to include Enzo's name, in case they feel moved to probe further."

"Is this support chappie still coming?" she asked.

"Yes, I'll make sure he's there by midweek. His name is Quentin Taylor. I'll get him to call you between now and then to introduce himself."

There was a loaded pause.

"Miles?"

"I feel I should give you a heads up. Quentin is old school. He thinks any and all investigations ought to be carried out in-house. He usually refuses to collaborate with outsiders, however qualified. He was dead set against the whole thing until he heard about Cris' involvement, which prompted him to suggest there ought to be a rep from our office too. You know, joint cooperation and all that."

"Joint cooperation? What are we, Scotch mist? Wait, are you saying he'll interfere? Scuttle our scheme?" Hannah's voice took on a cool edge, prompting Cris, to mouth 'What?' She replied in the same manner, 'I'll tell you in a sec.'

"Nooooo..." Miles dragged out the word, and Hannah could picture his expression. Rabbit trapped in headlights, came to mind.

"Don't stress, Miles. We'll figure it out," she consoled. "He does know not to mess with us, right?"

Miles' sigh whooshed down the connection. "He does.

Not saying that'll stop him trying but he is, under protest, prepared to acknowledge you and Bryony know what you're doing.

"Goodness, I'm flattered."

"No need to be sarky," he tutted. Now..." They chatted a moment longer, fine tuning one or two details, then ended the call. Hannah handed the phone to its rightful owner.

"Thanks, Cris," she smiled. "I feel relieved and on edge."

"I understand. Until we have that artefact in our possession, I do not think I will rest easy."

"I am glad it's you," she said cryptically.

"May I ask what you mean?"

She blushed a little. "You are exactly the right person to have on side for this kind of thing. I know this isn't our first rodeo... time doing this," she clarified at his visible confusion, "but I feel..." she paused, "...apprehensive, as does Bryony. Not sure I can explain it. It's nothing concrete. More a sensation, a subtle awareness of something on the periphery. Something ominous, sinister even."

"Hannah if this is frightening you, please do not feel obliged to continue. The last thing either Miles or I want, is for you to feel in any way vulnerable. None of this is new to me. I deal with it in one form or another every day.

"Yes, you have solved a few cases for Miles, but this one is atypical. Trust me. I know how scary the people dealing in stolen artefacts can be. They make the Mafia look like a group of kindergarten children on a day out at the zoo."

Hannah giggled at his analogy. "I'm not scared as much as unnerved. Almost as if something else entirely is going on." She shrugged. "Never mind, it's probably nothing."

For no reason Cris could think of, Tomas Durante came to mind. A man who believed in the vengeance of the dead. He shook it off.

"Okay, but promise me that if this becomes too much, you

will tell me." He held her gaze, until she bobbed her head. "Good girl." He grinned and the two trailed back to the office, where they briefed Bryony about the telephone conversation with Miles.

Drenched in sweat, Cris bolted upright, momentarily disoriented. *Where was he?* Then he remembered. He was in his bedroom, in a cottage not far from Hadrian's Wall. He flung back the covers and got out of bed, padding over to the window to stare out into the inky darkness.

The air was still, not even the hint of a breeze.

The dream lurked, taunting him.

For much of his life, Cris had found an untroubled sleep, elusive. He put it down to an over-active imagination, exacerbated by hours of studying historical documents, some of which were fiendishly gruesome.

Until recently, his dreams were nothing more than fragments of information, like watching a movie on fast forward. Since arriving in Northumberland, they had increased in frequency and were becoming more detailed.

This was the sixth night in a row that his sleep had been disturbed.

It never changed.

Fractured sensations, fleeting images, a pervading sense of abject terror and loss, maybe even grief. Stifling heat, the stench of sulphur, and a ceaseless roar. Moonlight glinting across an expanse of black water, its subdued glimmer illuminating a flotilla of assorted boats which keeled alarmingly on choppy waves.

A man stood on a wooden jetty. He seemed to be in

charge but, of what, Cris could not fathom. Around him, people shouted and pleaded, but Cris could not decipher their words. Over the cacophony, he heard a voice. One he was drawn to, felt he ought to recognise, along with the oddest impression he was being summoned, deliberately.

The roar became deafening. A thick cloud of something impenetrable engulfed the scene and the voice was drowned out.

In that instant, the setting changed, morphing into an idyllic rural landscape. He was approaching a Roman fort, bustling with soldiers, merchants, and local tribespeople. It came to him that this was his home. He entered the huge wooden gates, and people greeted him, deferentially.

A young woman was crossing the central quadrangle. She glanced in his direction. Her face lit up and she headed towards him. Her dark blonde hair was caught in a neat plait, her grey eyes sparkled. His heart thudded. This woman was vitally important to him.

She was almost in his arms...

...and he woke up.

The dream never varied.

Generally pragmatic — an essential trait in his job — Cris also accepted there were things beyond his comprehension.

The world of ancient Rome was littered with curses and superstitions, rituals, and omens. One in which he immersed himself at every opportunity, and the reason he was here in Northumberland, but it was also a world which retained much of its mystique.

Modern historians took pains to provide rational justifications, but it was widely accepted that some things might remain inexplicable.

. . .

Cris felt confined. Shrugging into a pair of jeans and a T-shirt, he slipped silently down the stairs and out through the door leading to the back garden. Barefoot, he walked up the slight slope to the wall, the cool grass between his toes, reassuringly normal.

He perched against the stones and looked up at the sky. The stars were out in abundance; so far from urban pollution, they seemed close enough to touch. The serenity of the night, at odds with his inner turmoil.

Cris let his thoughts roam. The dream badgered his brain.

The first part seemed ephemeral, more an echo than anything substantial. *What did the ghost hunters on those American TV shows call such phenomena? A residual haunting, a moment trapped in time, destined to play on repeat.* Someone long dead, still desperately trying to send a message or relay a warning. Not something in which he was directly involved.

The second half was more... tangible. He felt a strong connection to the person through whose eyes he had become a spectator to the daily life of a fort. He chuckled quietly at the fantastical direction of his thoughts, then gave a very unmanly squawk when a voice spoke out of the darkness.

CHAPTER 12

"Can't sleep?"

"Hannah, you nearly gave me a heart attack," Cris remonstrated, catching a gleam of white when Hannah grinned unrepentantly and came to balance on the wall next to him.

"Sorry. I ask again… can't sleep?"

Cris did not answer immediately. "Something like that," was all he offered.

"Wanna talk about it? Is it the auction? Are you concerned?"

"No, not about that. While I deplore the idea, I am reduced to bidding on an artefact which by rights should be safely in a museum, the method of reacquiring it does not daunt me. No…"

Hannah, who knew more than he realised, went out on a limb. "Is it anything to do with Magnis?"

His head spun around. His expression wary. "Why would you ask that?"

There was a protracted silence.

"Do you want me to be honest, or would you prefer I fabricate something to soothe your mind?"

He swivelled to face her, leaning his hip on the rough stone. "I believe you English have a saying: honesty is the best policy." He quirked a brow.

"We do, but I ought to mention, my honesty might freak you out."

Those perplexing moments when Hannah seemed distracted by something unseen, popped into Cris' head. *He knew there was more to this woman than met the eye.* "I believe I can handle it." He smiled slightly.

"Okay, so how about this. I tell you something I believe will help, and you tell me what bothers you. Deal?"

"Deal," Cris agreed.

"Two people in our world are privy to this information, and only one of them knows the full extent. The sole reason I feel it necessary to reveal this part of me is because I think you will benefit from the knowing. Something is stirring and, in this case, a lack of awareness might prove detrimental to the outcome."

Hannah's enigmatic comment piqued Cris' curiosity. *Our world? What did she mean by that?*

"What I am about to disclose requires three things." She held his gaze.

He dipped his head in acknowledgment.

"Do you trust me?"

"I do," he answered without equivocation.

"Are you prepared to listen with an open mind?"

"I am." He hid a smile. It sounded as though he was affirming wedding vows.

"Do you promise never to speak of this to another soul, unless I grant you permission?"

By now, Cris was so interested in what she had to say, he

would have agreed to run naked through the Forum Romanum. "I promise."

"Are you okay to sit out here or would you rather go indoors?"

"Here's fine, it's not cold… unless…" He did not need to spell out his inference.

"I'm warm enough. Let's grab a chair though, this may take some time. Good job it's Saturday tomorrow, well today actually." She winked.

They made themselves comfortable on two of the patio chairs. Cris watched Hannah corral her thoughts. Then she started to speak, and the story she told him all but blew his mind.

Riveted, Cris lost all awareness of place and time while Hannah wove her tale. It bore all the hallmarks of a Hollywood movie, or a paranormal television series, yet he knew without an iota of doubt this was no fantasy.

By the time she finished, his head was spinning with the ramifications of what her knowledge could do for ancient history.

There was a strained hush when Hannah fell quiet, one neither speaker nor listener felt the need to break. The plaintive hoot of an owl as it flew over the cottage heightened the surreal atmosphere.

Although Cris had perceived there was something different about Hannah, to hear her calm description of a life two thousand years in the past took some swallowing.

He questioned whether this was a continuation of the visions which stalked his slumber and, closing his eyes, pinched his thigh in an effort to wake himself up. Opening his eyes, nothing had changed.

It was still dark, and Hannah had not moved.

This was no dream.

The quiet lengthened

"To be clear, your mind melds with another woman's, also called Hannah who lives... lived in the first century AD? You witnessed the aftermath of the massacre of the Roman garrison on Masada, subsequently marrying one of the soldiers whom you also healed? You travelled to Pompeii where you worked with gladiators and saw Vesuvius erupt? Then came here to Hadrian's Wall?" His incredulity was unmistakeable.

Hannah gave a low laugh. "Hadrian's Wall as we know it wasn't constructed for several decades. None of the main forts we see today existed when we... she first arrived." Hannah caught herself. "Not even Vindolanda, it's construction began five years later."

She sought to elucidate. "I did not *physically* do any of those things. I don't leave here and travel back in time. We... she and I, connect at a subliminal level. The simplest way to process it, is to think of it as being on the lines of second sight in reverse.

"I cannot predict my future but am able to inform my ancestor what is going to happen in the past, in her era. I see, feel and hear everything she sees, feels, and hears but her actions, emotions and so on are hers not mine."

Hannah saw the bewilderment in Cris' face.

"I know how hard this is to digest. It took a long time for Max to accept what happens is not because I ate cheese before I went to bed, or my vivid imagination or some weird out of body episode resulting from the head injury I received on Masada.

"It *is* far-fetched, preposterous, and ludicrous but, whatever anyone says, I know it to be real. I have lived," she made air-quotes at the word, "more than a decade with my ancient family, even though I never left the modern world."

"Why have you trusted me with this?" Cris ventured. "You barely know me.

"Before I answer that, will you tell me why you can't sleep?"

Cris nodded slowly. "I did agree to enlighten you." He provided a synopsis, fleshing out details as Hannah pushed him to describe the scenes and any people therein.

Her intuition correct, Hannah shocked her guest. "I think you are connecting with my ancient family. Wait..." when Cris started to splutter a strenuous denial. "...the other day you called Bryony, Senna, and you are dreaming about an, as yet unidentified, woman. One with whom your dream-self shares a profound emotion, which I know to be love.

"Senna is the wife of Gnaeus Marcus Aelianus, my... Hannah's... adopted brother and Maxentius' second in command. She is not Roman. Her family are local tribespeople. She worked for Hannah, through whom she met Marcus."

A trifle unsettled to hear Hannah speaking of people long dead, in the present tense, Cris rolled the name around in his mind. "Senna..." A face swam across his vision, a delicate countenance pulling at something deep within. It was the face from his dream. "How...?"

"I cannot tell you. What I *do* know is, it is not related to some earth-shattering event... equivalent to the massacres on Masada, the eruption of Vesuvius, or me believing Max had been killed. This is something else entirely, and thus far remains out of my reach. Even my other self has no idea, but…" There was the other matter, but Hannah was concerned it was an exposure too far.

"What?" Cris demanded.

"Marcus has seen you."

"I'm sorry… how can he have seen me? He is, was, lived," Cris did a swift calculation, "one thousand, nine hundred, and twenty-five years ago."

"The day you arrived, and we showed you Carvoran… Magnis. He saw the three of us. He described us to Hannah."

"I am confused. If I am this Marcus, or he is me, how am I seeing things through his eyes, but he is not seeing this world through mine?" Unable to credit he was having this discussion, Cris rose from the bench and began to pace. Back and forth, back and forth.

Hannah said nothing.

"What about Bryony?" he bit out.

"I am loath to say." Her reticence was obvious.

"Really? Why stop now?" For the life of him, Cris could not mask the faint jeer in his voice.

"It is late, and you are tired. Perhaps in the light of day, you may wish to revisit this conversation. Mark my words, Cris. Whatever is about to happen affects all of us, but mainly, you and Bryony. Whether it is for good or for evil, I am unable to distinguish, nothing save a repressed anger." Her voice was flat, hard, with the merest hint of disappointment.

"Do you think me a fool? I know how bizarre it sounds. Do you suppose the telling is straightforward? That I enjoy sounding like a crazed loon…"

"No one dragooned you into telling me. I didn't need to know," he sniped.

Hannah carried on as though he had not interrupted. "… but I believe the more information you have the better able you are to handle what is to come. And yes, you do need to know," she moderated her tone. "Your life could depend on it."

She got to her feet. "Try to get some rest. We will talk again tomorrow." Hannah stared at him for a long moment, then walked away.

Cris watched her go, hearing the metallic click of the latch when she closed the back door.

He felt like a heel. He had been rude to his hostess, a woman he already considered a close friend despite their brief acquaintance. A woman who — if her story was to be believed — in a previous life was as a sister to him.

He ruminated over their conversation.

Farfetched though her account was, it rang with veracity. For a start, Hannah could have kept it secret and allowed him to go on thinking his dreams were just that... dreams, not a portent. She had risked more than a burgeoning friendship to tell him.

For a split second, he wished he had never agreed to Miles' proposition. *Wait, was* he *the other person who knew? Was that why he trusted Hannah implicitly?* It was possible. Another thought emerged. If he had not come to the wilds of Northumberland, he would not have met Bryony.

His head whirled. Thoughts, images, and emotions careened around his skull. In an effort to calm his mind, he looked up at the sky, wondering, absently, who else was admiring the celestial display.

How did all this affect or relate to Bryony? Did Hannah think she was this Senna person, or was that pure coincidence? His brain scorned the theory. Bryony's remark about being descended from the Border Reivers came back to him. *Was it possible her heritage went further back... much further back?*

Exhausted and confused, he trudged back to bed, trying to come to terms with the fact that everything he knew had been summarily tipped on its once logical head.

Magnis - AD 91

"Marcus, wake up."

Marcus felt a hand on his shoulder, rocking him. He ignored it, but the quiet voice was insistent.

"My love, wake up. You are having a nightmare."

Groaning in resignation, Marcus rolled onto his back and peeled his eyelids open. Senna's face floated above him. He mumbled something unintelligible, his mouth not yet connected with his brain. His wife repeated her plea and this time her words registered.

"Nightmare?" he griped. "That is an understatement."

He sat up and stared around the room. It was still dark. Fingers of moonlight filtering through the slats in the shutters.

"Aelia,"

"She sleeps, you have not disturbed her."

That mollified him, but the nightmare did not recede, tormenting.

"Shall I bring you some of Mabina's tea?" Senna asked.

His lips were dry. He nodded and, while his wife disappeared to locate said tea, made a concerted effort to pull himself together. His dreams had taken on a malevolent tone.

What had seemed a tenuous and, he hoped, fleeting link to an unfathomable world was mutating into something which might spiral out of control.

He did not want to burden Senna, but not telling her went against every instinct. *How would she react?* His heart ached at the notion of shattering her perceptions, of ruining what she thought was inviolable.

Once she knew, there was no going back. Everything changed. Even if you tucked it out of the way at the fringes of your mind, you could never lose it. Never return to that moment before the words were uttered.

Perhaps if he told her while Hannah was with them, it might be less confronting. Maxentius' presence would help also; he knew of Hannah's connection. They could answer Senna's questions — and he knew she would have many — far better than he was able.

Still, he vacillated. *Was it fair?* Senna's world was enviably simple. Even though her people had been party to strife, she hardly recalled it. The peace which had prevailed for almost two decades had lulled the populace. Another thought nudged at him… *was it about to be ruptured?*

At that moment Senna returned with two beakers of tea. Marcus sipped the warm drink, welcoming the diversion from his darkening thoughts.

"Tell me," Senna entreated, kneeling in front of him, and leaning against his legs.

Marcus began to shake his head.

"Please do not pretend it is nothing. This is not your first nightmare. Your slumber has been broken of late. You think I do not know how often you get up to roam our quarters?"

"Aelia…"

"…is not the reason for your insomnia. I concede, if she

wakes, she settles quickly in your arms, but she is not the cause. Marcus, you are exhausted. Your temper is fraying. My love, do not shut me out."

Marcus speared his fingers through his hair, as Senna reached out to grasp his free hand, her dove-grey eyes searching his.

Lifting their joined hands, Marcus kissed her knuckles and, holding her gaze, said, "I love you, my Senna. I promise I will tell you, but would you be offended if I asked you to wait until the morrow? I believe Hannah and Maxentius ought to hear what I have to say." He stopped, unwilling to enunciate why. "Trust me?" He made it a question.

"I always have, and I love you too. Here." Senna took his beaker and placed it on the little table beside the bed. Inching closer, she angled her body until her lips met his. "Time to sleep," she kissed along his jawline, hearing his sharply inhaled breath.

She smiled in the gloom. That she elicited so immediate a response to her touch a decade since they had first kissed, never failed to thrill her.

"But first…" light fingers tiptoed down his body.

With a guttural growl, Marcus halted her provocation. "Senna," he husked.

"What?" Her eyes gleamed wickedly.

"It is almost dawn."

"And…?" Her free hand teased over his naked chest. Capitulating, not that there was ever any doubt, Marcus swung her around, his hands and his lips weaving their seductive magic until she was begging for mercy.

Uncaring that the household would be rousing, but mindful of the sleeping infant, husband and wife lost themselves in each other and Marcus' nightmares were banished for a little longer.

CHAPTER 13

I t was mid-morning before Marcus had the chance to talk to Hannah.

"I must tell Senna, Hannah. I think part of the reason for my disturbed rest, is because I am keeping this from her."

Sympathetic to his quandary, Hannah affirmed she would be happy to offer any support he needed.

"I am prepared to tell her, if you think might be better coming from me." She smiled up at the tall man.

"I feel I ought to be the one…" His expression proclaiming, he would be happier to face wild animals in the arena.

"Perhaps we both take a part," Hannah proposed, gently. "Between us, she might gain a better understanding without feeling the urge to run for the hills."

She pressed her point home. "Remember how it affected you? To try to persuade someone that I share a bond with a descendent who lives centuries in the future is both a challenge and a risk. It undermines your whole belief structure, and I suspect could cause insanity.

"I have been fortunate indeed. When I told Maxentius, he accepted my words to be the truth, as did you. Unimaginable though it sounded, you knew I would never deceive you, or speak in falsehoods. Let us trust Senna knows this too."

"Shall we discuss it after *cena*?" Marcus suggested, referring to their evening meal.

"I think that would be best. We have call on our time during the day, and this is a discussion which ought not to be rushed. Moreover, the younger children will be in bed and out of hearing range. I shall ask Liora to invite her sister to their quarters. Claudia is not ready to be acquainted with this facet of her life yet."

Arrangements in place, Hannah sped over to the hospital, while Marcus joined his commander in the principia.

Remnants of the meal removed, their goblets refilled with calda, four adults made themselves comfortable around the low table in the triclinium. An air of anticipation enveloped the quiet room. Marcus glanced at Hannah who inclined her head.

He faced his wife and took her hand. "Senna, you asked me to tell you the details of my nightmares." He waited until she nodded, her gaze darting between the three sitting around the table.

"I am party to a secret, one which I have not been courageous enough to impart. In truth it is not my secret to impart, but circumstance has left me no option. I asked you last night whether you trust me. I repeat my question now. Senna, do you trust me? Do you trust us?"

He waved his hand to include Hannah and Maxentius.

At his words, Senna paled. She tried to disentangle her fingers, but Marcus refused to let go.

"Why am I beset with an irrational compulsion to run away?" she whispered.

"Because I think you have always known there is something of which you have not been apprised. Something you chose not to question for fear the answer would be too terrifying to comprehend," Hannah interposed. "Senna, have I ever given you reason not to trust me?"

"No," her reply although quiet was firm.

"I acknowledge what you are about to hear will sound as though I am narrating a tale from myth, but it is not fiction. I am the catalyst, the one with whom the connection is made. Marcus' dreams indicate another thread is unravelling."

Senna stared at Hannah, utterly mystified.

"All I ask is that you listen carefully and hold your questions until I have concluded." Hannah gave her listener a warm and loving smile. "I would prefer not to encumber you, but I believe Marcus will need your strength before this is over."

"You think I am strong?" Senna sounded dubious.

"Of course. You are one of the strongest women I have ever met." Hannah's words were upheld by swift agreement from the two men.

Marcus drew Senna into his embrace. He felt the apprehension in her body and his heart ached. "I love you," he said in undertones.

She moved her head slightly, so their eyes met — rich brown on smoky grey. "I know." Her lips curved in a sweet smile.

Facing Hannah, Senna straightened her shoulders. "I am ready."

Hannah closed her eyes and sent out a plea. Awareness seeped in as her other self merged, hovering on the threshold of her consciousness, imbuing her counterpart with the necessary fortitude.

Gathering herself, she began to talk. For only the third time — in this era — Hannah unveiled her dual lives. How her descendant, who lived two millennia in the future had somehow connected, sharing what she knew to keep them safe, without changing history.

The last time she had spoken of her other life, more than the odd occasion with Maxentius, was when she told Marcus, in Pompeii. That was over a decade ago. Much had happened since then, not least being the troubles which had plagued the fort during their first year at Magnis.

Inevitably, this meant the tale was lengthy, and emotionally taxing. When Hannah finished her account, she was trembling. Maxentius held her hand throughout, his thumb rubbing her palm, a gesture which never failed to comfort.

Nobody spoke.

Senna gawked at Hannah, her eyes rounder than the platters from which they ate their meals. She shook her head and nipped her skin to determine whether she was indeed awake. *Perhaps this whole thing — including her husband's nightmares — was naught but her own bad dream.*

She spotted Hannah's lips twitching.

"What is so funny?" She pinned her friend with a piercing look.

"I did exactly the same thing the first time I was witness to the past."

"This... wait... you are the other Hannah? Speaking through..." Senna croaked, blanching. She started to stand, then thought better of it. Her legs were wobbling. She sank back onto the sofa, clutching Marcus' hand like a lifeline.

"Forgive me, Senna. I had no mind to frighten you. We... your Hannah and I... deemed it necessary to divulge what we are, what we know. Please understand, while our minds fuse, that is all. In basic terms, your Hannah gains an extra sense, and I am privileged to be part of your lives, if only temporarily.

"Yes, it is confounding, but it is also an honour, for which I shall remain forever grateful. This is the first time we have joined, other than subconsciously, since the day Hannah's children arrived at Magnis with Maxentius' mother.

"Various factors, primarily my being here, corroborate my conviction that what is about to happen involves Marcus, and a man of my time called Cristiano. Your Hannah and I have yet to fathom what this is, but my heart tells me it will be soon, and that there is an element of danger. There is also an underlying rage, but I cannot determine its source."

Not quite steadily, Senna rose and walked to where Hannah was sitting. Balancing on the edge of the table, she scrutinised the woman who had become as a sister to her. "What do you look like?" she asked. Intent on tracing Hannah's face, her hand lifted then dropped back onto her lap.

Stretching around Senna, Hannah plucked the larger of two coils of papyrus off the table. Unrolling it, she handed it to the younger woman. "Here." She indicated the etchings.

Recognising the artist, Senna glanced at Marcus, then back at the drawings. They were astonishingly life-like. She studied the illustrations carefully. The taller of the two women depicted — who were wearing the oddest attire — resembled Hannah, but there were subtle differences, specifically her height and her hair.

The second woman was diminutive, her hair short and spikey. There was something infuriatingly familiar about her stance and her features, but Senna couldn't place them.

She looked up to see Hannah watching her. "This is the other you?" She pointed at the taller figure. Hannah nodded. "Why do I feel I know the smaller woman? Listen to me... I cannot believe I am having this conversation." Her stupefaction was obvious.

The other three chuckled.

"What?"

"We have all said the exact same thing, on more than one occasion," Maxentius spoke for the first time. "I think it was less problematic for me than for either of you. When Hannah confessed her duality, I already knew there was something different about her. Initially, I presumed her words, the way she phrased certain things, her curious terminology and unusual responses were because of her upbringing."

He had no need to elaborate, Senna knew Hannah was trained in Jerusalem by her physician uncle and had lived among rebels.

"Her explanation, when it came, while outlandish in the extreme was also plausible. Everything clicked into place. Moreover, her knowledge has saved us numerous times. If not for her future self, none of us would be sitting here."

Hannah beamed at her husband, and he twinkled back at her, their love a tangible thing, undimmed since first they met.

"Returning to your question. What about this woman teases at you?" Hannah asked.

Senna twisted the papyrus this way and that, hoping changing the angle would help. Her nose crinkled in concentration, and it took great effort for Marcus not to kiss it.

Unexpectedly, the face of the woman was highlighted by the glow from the oil lamps.

"Not possible," Marcus gasped.

A wave of relief washed over Hannah — persuading him of her suspicions might have been a trial.

"What?" Senna repeated, slightly embarrassed that this seemed to be the only word she could formulate.

"She is you, or you are her, or…?" He swung an astounded gaze from Senna to Hannah.

"I think you are correct. I think this is why you have connected with Cris. I am of the opinion that he and Bryony, yes that is her name, are your descendants. Similarly, my Max and I are descendants of your Hannah and Maxentius."

The sheer convoluted nature of her two worlds and how to discuss them with any coherence, made Hannah want to laugh. It never got easier. "I expect there are things you wish to ask or require clarifying," she invited.

Hesitantly, more because she was unwilling to sound foolish, Senna soon relaxed and interrogated Hannah in the manner of a soldier grilling a captive. Dazed by her new-found knowledge, nevertheless, Senna realised she was not unduly ruffled.

"Did I not say you were strong?" Hannah reminded when the barrage of questions came to a halt.

"I am glad you think so." Senna smiled. "I admit to a sensation of falling, you know the way it is sometimes in dreams when you plummet to the earth but wake up in that split second before your body slams into the ground."

"*Yes!*" the other three stated, in unison.

For no apparent reason, this caused a bout of merriment… and the tension dissipated

Annant appeared to ask whether they would like more refreshments — which they did — and, by tacit consent, their conversation moved onto other things.

Before saying their goodnights, something Hannah had said prompted Senna to one last question… for now.

"Hannah, you said there is an element of danger. Are we in danger? Our children…" A hint of dread laced her tones.

Hannah, her future-self retreating, pondered that for a

moment. Ever honest, she replied, "While I am not certain, my instinct tells me the danger is confined to the future. I would never wilfully place you or your children in jeopardy, Senna."

"I know, it is just…"

Hannah drew her friend into a warm hug. "Have a little faith in me. I cannot stop what is happening, but I am not reckless, especially where the lives of my nearest and dearest are concerned. Go, sleep well, and try not to worry. If you want to talk tomorrow, you know where to find me."

She kissed Senna's cheek, and pushed her gently towards Marcus, who slid his arm around his wife's waist.

"Come, my love." He smiled his thanks over his shoulder at Hannah and Maxentius, and the couple headed to their own wing of the residence, talking quietly.

"I hope I did the right thing, telling her," Hannah said when the connecting door swung closed.

"As far as I can see you had little choice. I know you dislike sharing your link, but in this instance it was imperative. If Marcus is to play a part, Senna should be made aware. Not enlightening her would be unfair.

"I know…"

"Enough now, it is time we sought our bed. You cannot untell her. It is done. Try not to fret. Senna is a sensible woman, not disposed to mania. You asked her to trust you, you need to afford her the same courtesy." Maxentius' practicality settled Hannah, as he knew it would.

Thanking Annant, who appeared to clear the table, Maxentius ushered his wife to their chambers.

Soon, the huge building was quiet, its occupants lost in slumber.

CHAPTER 14

At breakfast, Hannah behaved as though her night-time conversation with Cris had never happened. She was her usual blithe self, chatting about their weekend plans, while making sure the twins didn't wear their food.

For the time being, Cris let it lie. A revisit was essential; he had many questions, but he had no mind to upset the Valliers. He reckoned Hannah would broach the subject when she was ready. When she handed him a plate of eggs on toast, she held his gaze, and he was reassured by what he read in her expression.

"Coria today?" she suggested, while they sipped a second cup of tea. This was the fort on the outskirts of Corbridge, also known as Corstopitum. "I know you missed seeing it last weekend."

"I would enjoy that very much," Cris smiled his appreciation. "If you are sure you can spare the time. I expect your weekends must be precious and I do not wish to monopolise them."

"Of course, we can spare the time. We would be rubbish hosts if you missed seeing as much as possible of the area.

We love exploring. It doesn't matter how many times we go to Coria, there's always something different to see and the twins love it. It's an undemanding site for short legs. Then there's Corbridge itself. Ohhh, I can feel a pub lunch coming on," Hannah replied.

"Lunch? We've barely finished breakfast." Max felt moved to comment.

"Bryony will meet us there," she said airily, ignoring her husband's gentle barb. "Okay, let's get sorted. Meet by the car in ten…" she glanced at Claudia and Luc, whose faces were smeared with egg yolk, "better make that fifteen minutes." She shook her head in mock dismay at the twins who beamed back.

"Come on you two monsters." She helped them down from the table and shooed them out of the kitchen. "Max, please will you stack the dishwasher?" Her request drifted back from the bottom of the stairs.

Mirth playing around Max's mouth, he did as she bade and, with Cris' help, ensured the kitchen was returned to its usual tidy state.

About to follow Hannah, Max paused to face Cris. "I know she has told you. I expect you are besieged by a gamut of emotions ranging from disbelief to frustration to bafflement, hopefully interspersed with a pinch of fascination.

"Let them sit for a while. Give your mind some time to wrap around this knowledge you are privileged to share. How about we discuss it later over a beer?"

Startled at Max's words, Cris found himself nodding.

Max gave a laconic smile. "Great, and I know exactly how you feel. It took me a considerable amount of time to accept what Hannah experiences is real. But it *is* real. Put it aside for now and relax. Plenty of time to deal with ancient families." He gave Cris a brotherly slap on the shoulder and bounded up the stairs after his wife.

Ascending more slowly, Cris felt a strain he was unaware he carried, lessen, Suddenly, he was okay with his new world order... *or was that disorder*? He grinned to himself and, entering his bedroom, prepared for the day.

The weekend disappeared in a flurry of ruins, sightseeing, picnics, and fun. Between them, the Valliers and Bryony organised a variety of interesting activities, without overwhelming their guest.

They took the whole of Saturday morning to wander the ancient site of Coria. Built to protect a river crossing, it went through multiple phases and remained an active fort almost continually, from its construction until the Roman legions were recalled in the early 5th century.

Cris was interested to note that although Claudia and Luc scampered around in the manner of small children, they were deferential of the ruins. He remarked upon it to Max.

"Start 'em young," Max said, good humouredly. "Hannah cannot abide people who don't respect the past. You wouldn't believe how many times I've had to stop her barging in on groups of people climbing walls or helping themselves to bits of tesserae."

He shook his head tolerantly. "She's right, but one day she'll accost the wrong person..." he opened his palms, implying 'and you know how badly that will go', making Cris laugh.

"Yes, I can believe it, but I happen to agree. There's enough damage caused by the weather and mismanagement. We don't need it destroyed further by ignorance. I wish there were more people like you and Hannah. Once it is lost, that is it... no more. We cannot turn back the clock."

As the words left his mouth, images from his nightly

visions surfaced. With an effort, he pushed them back. *Not the time.*

Sunday night, leaning on the window frame, Cris reflected how welcome he felt among these new friends, in this remote landscape, to which he was now drawn.

Italy was his home and, until recently, he could not imagine wanting to live anywhere else.

That said, if Hannah was correct and he was indeed somehow connected to this Gnaeus Marcus Aelianus person, the sentiment was not without foundation.

He had found time to discuss Hannah's revelations in more detail. Bryony had declined Hannah's dinner invitation that evening, citing a prior engagement with an old school friend. Much as Cris missed her company, it provided the ideal opportunity to talk without constraint.

After the meal, and once the twins were in bed, the three adults sat in the garden, chatting over a glass of wine. Hesitant to revive the subject, bearing in mind his heedless comment, he was heartened when Hannah raised it first, acknowledging his reaction was partially her fault.

"I should have been more sensitive when I introduced the topic. It is so much a part of my life, I forget how mind-bending it must be to hear it for the first time," she said ruefully

"I confess, I am still confounded, but your disclosure solved several puzzles.

Hannah arched a brow.

"You thought we had met before. You often seem to be listening to an inner voice. There are moments when I swear you are seeing an entirely different scene from the rest of us. Inexplicable expressions, the odd turn of phrase. Your knowledge about things even the most obsessed historian would struggle to possess. The principal one being that you talk about certain events in history as though you were a participant... which I know now you are... were..." he faltered.

"To be honest, it was as much as a shock to me when I worked out what was going on. Such knowledge can be a burden. One I would not be without, but it is a challenge. I have been privileged to see, take part in some of history's pivotal events, but cannot repeat what I have seen, save with you two and one other," Hannah said.

"There have been times when I questioned whether I was going mad, whether the whole thing was a fantasy I'd conjured up in a moment of delirium. In my head I have lived over a decade with my ancient family, but the time lapse in this world was mere weeks in total. To encumber another is a huge gamble. It stretches the tightest of bonds almost to breaking and could easily be too much to process. Unfortunately, your dreams took the decision out of my hands."

She sipped her drink. "Okay... let's review this logically. We rarely connect more than subconsciously unless there is a significant reason, particularly when it happens during a period of time I know to be relatively peaceful. I am usually the one to whom Hannah reaches out, although Max has met, for want of a better word, Maxentius.

"This time it's Marcus and it's you, which I believe is crucial. The other Hannah cannot figure it out, and Marcus is not only stumped, but also kinda spooked. We have told Senna." She grinned when she noticed Cris' expression.

"Get used to it. This will become your normal." Max

raised his glass in a droll salute, which Cris mimicked. The three fell quiet while they enjoyed the crisp white wine.

"I think we need to delve deeper," Cris, who had been mulling over the conundrum on and off, suggested. "If this scenario is uncommon, then perhaps we need to re-evaluate everything from a different angle. What if it relates to the auction?"

Hannah was about to scoff at this. It was too far-fetched. Something made her swallow her words. She ran her mind back over the last few weeks. Everything had lain dormant until Bryony stumbled upon this latest sale. Even then, nothing untoward had happened until Cris arrived.

"I think it's you," she said forthrightly.

"What do you mean, *me*?" Cris demanded.

"You're the trigger. Whatever this is, has some association, or link to you." She sat back, a satisfied smile playing around her mouth.

"Okay, accepting your premise… not saying I do, necessarily… I am at a loss as to how or why, *I* instigated this. Prior to my arrival, we had never met. I have only been here a few weeks. You have had this connection for years. Is it not more likely that my arrival precipitated something already brewing? Good grief, I cannot believe I am having this conversation," he contended, amazed by his sangfroid.

"You proposed we delve deeper. I think we need to do exactly that. I'll get Bryony on it tomorrow. I'm pretty savvy, but she lives and breathes this stuff."

"What if the reason I called her Senna was more than momentary confusion? Ought we to tell her? To ask her to scour databases without any real reason might seem irregular."

He saw Max and Hannah exchange a look.

"Come on, out with it," he coaxed.

There was a lengthy pause.

"Okay... I apologise now if your brain explodes, but you asked." Hannah winked. "Max and I, are descended through Hannah and Maxentius..."

Cris' face scrunched up into an 'ewwwww' expression.

"...let me finish, and no, it's not incest, sheesh," Hannah chided. "Max is descended though Luc's bloodline, I through Claudia's. There are hundreds of generations between us, it's not like we are cousins." She shook her head in exasperation.

Cris grinned.

"By the same token I fancy you and Bryony can chart your individual family trees back to Marcus and Senna. There can be no other reason for your visions."

Cris' jaw dropped. It was one thing to have a faint suspicion, quite another to hear someone else articulate it unequivocally. He started to reply, then thought better of it.

"What?" Hannah pressed.

"It was something Bryony said about being descended from the Border Reivers. It made me wonder..." he broke off, his reluctance evident.

"Let's not get ahead of ourselves. I might be wrong," Hannah mollified.

"But you do not believe that?"

"Regrettably, no, I do not."

"Neither do I," Max interjected. "I have come to realise, when it comes to her ancient family, Hannah is never wrong. She might not always be in possession of all the pertinent details, but her gut instinct is to be trusted."

Hannah smiled at her husband, and stretched across to take his hand, her heart in her eyes. Max responded with interest.

Cris felt like the proverbial third wheel, whilst wishing he might get the chance to share such devotion with Bryony.

The moment passed.

There was little more to be gained until they had more

information at their disposal, and Max turned their conversation to less dramatic topics.

Monday was overcast, and rain threatened. Once Bryony arrived in the office, Hannah, somewhat circuitously, explained what she needed.

"I know this sounds unorthodox, but please will you map out Cris' family tree. He can get you started with what he knows and then go for it. As far back as possible."

Bryony swung a sceptical gaze between Hannah and Cris. "That could take weeks," she grumbled, miffed. "Isn't it more important to keep an eye on traffic to and from the auction site?"

"Can't you do both?" Hannah quizzed with apparent nonchalance.

"Well, yes, but…"

"So, don't stress. I know you won't neglect our current case, but I think this might end up being of importance and possibly connected. Go for it," she repeated without detailing her reasons.

Recognising her friend's expression, Bryony didn't push it. If Hannah wanted to enlarge on her request, she would.

Going for it, Bryony spent an hour or so hassling Cris in a bid to extract what she could, inputting names and approximate dates of birth onto a spreadsheet. Once done, and despite her grousing, it wasn't long before she was oblivious to all else around her, buried in databases, while occasionally muttering at the screen.

. . .

Sometime in the afternoon, Hannah's mobile chirped in the peace of the office. Grabbing it, blindly, she answered. "Hello, this is Mrs Vallier."

"Good afternoon, Mrs Vallier. My name is Quentin Taylor, and I believe you are expecting my call." The voice was a nasal whine.

Hannah pulled the phone from her ear. Gesticulating to the other two to listen but say nothing, she hit the speaker icon and placed the phone on the table.

"Mr Taylor, how lovely to hear from you. Miles did mention that you are travelling up for the auction." She glanced at the other two and gave a 'what else can I say?' shrug.

"I am leaving London tomorrow. I have booked a room at Langley Castle. Perhaps we could meet at your offices on Wednesday morning, say ten?"

"That sounds perfect." Hannah smothered her astonishment at his choice of hotel with aplomb. Langley Castle was magnificent. Max had taken her there for their first wedding anniversary, a gift he repeated every year.

While a marvellous place to stay, it was rather grand for a government employee who surely ought to be less extravagant with the budget.

As though he had read her mind, Mr Taylor remarked, "I have stayed there before, the staff know me. Moreover, it is a good cover. Hiding in plain sight so to speak." His tone was nothing short of snippy.

The staff know you, do they? Very la di dah. Oh boy it's going to be a long week. Hannah rolled her eyes. "I am sure you are well versed in protocol, Mr Taylor." Was all she could think of to say in response. Before he had chance to counter her comment, she affirmed they were looking forward to meeting him on Wednesday and hung up.

"Well," she exclaimed, "he sounds…"

"...like a right pain in the butt," Bryony finished with a pained grimace. "Why couldn't Miles be the one to come up? He's cool."

Hannah nodded absently, her mind churning over the upcoming days.

Cris, on the other hand, felt a pang of irrational jealousy. He caught Bryony's eye, heat creeping up his cheeks. He looked down and studied the desk, *he was worse than a lovesick teenager*, only to feel cool fingers skim the back of his hand. He lifted his head to meet her shrewd tawny gaze.

Bryony didn't speak. She had no need to. Her eyes told him all he needed to know.

He was wholly unable to stop the goofy grin which spread across his face.

CHAPTER 15

Mr Quentin Taylor duly arrived at Langley Castle Hotel on Tuesday evening, where he was greeted with warmth. Shown to his favourite room, he settled in, unpacked, and opened his laptop.

Waiting for it to boot up, he pondered the next few days. He would need all his wits about him, surmising this Mrs Vallier and her sidekick were no slouches.

Quentin's lip curled. He did not expect the Italian fop to obstruct him, but if he did... well, there were ways to deal with minor irritations. His screen came to life and he tapped at the keys, activating multiple pages.

He navigated through each one, meticulously checking and double checking. Half an hour later, he closed each tab in a specific and pre-arranged order, satisfied his instructions had been carried out to the letter.

Placing the computer, along with one or two other items in the safe, he punched in his usual code. Pressing the door closed, he waited to hear the satisfying whir of the mechanism as it locked.

A glance at his watch, and he changed into his workout

gear. An hour or two in the gym was just the ticket after a day's travel.

Bryony was elated. So far, she had mapped Cris' heritage to the sixteen-hundreds. Her task expedited because once she had gone back a few centuries, the family did not appear to move beyond the tiny village in the hills outside Rome.

Someone, and Bryony was in awe of their dedication, had painstakingly uploaded every single recorded birth, marriage, and death, into an internationally renowned and vast database.

The more she searched, the more interested she became. Some entries had extra snippets of detail, such as — Antonio Rossi died on the 23rd day of January 1632; cause: froze to death during winter storm, or Luciana Toiati died in child-birth on the 14th day of August 1596.

The human element spurred Bryony on. She had to be careful because of mis-spelled names or the occasional dupli-cate entry, but it was riveting and created a narrative about life in the remote rural community throughout the generations.

Her search was aided by the fact that, historically, there were a limited number of residents. The population of the village fluctuated, and had multiplied in modern times, but the further back she went, the fewer the family units.

With Vincente — Cris' brother — acting as translator she had been privileged to talk to Cris' grandparents, who were excited to be included in her investigation. It transpired they possessed a swathe of documents, of which Vincente had generously taken photos and emailed to Bryony.

She was secretly thrilled to have spoken with members of his family. It added another level to Cris, another layer peeled back. Unsure how far she would be able to go, Bryony persevered. It would take time, but she had no intention of giving up.

Wednesday morning saw the trio in the office by half past seven.

Hannah had woken around dawn, the upcoming appointment with Quentin Taylor playing on her mind. Seemingly, Cris was equally disquieted, for he trudged into the kitchen a little after five.

"Morning." Hannah waved her cup but didn't move. "Want coffee? It's fresh."

Cris nodded with a weary smile. "I'll get it." He poured himself a shot from the Moka pot on the stove and topped it up with hot water. "I need more than an espresso," he explained at Hannah's inquiring expression. "Or at least, this will slow down my caffeine intake for the day."

"This meeting is plaguing me," Hannah admitted, after a few moments of quiet during which the coffee began to work its magic.

"Me too, although I can't think why it should. From what Miles told me, I have seniority of rank over this Mr Taylor, yet I am of the opinion he delights in lording it over those to whom he is assigned."

"That was my feeling too. Miles was a bit circumspect in his caveat. Reading between the lines, I'll hazard Quentin Taylor might try to override our authority." She shrugged. "Nothing we can do until we meet him, but..." she didn't need to finish her sentence.

"Agreed." Cris sipped the aromatic brew. "This coffee is delicious."

"Italian." She beamed. "Of course. We order it from this excellent coffee place near the Pantheon. It became our favourite the first time we visited Rome. We drop in at least twice a day when we're there. Best coffee."

"Don't tell me… Antigua Tazzadoro?"

Hannah gaped. "How could you possibly guess that?"

"It's one of my favourites too."

The pair chatted about other eateries scattered across the Eternal City, while Hannah pottered around the kitchen preparing breakfast. Cris was surprised to discover how many both were familiar with.

"You certainly get the most out of your holidays there," he observed.

"It's Rome." Hannah said, which was answer enough.

Max appeared and joined the conversation. By the time they had eaten, the twins were rousing, and Hannah went off to see to them. The two men dealt with the pots and re-laid the table.

The clock chimed six-thirty.

"Fancy going in early?" Hannah asked, coming back into the kitchen, Claudia on her hip, and holding Luc's hand. "I want to be prepared. Not sure why, but I do."

"Absolutely," Cris replied.

"That okay, Max?" Hannah checked with her husband.

"'Course." He smiled. "I'm here all day." He tickled Luc who chortled with glee.

"Me too, me too," Claudia pleaded.

By the time the twins had munched their way through breakfast, Hannah and Cris were at the office.

.   .   .

Shortly after, Bryony arrived travel mug in hand. "Seems none of us could sleep." She chortled.

"It's this guy." Hannah stopped. "I don't know why he's bothering me, but he is."

"Don't stress, let's wait and see. Three against one, we'll be okay. He needn't think he's taking over. Liaison that's all he's here to be. Nothing more." The light of battle glinted in Bryony's eyes, inspiring some good-humoured ribbing from the other two.

With nearly three hours before Mr Taylor was due, they got on with the business of the day.

Bryony was making decent progress with her search although it was becoming more difficult the further back she went. This was inevitable because there were lengthy periods when records were sparse. Bryony wasn't discouraged. If anything, it acted as a motivator.

In his hotel room, Quentin Taylor studied his reflection. Looking back at him, a man of above average height, with close cropped, wavy, dark-blond hair, wearing a charcoal grey suit, snowy white shirt, and a flamboyantly patterned silk tie. A vain man, Quentin admired what he saw, aware he looked good for his age.

Dropping his phone into his briefcase, and room card into the breast pocket of his jacket, he picked up his car keys, and left. The drive to the museum took less than half an hour, and he was pleased to find a parking spot in the shade.

He retrieved his phone, about to call his contact, when a voice hailed him.

"Mr Taylor?"

He turned to see a woman strolling towards him, a welcoming smile on her face.

"Yes," he replied with little warmth.

"I'm Hannah Vallier. Pleased to meet you." She stretched out her hand in greeting.

"Quentin Taylor and the feeling is mutual." He shook her proffered hand.

Hannah led him through the side gate, into the administration block and upstairs to her office, where she introduced him to Cris and Bryony. She watched the latter's face carefully, wondering whether she too felt her skin crawl when their palms met.

To a casual onlooker, Bryony seemed unmoved, but Hannah caught the slight pinching of her friend's eyes, oddly heartened she wasn't the only one adversely affected by this man's touch.

Once all four were supplied with a good strong coffee each, they discussed the auction.

"Piece of jewellery for this one, Miles reckons," Quentin stated.

"Apparently so. Usually, the invitee receives an emailed photo of the item, the morning of the auction. It's viewable for about fifteen minutes then automatically deletes," Bryony affirmed.

"This is not my first auction. I expect to be here when the email is opened."

"I hardly thought otherwise," Hannah intervened placidly, spotting Bryony's affronted expression. "What are your suggestions for the auction itself?"

"Firstly, neither of you two can be there." He pinned Hannah and Bryony with a flinty glare. "It is only because Miles deems you trustworthy, that I agreed to this farce. This is Art Squad business, not a job for women working in historical archives."

Bryony opened her mouth to object, but Cris spoke over her, smoothing the very ruffled waters.

"We understand and acknowledge your consternation, Mr Taylor," he placated. "Nevertheless, I must remind you, had Bryony here not been monitoring activity on the dark web, this auction and the subsequent two, would have passed us by. Perhaps we would be better employed developing a plan of action for Saturday evening, instead of arguing over who should and should not be involved."

He held Quentin's gaze, trying to ignore a jostle of unease.

"Fair point," Quentin acceded, grudgingly. "My apologies ladies, I had no mind to offend."

Like hell you didn't, Bryony groused inwardly. "Whatever. I have work to do. Doubtless, Hannah will update me with any pertinent details later."

She looked at Hannah, who dipped her head. With as much of a flounce as she could achieve, bearing in mind she was seated, Bryony snatched her iPod, stuffed in her earbuds and turned her back on the three at the table. Family trees called.

Hannah bit her lip, to disguise her mirth. Bryony did not suffer fools gladly and Mr Quentin Taylor was proving himself to be a consummate fool in temperament. Hopefully, he was less so when doing his job.

"Right, let's get on with it." She bestowed on Quentin a dazzling smile, causing that man to blink.

Diverted, the newcomer outlined his plan for the auction.

Attempting to conceal a squad of policemen around the venue was impractical, the probability of detection, too great. Typically, the organisers engaged a small army of security to keep away unwanted visitors or nosey parkers. Those attending, did so because their anonymity was guaranteed. The last thing the auctioneers wanted was either to lose their clientele, or have their event plastered all over social media.

Secrecy was key.

Quentin gave a litany of dos and don'ts, his tone patronising. It was plain he thought them simpletons instead of the highly qualified and astute people they were.

Catching Hannah's eye, Cris shook his head imperceptibly. He could tell she was cross at Quentin's attitude, but it was better to let it lie than take umbrage. The man would be gone by the end of the weekend. It was not worth the surge in blood pressure.

Cris had years of experience dealing with men of Quentin Taylor's ilk, and he wasn't intimidated in the slightest. He preferred to let them think they were superior. It made it all the more fun when they were brought down to size.

Presuming Quentin might be more forthcoming without her presence, Hannah excused herself and, motioning for Bryony to follow her, left the office.

"I'm sorry, but the man is a dickhead," Bryony huffed, as they headed down to the cafeteria, "and he gives me the creeps."

"I know what you mean," Hannah replied slowly. "I can't work out what it is about him, but..." she let that dangle. "Come on, I'll treat you to a slice of Edie's luscious lemon cake, if it hasn't all been snaffled by this lot." She waved her hand in the general direction of the other offices.

"Yummo, thank you," Bryony whooped, and the two put Quentin out of their minds for the next little while.

Cris was doing his best not to punch the visitor. Only his friendship with Miles stopped him. That Quentin believed himself an expert on all things relating to the peddling of stolen artefacts was plain, and nothing Cris suggested was suitable or credible.

In the end, Cris shut up and let the man talk. Quentin wasn't the one entering the fray, so to speak, that was Cris' job. It was his photo and his backstory Bryony had uploaded, not Quentin's.

His mind wandered... straight to Bryony. Saturday evening marked the official end of his time here. There was no legitimate reason for him to extend his visit, but he didn't want to leave.

Since their first kiss in Sele Park, the two had spent many hours together. They scarcely knew each other, but to Cris, there was something tantalisingly familiar about Bryony.

There had been no declarations of undying love, but it underwrote every kiss, every touch, every glance. They had not slept together but their desire, their passion was undeniable.

Not prone to flights of fancy, and regardless of Hannah's theory that he and Bryony were somehow linked to an ancient couple — implying their connection was inevitable... *damn* — Cris believed he had found his soul mate. *But what did Bryony believe? Did they have any chance of making a long-distance relationship work? Did he **want** a long-distance relationship?*

They hadn't discussed anything beyond the auction, but Cris wasn't blind. Not only was he intensely aware of Bryony's every mood but also, he would have to be a total idiot to have missed the sadness which occasionally swept over her expressive face, or the shadows lurking in her striking eyes.

A nasal voice penetrated his thoughts. Cris pushed everything else aside for now and applied his concentration to the discussion. Certain aspects of Quentin's plan sounded a bit dubious, prompting Cris to throw out a few questions, and demand further detail, which Quentin provided without discernible rancour.

Even so, one or two statements did not fit the scenario the liaison was presenting. Cris couldn't be sure whether it was his own imagination playing tricks because they seemed too random, but they badgered him throughout the conversation.

Making a mental note to mention them to Hannah, or even Miles, Cris was content to let Quentin talk uninterrupted.

CHAPTER 16

Quentin left the office mid-afternoon. When the door swung closed on his retreating back, there was a sense of equilibrium being restored, of being able to breathe easily again, liberation almost. In itself, mildly disconcerting.

"Okay then," Hannah broke the silence. "Errrr... nope... no words." She looked at the other two, her nose wrinkling, partly in indignation and partly in amusement.

"I am exhausted," Bryony grumbled, "and I hardly said two words to him. It's as though he's sucking the life out you."

"I am inclined to agree." Cris flexed his tired shoulders and ran a hand around the back of his neck, kneading tight muscles. "The man is draining. I..."

"What?" Bryony entreated at his hesitation.

"I am not sure. I am going to think out loud if you do not mind?" He was rewarded by two heads nodding. "He does not approach the assignment, or mission or whatever you wish to call it, sensibly. For a man who purports to do things by the book, and who thinks we are out of our depths, his

strategy lacks cohesion. If I did not know better, I would…"
he paused again.

Those disturbing niggles which had pestered throughout
the morning, the ones that refused to be dismissed,
coalesced. No. Surely, he was overreacting, inventing problems which weren't there. Then again, if his fears were
realised, they might all be in grave jeopardy. *Porca miseria, this
was the last thing he expected.*

"What?" Hannah echoed Bryony.

The women looked at each other and shrugged. Cris'
genial expression had transformed into a sombre mask.

"Cris, what?" Hannah reached across the table to press his
hand.

He lifted his head, suddenly aware of the quiet room. "I
am afraid to enunciate what rattles me. What is that saying?
Hmmm… if you eliminate the impossible whatever is left
must be the truth, however improbable." He cocked his head.
"That is correct, yes?"

"Yes, but what is improbable?" Bryony quizzed.

"That Quentin is involved."

"Well, of course he's involved. He's the department liaison. Probably their go to guy for these auctions, but this
time… oh." Hannah's brain caught up with her mouth.

"Quite," Cris said.

"Come on, people. What are you talking about?" Bryony
wailed.

Cris swivelled to face her. "I think the reason we have
failed to apprehend the organisers, or at least their front
men, in the act is because they were tipped off."

"By whom?" Bryony was puzzled.

"Quentin Taylor," Cris and Hannah answered in unison.

. . .

135

"Oh. My. God." Bryony gawked at the other two. "No way. God's Gift? Nah, he wouldn't have the balls."

Hannah chortled at Bryony's flippant description.

"God's Gift?" Cris was completely at a loss.

"Yeah, ya know... up himself."

Cris' bemused frown gave Bryony the giggles.

"Sorry, I forget you speak proper English. So, God's Gift, means you think you are irresistible, primarily to the opposite sex. In our esteemed Mr Taylor's case, it has made him preen like a peacock, while expecting us to wait with bated breath for the pearls of wisdom to drip from his oh so perfect lips." She fanned her face dramatically. "Basically, a dickhead."

"*Testa di cazzo*," offered Hannah helpfully, "or possibly, *segaiolo.*"

Cris stared at his usually polite hostess, who pulled an impish face.

"Hannah..."

"What, you think I am too refined to swear? You should hear me when I stub my toe."

Bryony who had been privy to Hannah's stream of expletives many a time, chortled. "She could teach most guys a thing or two."

"I am simply stunned you know how to swear in Italian."

"It's such a beautiful language to curse in. It sounds so lyrical, my victim usually thinks I'm giving them a compliment," she quipped.

"I still say it's not him. He wouldn't risk anyone messing up his face," Bryony stated. "Crap, what if it's Miles...?" She looked at the other two in horror.

"No, Max has known Miles since uni. He's honest as the day is long. Max told me, he once turned himself in at his local police station because he'd driven through a red light by accident, in the middle of the night. The road was completely empty, but he wasn't happy until he'd confessed. Even thought he ought to be fined." Hannah palmed her forehead. "Trust me, it's not him."

She thought for a moment. "It would explain him choosing to stay at the Castle. No way would Miles' department stump up for that bill when there are plenty of cheaper and eminently suitable places hereabouts. Hang on."

She dialled Miles' number, relieved to find he was still in his office. She put her phone on speaker.

"Hannah, good afternoon, what's up?" Miles sounded surprised. Hannah never called him unless it was important.

"Is this line secure?" she asked.

"No. Why?" His tone sharpened.

"There is something we need to discuss, and I don't want anyone, anyone at all *overhearing*," she emphasised the last word.

"Give me five minutes. I'll ring Cris' number." The line went dead. The three looked at each other. Bryony felt ice slink down her spine, as foreboding gripped her.

"This is bad," she fretted.

Cris rested his hand on her knee. "I promise no harm will come to you, either of you." He held her gaze.

She felt heat wash up her cheeks and bent her head. Uncaring that Hannah was right there, Cris cupped her cheek, lifting her face until their eyes met once more.

"I promise." He leant across the gap and brushed his lips to hers. "I would die before I let anyone or anything hurt you."

"Cris, I..."

Whatever Bryony was going to say was swallowed in the shrill ring of Cris' phone. "Later," he mouthed.

"Miles?" he answered on the third ring.

"Go outside the building, all of you," Miles instructed.

They trooped into the car park.

"Okay, we're nowhere near anyone," Cris affirmed.

"Good... now what's up?"

As if he was discussing nothing more exciting than a shopping list, Cris explained their qualms. "I trust my instinct, Miles. It has never led me astray," he said as he concluded, "and currently it's on high alert. Quentin Taylor might not be the brains behind this ring, but he's definitely involved."

Miles did not reply immediately.

The quiet lengthened.

Hannah, for want of something to do, picked up a leaf and twirled it in her fingers.

Cris remained motionless, phone in hand.

Bryony wanted to scream.

Miles' bitter sigh was heard by all three. "You can't be serious? No, wait," before Cris could respond, "yes, I know you are serious. This is nothing to joke about."

His listeners could envisage Miles' expression. The knowledge that one of your own has been playing both sides. The gross breach of trust. Worst of all, the loss of numerous artefacts and the years of meticulous work evaporating in front of your eyes.

"Sorry, Miles," Hannah spoke quietly. "This stinks, and maybe we're jumping to conclusions..."

"But you don't think so?"

"No, and it is better to assume the worst and be proved wrong, than the other way around," Cris observed. "If he's innocent, then there's no harm done."

"God dammit, Quentin's been in this department for years. He's like a fixture, you know. The guy who could be relied upon to dredge up the details without needing to check a file or a database. The one who remembered the odd twists from old cases. The names of the culprits, how they were linked to the underground. *God dammit,*" he repeated, and they heard the loud slap of a palm hitting something solid. "How do you want to play this?"

"I think we ought to carry on as though this conversation never happened. Treat Quentin as your liaison, while we make a counter plan. I can't believe he hasn't slipped up before now. It must be exhausting behaving in the manner of a trusted employee for his day job, knowing he is doing the exact opposite behind closed doors." Cris sounded almost impressed. "I wonder what possessed him to do it?"

"Greed," Bryony interposed. Cris glanced at her. "Gotta be," she shrugged. "What other reason could there be? If he's not the head honcho, he'll be getting a massive kick back for passing on information."

"I'm going to have to start looking at all the cases with which he's been involved," Miles groaned. "This could take years."

"Pleeeeeeease let me help," Bryony piped up, sensing an opportunity.

"I take it, on top of your suspicions, our Mr Taylor has failed to make friends," Miles said dryly.

"He's an ars... idiot," Bryony amended.

"I know he's stuffy, but until today, I thought he was honest. I am..." Miles stopped speaking. "Okay," he continued after another lull. "I'll ask Todd to start digging at this end. Bryony, if you don't mind running some checks, but please, and I cannot emphasise this enough, *please* be careful. If he is who you think he is, he knows he will be subject to some kind of surveillance, and how to cover his tracks. Do not, I repeat do not, underestimate him."

"That's the last thing I'd do," Bryony asserted. "I'm used to people like him. In fact, I think I detest him less now I know he's a crim. Catch ya." She waved at the phone and sauntered off whistling a cheery tune.

"Lordy, now you've done it," Hannah said. "You know how she gets when you gift her a riddle."

"The proverbial dog with a bone." The hint of a smile in Miles' voice, hardened slightly with his next words. "Watch her."

"Fret not," Cris said. "Don't worry about us, Miles. We'll keep you informed."

"Anything else… and please, do not feel obliged to add to my woes," Miles asked, tongue-in-cheek.

"Not yet," Cris replied, his lips twitching.

"Maybe I need to come up."

"We'll be fine. Quentin has no clue we are onto him. I reckon, he thinks we are next to useless, so we'll use that to our advantage. Go home, have a beer," Hannah suggested. "It's late so there's nothing we can do 'til tomorrow anyway."

"Keep me in the loop. We'll use this method."

"Where are you?"

"In a phone box, a street away from the office." Miles chuckled. "Okay, talk tomorrow?"

"Absolutely."

Cris heard the dial tone as Miles hung up. Hannah and he stood without speaking for a moment or two, each lost in thought.

"I need a drink," Hannah broke the quiet.

"Me too," Cris agreed, perhaps a trifle too eagerly, prompting Hannah to laugh softly.

"Let's find out what Bryony is up to, then I think we call it a night. Come at this fresh tomorrow," she said.

Bryony was in a world of her own, her earbuds in, swaying gently to whatever music was playing. Hannah went round to the other side of her desk and waved over the top of the computer.

"Yep?" Bryony removed the earbuds expectantly.

"Home."

"But…"

"No buts, we've done enough for today. Come round to our place for dinner?"

"I'd love to. Give me…"

"Nope, we're done. We can hash this out later. We deserve a break."

A glance at Hannah's expression told Bryony there was no point arguing. In truth, she was tired. No — more wearied, from Quentin's visit and Cris' subsequent epiphany. *Dang, it was so much more straightforward when their involvement was from a distance.* She packed away her laptop, then gathered the cups and went to wash them, while Hannah shut down the computers.

The door secured, the three trudged back to the car park.

Shortly thereafter, they were sitting on the Valliers' terrace sipping chilled Peronis and nibbling on Hannah's favourite chips and dips.

It wasn't long before the four adults were dragged into silly games by Luc and Claudia. Their ridiculous antics were the perfect diversion, and for a while the lurking anxiety was extinguished.

To Cris' badly concealed delight, Bryony was invited to spend the night. A relatively common occurrence, since

Hannah and she often worked late.

When the twins were babies, Max had decided a bedroom downstairs might be useful. Somewhere out of earshot one parent could take the babies if they woke at night, reducing the chance their cries would disturb the other.

Purloining the small room adjacent to his study, he managed to find a sofa-bed to fit the space, then had a plumber install a basin. Although basic, it was comfortable and had been a godsend during the twins' first year.

No longer required for its original purpose, it had become a useful emergency bedroom. Hannah, contending that you never knew when the need might arise, had persuaded her friend to store a few days' worth of clothes and necessary toiletries in the linen cupboard — just in case.

Given the times Bryony had stayed over, it was a behest merited and appreciated. It also meant she could relax and have a second beer, without worrying about being over the limit to drive home.

Hannah and Max retired early, but Cris and Bryony stayed in the garden, savouring the mild evening air. Although pale at the horizon, above them, the sky was fading through shades of pink and purple to the darker blue of the encroaching night.

"I find it hard to believe how peaceful it is here." Cris had slung one arm around Bryony's shoulder, tucking her against his body, their heads touching.

"I know. It must be strange for you, coming from Rome, where I daresay it's never quiet."

"At certain times of the year, very early in the morning, before the delivery trucks begin their rounds, the city is almost empty. I like to walk along the Tiber or past the Forum towards the Colosseum to watch the sunrise. Better still, Herculaneum. To witness the sun bleeding light into the ruins is spectacular. You really ought to visit."

"Is that an invitation?" Bryony teased.

Cris twisted to face her. He studied her dainty features, her sparkling amber eyes and cheeky grin. His heart gave a jolt, as the emotion which had been taunting him from the day they first kissed, took root.

"A visit will never be enough," he said gravely, stroking her jawline with a gentle finger.

"Errrr..." Bryony gulped, lost in the rich, dark brown of his eyes.

"I love you, Bryony Emerson." The words were out before he could get his brain into gear. *Merda, that was precipitous.* He held his breath.

Bryony's eyes widened in shock and her jaw fell open. "You do?"

"I do." His expression indicated he expected her to doubt his admission.

A wide smile began to form, and she shuffled around to straddle his legs. Bending slightly until her left cheek skimmed his right cheek, Bryony's lips grazed the lobe of his ear.

"I love you, too."

Cris jerked backwards, his face a picture.

Bryony's smile sent tingles right down to his toes.

Gently, he drew her close until their noses brushed before stealing her lips.

His kiss — sweet and seductive, tender and fierce — was a beginning, a future, a lifetime.

It might not be easy. They had much to resolve, not least their jobs and where to live, but suddenly, none of that mattered. For now, it was enough that they had dared open their hearts... if it was meant to be, everything else would fall into place.

CHAPTER 17

T he two days prior to the auction were crowded.

Buried in the bowels of numerous databases, Bryony was balancing three separate yet interconnected investigations. The one pertaining to Cris' family tree, the one relating to Quentin, and the one concerning the auction.

On Thursday morning, Cris and Quentin discussed their plan of action, but by lunchtime the latter excused himself. It appeared he preferred the amenities of the hotel, to doing his actual job — not that any of those left in the office were complaining.

While Hannah appeared to be busy archiving and cataloguing, her brain was focused on how to outmanoeuvre Quentin. Not necessarily within the bounds of the law, it must be admitted.

The biggest concern for Cris was Quentin's role in the auction. If, in fact, he was the brains behind the whole thing, how did he ensure the artefact went to his chosen buyer? Were the bids themselves fraudulent? It was a reasonable assumption. Miles had confirmed Quentin was, to some degree, involved in every operation during the past two decades.

Yes, some of the artefacts had been recovered and, either returned to their rightful owners or loaned to a museum, but the majority had not. To Cris, that meant Quentin was allowing the department to win enough that they didn't question the loss of those they missed out on, too rigorously.

He really wanted to know what was being auctioned on Saturday. His, or rather, Enzo's initial bid had been £11,000. A significant sum for something they had yet to see, bearing in mind the actual item might be worth less than half that.

An aggrieved sigh wrested his thoughts back to where he was currently sitting.

"Something wrong?" He glanced at Bryony, who was glaring daggers at her screen.

"It's this Quentin guy…"

"What about him?" Hannah spun in her chair.

"He doesn't exist."

"What, he's a figment of our imagination? That's a relief," Hannah sniggered.

"No, silly. Well, he's figment all right, but of his own imagination."

That caught the attention of the other two.

"Please explain," Cris begged.

"Superficially, even digging down two or three levels, Quentin Taylor is as he appears. Fifty-seven years old, he joined the police at nineteen. Fast-tracked into the detective division of the Met from where he was noticed by his superiors. Invited to join Interpol, he was seconded to the Art Squad shortly after.

"It all looks perfectly legitimate, until I ascertained that the Quentin Taylor with whom we are purportedly liaising, died thirty-nine years ago."

Bryony's dramatic announcement was worthy of a BBC murder mystery.

Cris and Hannah gaped.

"No way, you're joshing us," Hannah said with a nervous giggle.

"Joshing?" Cris quizzed, for want of something to say.

"Joking," Bryony clarified.

"Craaaaaaaaap," Hannah groaned. "Miles will have a conniption."

"Connip… never mind." Cris brushed aside the second incomprehensible word in less than three seconds to demand, "Okay… can you substantiate this?" He moved his chair alongside Bryony's.

She talked him through her findings.

At first, Cris could not see how Bryony had come to her conclusion. All the details matched the record Miles had sent. Date and place of birth, National Insurance Number, education, parents, friends, jobs, everything.

"I am confused. How does this tell us he is not who he purports to be?" Cris was lost.

"Because I believe *this* is the real Quentin Taylor." With a flourish, Bryony hit a key and a picture filled the screen.

Cris stared.

"Let me see." Hannah came around the table.

The image was slightly out of focus and, clearly not a recent photograph.

The man depicted, was not unlike Quentin. All three studying the image knew eye and hair colour could be altered, but to overcome age and disabilities was extremely difficult. The individual was not young and looked to be suffering from some kind of wasting disease. His body was twisted, and he was in a wheelchair.

· · ·

There was an odd hush.

"Oh, the poor man," Hannah whispered, sorrowfully.

"He died in 1976, aged forty-eight," Bryony elaborated.

"Double crap," Hannah wailed. "Dammit all, this is a great, big, enormous mess. Are you sure, Bryony? This couldn't be a simple coincidence?" She knew the answer before she finished asking. Bryony didn't rely on guesses when it related to work stuff.

"As sure as I can be. Our Quentin has combined their statistics ingeniously, at least those that are searchable."

"Wait, before we start panicking, he doesn't know *we* know. Bryony, what is Quentin's real identity? The Quentin we have here, I mean. There are discrepancies. Why were they not picked up during background checks? For instance, if our Quentin was born in the same year as that guy, he would be..." Cris did some rapid maths in his head, "... eighty-seven, not fifty-seven. Do you think it's possible to unearth who he really is?" he asked.

"Of course. I just need a bit of time." Bryony grinned.

Cris looked at his watch, it was coming up to two o'clock. "Okay, we may need to stay late tonight if you want to let Max know." He caught Hannah's eye. She nodded and picked up her phone to ring her husband.

"Best not call Miles until we have everything," he added.

"Nothing spoiling," Bryony said, distractedly, replying to his unspoken question.

They hunkered down.

Hours ticked by. Coffee was drunk and replaced, drunk and replaced, until Hannah remarked they would be flying before long. Someone thought to run down to the cafe before it closed to fetch a pile of sandwiches. Still they worked.

The sun set, lights came on, the building fell silent.

"Got him," Bryony's gleeful declaration pealed around the quiet room.

Too tired to move, Cris and Hannah raised their eyes from what they were doing and waited.

"His name is Timothy Bryce Lawton. He *is* fifty-seven and grew up in a tiny village on the south coast." She grinned. "Want to know more?"

"Yes," the other two chirped in unison.

"Okay, our luverly Mr Taylor has been very diligent, all but eradicating his alter ego's existence."

She pointed at the photo she had shown them earlier. "This is the only image I can find of the real Quentin Taylor. I was ferreting about in the newspaper archives around where *our* Quentin allegedly grew up, wondering whether there was any connection between him and the real Quentin.

"You know, why *thi*s man? Why steal *his* identity, particularly given the difference in ages? From what I can figure out, people usually find an old grave of someone who died at birth and create a new identity from that." She shook her head.

"Anyway, by sheer fluke, I came upon a brief article about this guy." She waved at the screen. "It transpires, the original Mr Taylor inherited a fortune from an uncle, who had made it big in mining, or some such thing.

"The substantial residue of which, after his medical bills were paid, was bequeathed to the son of his best friend. The *only* person ever to visit him in the hospice. Bet you can't possibly guess who that visitor was?" she posed slyly.

"Timothy Bryce Lawton," her audience chorused.

"The very same."

"How did Miles not uncover this?" Hannah wondered out loud.

"Because Quentin... Timothy... is your consummate mastermind. Probably using a similar method as I did when I invented Enzo here, he invented Quentin. He blended his own details with that of Mr Taylor. To a certain extent, the early life of the man in the photograph mirrored Timothy's, even down to the schools they attended, despite the decades separating them.

"All Timothy had to do was delete what didn't fit, and doctor the rest, so it appears legitimate, even to an extensive and detailed search. Bingo. Mr Timothy Bryce Lawton becomes Mr Quentin Taylor. It's not too difficult if you know how. It also explains why he can afford to stay at places like the Castle."

"And how he has stayed under the radar for so long," Hannah observed. "He's a ghost."

The three stared at the grainy photograph as though somehow all the answers would leap out of it. While intriguing, Bryony's discovery didn't address the more urgent issue as to how they were going to thwart Quentin's intentions at the upcoming auction and put an end to his trade in stolen artefacts.

"I need to talk to Miles," Cris muttered reluctantly.

"Leave it 'til the morning," Hannah suggested. "We're exhausted. Let's sleep on it. Maybe overnight one of us will get a brainwave."

Making sure everything was switched off, and the building secured, they trooped out to the car park.

"You gonna stay over again, Bryony?" Hannah asked when they reached the cars.

"You sure it's not an inconvenience?" While the invitation was too good to resist, Bryony felt she ought to make a token objection.

"Don't be daft. No point driving all the way to your place this time of night." Hannah grinned. "Leave your car here, too."

Bryony nodded, so drained she couldn't be bothered to form an argument.

Warned by Hannah of their imminent arrival. Max served up a crisp chicken salad accompanied by a glass of white wine. The three devoured the meal almost without tasting it, updating Max on their findings between mouthfuls.

The latter felt a nagging unease at what they had uncovered. He was conversant with the tactics these shady groups used to disguise their existence. He needed a chat with his wife when they were alone.

For now, he listened, asking questions here and there until he had the whole story.

The dark red numbers on the clock mocked him. Four a.m. — it would be dawn soon. Frustrated, Cris flung himself back onto the pillows. He had been tossing for well over an hour, watching the minutes tick over. He had tried all the tricks, but sleep eluded him, disturbed, yet again, by his recurring dream.

Instead of fighting it, he gave into wakefulness and let his thoughts stray. Inevitably they circled the last few weeks. So much had happened, not least being informed he was linked to an ancient ancestor. He felt a grudging smile tug at his lips.

Oddly, the connection was growing on him. Fascination regarding his past had overtaken the consternation he was losing his mind. Especially when he reflected on how insouciant Hannah and Max were on the subject.

His night-time visions had become substantive — like a computer software upgrade was the best definition Cris could think of — crystallising the physical aspects of his counterpart.

Perhaps not quite comfortable with the other man in his head, he was definitely less perturbed. *Marcus*, Cris corrected himself. Names gave their *relationship* a substance hitherto intangible, veiled by the centuries.

They shared certain traits. Their facial characteristics were the most obvious and marked them as kin, despite being separated by hundreds of generations.

They used identical mannerisms. Although his voice could not be mistaken for Marcus', their inflections were not dissimilar. He knew what Marcus was going to say before the latter realised he was going to speak.

The depth of emotion he, Cris, had for Bryony mirrored Marcus' love for Senna. Yet there were enough differences that one would not be subsumed by the other.

Being somehow linked to a man who had lived centuries in the past, no longer fazed him. On the contrary, it was congenial. He couldn't explain it to himself, and so simply accepted the premise.

He had to tell Bryony. Whatever her reaction, he could not keep something so elemental hidden. Worst case scenario, she would freak out and sever their budding romance. It would crush him, but it was better now than later. He hated secrets. Secrets destroyed trust.

Slivers of light glimmered through the chink in the

curtains. Dawn was breaking. Pushing back the bedclothes, Cris donned a pair of jeans and a t-shirt.

Padding silently down the stairs, he paused momentarily outside Bryony's door. The need to hold her in his arms, to kiss her, to trace her shape was almost palpable. An ever-present ache. He raised his hand to knock, then lowered it to his side. It was unfair to wake her. She had been slaving away over her computer for days.

Unlocking the back door, Cris stood on the threshold and stretched, breathing in the cool, slightly damp, morning air. Heading across the garden to the wall, he made himself comfortable on the cool stone to watch the world revive.

Far to the east, the first hint of the sun's rays cleaved the mauve-hued sky. Overhead, the greyness slowly yielded to a dusky pink and the last of the stars winked out.

As far as the eye could see, life was being breathed into the land. The sun broke the horizon, its golden beams rekindling the earth, gentle as a lover's kiss, and no less profound.

Movement caught his attention. He turned to see Bryony coming towards him. He blinked; not quite sure she was real. Her flimsy dressing gown creating the illusion she was an apparition. An hallucination induced by his desire.

Then she touched his arm and the sentiment fled. Neither spoke. Words were not needed. He held her gaze, ebony on amber. Drawing her close, Cris moulded her slender body to his, tangling his fingers in her silky hair. He tilted her head and their lips met.

He heard Bryony sigh, as her arms slid around him. Cupping her butt, he lifted her until she was able to hook her legs around his waist. She clung to him, scattering kisses wherever she could reach.

He recaptured her lips, and their kiss went on and on and on.

Passion simmered, but by sheer force of will, Cris kept it at bay. Not yet.

All around them, sounds of the morning pierced the quiet. The avian chorus tuned up. The distant hum of a tractor. Still, they kissed.

Eventually, Cris lifted his head

"Bryony," he husked. His all-consuming hunger exposed in that one word.

"Cris," she replied, her tone matching his.

"It's a good job our hosts are less than twenty feet away. I am possessed with the most ardent need to take you right here," he growled.

"Oh my, good sir, what a to do." Bryony placed the back of her hand against her temple and batted her eyelashes, making Cris chuckle. "It may please you to know, *I* am possessed with the most ardent need to let you." Her legs tightened around his waist and she shimmied provocatively.

"Bryony," Cris croaked, her gyrations undermining his scarcely held control.

Abruptly she released him and before he could stop her, was standing on the ground.

"Later." She promised. "Let's get the sonofabitch, then you can seduce me until I'm screaming your name." She blew him a kiss, hitched up her dressing gown and ran lightly over the grass.

Shaking his head at her sass, Cris waited until his body obeyed instructions and followed her indoors.

Only then did he register he had missed his opportunity. Blaming Bryony's bewitching body and mind-blowing kisses, Cris made a mental note to talk to Hannah before day's end.

CHAPTER 18

Bryony stood in the shower luxuriating in the jets of water pummelling her body, while replaying that breathtaking embrace. The indefinable familiarity of his kisses taunted her. She was at a loss to explain it.

They had not met prior to a month ago, and the idea he might remind her of an old boyfriend, made her want to gag — particularly the latter two, neither of whom had covered themselves in glory while dating her.

No, it was as though they knew each other on a subliminal level. To most, implausible, but Bryony believed in reincarnation. She reckoned what most people called déjà-vu were memories of a past life.

Of late, her dreams had reinforced her belief, specifically the man attired in the garb of a Roman soldier, who evoked in her a raft of sensations equivalent to those Cris elicited.

The only explanation, however irrational, was that they *had* been lovers in a former life. A notion which made her body zing.

Conceding her work with ancient artefacts, not to mention tracing Cris' ancestry might be augmenting her already fertile imagination, Bryony was not convinced her dreams were flights of fancy.

Their frequency had increased, and even when aware she was asleep, Bryony swore she had actually travelled into the past and was interacting with the people around her, not merely an onlooker.

Bryony towelled herself dry, infusing practicality into her brain. Dreams or visions were merely a manifestation of daily activities. Surely, a *lack* of them would be more surprising, bearing in mind her recent assignments.

None of this was enough to erase the inkling, however irrational, there was way more to the episodes playing out in her sleep than met the eye.

As had become their habit, Hannah, Bryony, and Cris were at the office well before seven thirty.

Coffee brewing, computers on, and databases open, the room fell quiet. They only had twenty-four hours until the auction and no plan in place to catch Quentin.

Cris' chance to talk to Hannah came mid-morning, as they drove to the airport to pick up the hire car.

During a lull in their conversation, he jumped in with both feet... figuratively, of course.

"Hannah, I need to tell Bryony."

Hannah shot him a startled look, then nodded slowly. "Okay, I guess that's only fair."

"I dislike keeping secrets and this one is beginning to weigh on me. Moreover, you indicated I might be a catalyst. If this is true, I do not want her to be caught unawares."

Hannah pulled into a parking space, switched off the

engine, and turned to face him. "Take my hand," she said, holding hers out.

He did as she bade.

For a few seconds there was nothing. Then a sequence of events began to unfold, like a waking dream, rushing through his mind, too fast to interpret. Just as he began to feel dizzy, Hannah relinquished her grasp.

"We are in agreement. There is malice afoot, but neither of us can pinpoint its origin. That said, Marcus believes it is close, a conclusion he reached because he is becoming more aware of you."

"Strangely enough, I concur with his opinion." Cris struggled to credit he was discussing what was essentially a miracle, as if it was an everyday occurrence.

"We, Hannah and I, have told Senna. She accepted our revelations with remarkable aplomb, bearing in mind the era in which they live. I think for her, it answered a number of seemingly inexplicable factors relating to Marcus, and my other family."

"Likewise. While half of my brain continues to insist this whole thing is nonsense, my heart knows it is the only credible interpretation for what I am experiencing," Cris agreed. "And why it is vital Bryony is told."

"How about we persuade her to stay at my place again tonight, and tell her then?" Hannah proposed. "That means there's three of us who have first-hand knowledge of this phenomenon. Hopefully, she won't think we're all barmy."

Cris, nodded, divining the meaning of her last word from its context, allowing himself a grin at the idiosyncrasies of the English language.

Hannah spotted it. "What's so funny?"

"Your colloquialisms. They are very weird."

Hannah rolled her eyes and pulled a hideous face. "We do pride ourselves on being weird."

Cris guffawed. "You are incorrigible."

"I know, isn't it fun?" She winked. "Come on, this hire car won't drive itself."

Locating the appropriate desk, the paperwork was dealt with in short order. Keys and the signed agreement handed over, it wasn't long before they found the car, at the far end of the designated row.

Entering the office, they were met by a sullen silence. Quentin was there, his ramrod-straight back and immaculate attire at odds with the casual ambience. He was perusing the file they had collated pertaining to the auction.

Hannah sent up a prayer of thanks that anything sensitive was either locked in the safe or, if online, protected by multiple passwords and Bryony's firewalls.

Bryony's face was darker than a thundercloud, and she was jabbing at the keyboard. A sure sign someone had riled her.

"Coffee anyone?" Hannah asked brightly.

Two heads turned.

One smiled politely. One looked morose.

"Ahh, Hannah that would be very welcome." Quentin shot a snide glance at Bryony, an oblique indication her colleague hadn't offered one.

"Bryony? Give me a hand?" Hannah requested, and looked at Cris in appeal. He grinned in acknowledgement and asked Quentin a question about the auction. The two men fell to chatting immediately.

Bryony shoved back her chair and stalked out of the

room, her nose in the air. Hannah was hard pushed to keep a straight face.

"Okay, what gives?" Hannah demanded, the minute they reached the privacy of the kitchenette.

"He's a tosser," Bryony ground out. "Swans in, all 'so what's the plan? Where are your colleagues? Not the time to be taking a break', blah blah blah," Bryony mimicked Quentin's twang with added petulance.

Hannah pressed her lips together, feeling a giggle threatening. "Don't let him get to you, hon. Yes, he's an asshat, but we only have to put up with it for another day. With any luck, by midnight tomorrow he'll be in handcuffs.

"He'd probably get a kick out of that," Bryony's face contorted into fierce scowl.

Hannah snorted, unable to restrain her mirth. "Bryony Emerson, you are priceless. Come on, let's sort these coffees. Try not to spill it on him."

By lunchtime, Quentin and Bryony's spat seemed forgotten.

Bryony was engrossed in her searches, while surreptitiously shadowing any movement on the illicit trading sites. Cris and Quentin finalised the details for the auction.

It was plain, Quentin believed his Italian counterpart to be lacking in the subterfuge required, despite the latter's documented success in the field. Cris, amused by the liaison's patronising attitude, took no notice. Quentin's underestimation was to Cris' advantage. The more the guy assumed him inept, the easier his role.

Hannah, while apparently focused on her own work, continued to create and discard scenarios in her head. A premonition prickled at the far reaches of her consciousness.

Instinct told her it was related to the auction, but as yet she couldn't determine how.

As far as she knew, the venue was not part of the land over which Maxentius had jurisdiction, making it unlikely to be a place her ancient family had visited in their time. The artefact had yet to be revealed. Save Cris and Quentin, the players were unknown. Still, the premonition of a looming danger, troubled her.

Unable to solve the puzzles, she gave up and concentrated on a batch of items to be archived.

Quentin left, shortly before five.

A welcome tranquillity enveloped the office when the door swished closed. Bryony opened her mouth to say something, then thought better of it.

Hannah leant back in her chair and stretched her arms over her head. "Wow."

Cris looked at the two women, with a lopsided grin. "Well now, if pomposity was a crime, Mr Timothy Bryce Lawton would be sentenced to life, without the possibility of parole."

His irreverent remark garnered a burst of hilarity, and the tension in the room subsided.

"Home time," Hannah said when they had regained their composure. "Bryony, it's curry night, you gonna join us?"

"Three nights in a row, Hannah. Maybe I should…"

"Come on, you know Max makes the best curries. I've got a bottle of Prosecco in the fridge and salted caramel ice cream for dessert…" she bribed.

"Okay, okay… you are a bad influence, Hannah Vallier." Bryony raised her palms in surrender. "My poor house will think I've abandoned it."

"Well, it's not the first time and I doubt it will be the last," Hannah teased.

Bryony grinned and nudged her friend's arm. "True nuff. Right." She stuffed everything into her bag and slung it over her shoulder. "Come on then, that Prosecco is not getting drunk while we are standing here."

"Oooof, I don't think I will be able to move for at least three hours," Bryony groaned, holding her stomach. "That was sooooo good, Max. Thank you."

She did not see the glance Cris shared with Hannah.

"My pleasure. Glad you enjoyed it." Max smiled and tipped his glass in her direction.

A few moments of quiet ensued, broken when Hannah said, "Bryony. There is something we need to discuss."

Bryony was lolling in her chair, but the gravity in Hannah's tone made her bolt upright. "What's up?" She frowned, adding pertly, "You gonna sack me?"

"Yeah right, like I could manage without you. No..." Hannah paused.

For no apparent reason, Bryony remembered her dream. Dread trickled down her spine, as though drawn by a ghostly finger. "What's going on guys?"

She looked at the three around the table. They wore matching expressions — affection mixed with concern. She felt Cris lace their fingers together, as Aggie, perhaps sensing Bryony's unease, nuzzled her knee. Absently, Bryony stroked the dog's downy ears with her free hand.

"Hannah... you're scaring me."

Hannah seemed to steel herself.

Bryony damped down the urge to bolt. This was getting freaky.

"Bryony, what I'm about to divulge *will* sound preposterous. You may or may not believe me, but I give you my word it is the truth. Max knows it to be so, as does Cris. It is not something I share without due consideration as to how it will be received. I think it is imperative you are made aware, but the reason why, I have not been able to decipher."

Eyes like saucers, Bryony studied her friend. "Errrr… Okay…" she stammered.

In a bland voice, Hannah repeated the tale she had told Cris. The one, prior to this moment, only six people in either of her worlds had been privileged to hear.

As ever, the telling took its toll, but, as she spoke, a weight began to diminish, an indication to Hannah, she was doing the right thing.

Her voice died away, and she relaxed against her husband, who draped an arm around her shoulder and dropped a kiss on the side of the head. She twisted to face him, and they exchanged a knowing look.

Actually feeling her jaw drop, Bryony gawked at Hannah. She shook her head as if doing so would disperse the scene and all its contents.

Had she but known it, her expression mirrored that of Senna when she was apprised. Something Hannah felt was better kept to herself right at that moment, in spite of the amusement value.

For want of something to do while she processed her friend's words, Bryony raised her glass and took a large gulp of Prosecco. The bubbles tickled her nose and she sneezed; once, twice, three times.

"S-sorry," she gurgled. "I can't s-seem to s-stop sneezing." Affirmed when three more followed.

Her mirth was contagious, and suddenly, the four of them were convulsed with laughter.

Calm restored, Bryony contemplated Hannah's revelations. She was correct, preposterous did not even begin to characterise them. Absurd, incredible, inconceivable, crazy, illogical, ludicrous, wholly and completely nonsensical. A veritable thesaurus of descriptions for what she had been told ran through her mind.

Only the solemn faces of her friends, stopped her from succumbing to another bout of hilarity, *or was it hysteria?*

"Hannah…" she started, then dried up. Her mouth opened and shut, twice. Pretty sure she resembled a stranded cod, for the life of her, Bryony could not stop herself from gaping.

"I know it's hard, trust me. To admit I am linked to an ancestor who lived, who in my head still lives, almost two thousand years ago, is not something I do for fun."

"It's akin to the plot of a book. You know where someone from a bygone era inhabits the body of someone in the present, intent on wreaking vengeance, for wrongs their poor unsuspecting target had no idea were committed." Bryony gave a nervous giggle. "S-sorry, I think I might be a bit hysterical."

Cris squeezed her fingers. A gesture she returned, grateful for his presence.

"This might help." From beside her, Hannah lifted up a small box, which Bryony hadn't noticed. From within, she retrieved an item wrapped in layers of cloth.

Unaccountably, Bryony held her breath.

Hannah removed the cloth to display what resembled a wooden ball.

"This was carved by Maxentius at Masada. Hannah took it to Pompeii and then brought it here to Magnis. It was lost when a group of rebel soldiers overran the fort. I had only been working at the museum a few months when I came across it. It was sitting there in an archive box, waiting to be catalogued. I couldn't believe it." Hannah stroked loving fingers over the object, her voice wistful.

"How come you have it, here I mean?" Bryony whispered.

"One of our friends persuaded the museum to let me keep it on permanent loan. I thought if you could *see* something which connects me to my past, it might help. I am not supposed to show anyone, but the circumstances are extraordinary and I daresay I can trust you not to blab it all over Northumberland."

Hannah handed the artefact to Bryony.

The wood, dark with age, had a soft lustre. It was a solid piece and although one half was smooth, Bryony realised it was not a ball. The other half had been carved into some kind of shape; she traced the elaborate design.

Amazed it had survived the centuries, she turned it this way and that, trying to figure out what it was. "Is it a piece of fruit?" she chanced.

"Well spotted. It's a pomegranate." Hannah smiled dreamily. "One day, I'll tell you why."

Bryony passed it to Cris, who inspected it with the avidity of an expert archaeologist.

"This is stunning, Hannah. You are fortunate indeed to be its custodian."

"It's mine," she stated with a shrug.

. . .

163

Lost for words, Bryony stared at her friend. What she might have denied as fantasy, delusion, had become indisputable. Her head buzzed with myriad questions, the answers to which she expected would blow her mind, but she still wanted to ask them.

She closed her eyes, waiting for the uproar in her head to abate. An image flickered behind her eyelids. A face, a smile and it was gone, like a leaf on the edge of a storm, but with it came an inexplicable serenity.

"Want a minute?" Hannah asked solicitously.

"Funnily enough, no." Floored she might be, but Bryony wasn't totally freaked out. She had grown up on myths and legends, fables and folklore.

Her parents had instilled in their only child an appreciation of the mystical, taught her to embrace the incomprehensible and revere the unfathomable. Hannah's story, the manifestation of all three.

To Bryony, history and the preternatural went hand in hand. To deny the latter was to reject the former. History was not a gentle stream, it was a raging torrent, mired by twists and turns. A constant battle to find the smallest crack among solid obstacles, to find momentary respite in a quiet pool before being catapulted back into the cataracts.

How could something so powerful, so tragic, so calamitous, leave nothing in its wake?

Ghosts were the least of it.

CHAPTER 19

Pulling herself together, Bryony — tentatively at first then in the manner of the Inquisitor General and, had she but known it, in a similar vein to Senna — began asking questions. To be sitting alongside someone who had witnessed history, been part of it was — while mind-boggling — to be cherished, not dismissed.

Satisfied she had extracted every possible morsel of information, Bryony kept coming back to one specific detail. The inconsistencies and arbitrary fragments began to form a logical picture. Her dreams, that perplexing glimmer of recognition when she met Cris.

"Senna is married to Marcus, yes?" she quizzed.

"Correct." Hannah nodded.

"You think Cris is somehow related to..." Abruptly, Bryony realised why Hannah had asked her to research the Rossi family tree. "Okaaaaaay, *now* I get it. You wanted to see whether there was proof Cris was descended from Marcus' or at least the Aelianus family."

"Forgive me for being circumspect when I asked. You are my friend. To keep things from you goes against the grain, but this isn't me sharing a snippet of gossip." Hannah opened her palms, contritely.

"I hoped I could avoid burdening you with this, for make no mistake, it *is* a burden. To know what I know, and not be able to discuss it with *anyone* except those to whom it is entrusted, takes a toll. Regrettably, it seems Fate has forced my hand."

"Fate?" Bryony squeaked.

"I think the item being auctioned tomorrow somehow connects Cris and Marcus. It is the only credible reason for their heightened awareness of each other. Your part in this is unclear to me, yet I feel it to be important."

"Why did Cris call me Senna?"

"You are her descendent. You resemble her, and because Cris is seeing Senna through Marcus' eyes, he spoke without thought."

"Cris and I were a couple in a past life?"

"Yes," Hannah replied without hesitation.

"Reincarnation, yeah, okay…" when Hannah started to correct her… "I know it's not reincarnation exactly, but it's pretty cool." Bryony directed a devilish smirk at Cris. "Seems you might be stuck with me."

Cris guffawed and pulled her close. "Well, who am I to argue with Fate? Plus… I'm not sure my rivals for your affection are equipped to handle your… errr… shall we say… uniqueness." Suffering a punch to the shoulder. "Hey, no need for violence."

While they bantered, Max topped up the glasses, and the conversation moved from ancient ancestors to modern auctions. By the end of the evening, the four had devised the inkling of a plan.

Magnis - AD 91

Marcus was feeling out of sorts. He stared at the pile of reports on his desk with unseeing eyes. He tried to focus, but after another half an hour of studying the same document, without taking any action, he conceded defeat.

"Something amiss?" Maxentius glanced across to see Marcus rolling up the papyrus sheets.

"I cannot tell, perhaps," was Marcus' less than satisfactory answer.

"Are the children unwell?"

"No, I do not think it is to do with anything…" he paused, "…here."

Maxentius inclined his head. "Do you require Hannah's counsel?"

"Maybe." Marcus shoved out of his chair and patrolled the room, relaying his, as yet obscure concern. "Something evil lurks, but it is not close. Like storm clouds in the far distance or the faint rumble of thunder." He shrugged. "A harbinger of danger."

"Go, find Hannah. You will not settle until you have spoken with her."

Marcus nodded and strode out.

Lips pursed, Maxentius watched him go, listening to the slap of his second's sandals on the wooden floor. He sent up a silent pray to Fortuna that this menace would either manifest or disperse.

It was worse than standing on a massive ramp waiting for the Roman Army to breach the wall at Masada. Despite Hannah's promise that they were safe, he would not sleep comfortably until it was done.

Marcus found Hannah at the hospital, discussing some remedy or other with Atius.

"Might you spare me a moment," he entreated when the pair broke their conversation to greet him.

"Of course." Hannah led Marcus out of the medicus' earshot. "Is something wrong?" She studied his face, his quick smile missing.

"This growing evil."

"It is also increasing in my mind."

"I feel so impotent. An encroaching menace we can do naught to prevent."

"At least they are aware, and while none of us knows the source, we are on our guard. It is all we can do." Hannah sought to mollify.

"Is it absurd being fearful for the well-being of this man Cris, and his woman, neither of whom I will ever know? At least not in the conventional manner." Marcus frowned.

"Not at all. It is no different from the concerns I have for Hannah and, by extension, her husband and children." She studied her adopted brother closely. Although his expression was schooled, she read agitation in his rigid bearing.

"I know it is difficult, and none of us chose this, Marcus, but we cannot change it. Try to view it as a blessing, not a curse. The incongruity or occasional consternation engendered by our connection is cancelled out by the merits.

"Moreover, she has been part of my life almost since I set foot on Masada. I struggle to recall a time she was not in my head. Even when the thread binding us loosens, it never breaks. To be without her is inconceivable." Hannah's tone became nostalgic.

"You and Senna are bound to Cris and Bri-oh-nee..." Hannah's pronunciation of the unusual name pulled a half-smile from Marcus. "...like Max and Hannah are bound to Maxentius and me. Once you accept that, the rest falls into place. The concept is not new to you, my brother, only this aspect of it."

"Senna..." Marcus struggled to define what tormented him.

Hannah placed her hand on his forearm and pressed gently. "Is not in danger, of this I am certain. The threat is in the future, and will not harm us physically—"

"So why...?"

"I might connect with a descendent, but neither of us have been granted the gift of foresight. All I know is that whatever is going to happen is close. We must be patient. Now," determined to change the subject, she spoke briskly, "am I correct in thinking Turi's birthday approaches? A celebration is in order. Five is an auspicious age, even more so for the little boy turning five."

Effectively diverted, Marcus discussed his son's birthday with enthusiasm. Hannah hid a grin at his fatherly pride, pleased to see his countenance lift.

Northumberland - July 2015

Saturday morning dawned almost too quickly. This was it... make or break. There was an air of barely suppressed excitement in the office. All on tenterhooks for the email which would allow them their first sight of the artefact.

Being the weekend, the building was unnaturally quiet. The the museum and ruins were open, but the administration side operated on a skeleton staff, and the majority of the offices were empty.

On the dot of eight forty-five, Quentin appeared. Bryony, her back to the door, felt a draft when it opened. Gritting her teeth, she plastered a smile in place.

"Morning Quentin," the three within, chorused.

"Good morning. Anything?"

"Not yet," Bryony replied for all of them. "Would you like a coffee?"

"Thank you, I would indeed." His formal speech matched his attire.

Bryony made the drinks in record time, all but flinging the mugs across the table to their respective recipients. Sipping the strong brew, she checked her email for the umpteenth time, before switching her attention to Cris' family tree.

The previous evening's revelations spurred her on. This was now her heritage too, albeit indirectly, and she was closing in on the era in question.

Her focus was interrupted by a loud ping.

The immediate silence in the room was palpable.

Everyone looked at Bryony, who expanded her email account to full screen, seeing the impatiently awaited message.

"Okay guys, this is it. Gather round... we only get one chance to see it."

With Cris on her left, Quentin to her right, and Hannah behind, Bryony opened the email.

"This had better not contain malware," she muttered, praying her firewalls were up to snuff.

Quentin made a strangled sound.

"Joke," she hissed. "Geez. Here we go."

She clicked on the attachment. In a format duplicating the invitation, the artefact shimmered into existence.

They stared at the object.

The picture sharpened. Underneath, a description appeared.

Gold and onyx intaglio ring.
Circa first century AD.
Although damaged and dulled, the design etched into the onyx is believed to be;
A crudely fashioned 'A'.
A depiction of Mercury alongside a ram's head.
The imagery suggests the ring was the property of a wool merchant.
The A — probably the family initial.
Intaglio rings were the equivalent of a modern-day signature.
Estimated value: £10,000.

There was no provenance.

No indication as to where the ring was 'found'.

Neither were to be expected.

The four stared. The tarnished gold setting was pitted and blackened in places. The band was broader than usual for the era, but well made. The carving on the onyx had been smoothed by time but, after reading the description, the details became discernible.

. . .

ROSIE CHAPEL

Without anyone noticing, Hannah whipped out her phone and took a photograph, thankful she had it on silent mode.

Riveted by the ancient ring, Cris was jolted by something skittering across his mind, gone before he could capture it. On its heels, a succession of scenes, and a smouldering fury. He heard himself whistle between his teeth, and saw Bryony shoot him a startled glance. He shook his head, unable to vocalise what was happening.

In his head, he heard frenzied shouts and mournful wails, accompanied by an almost suffocating smell of sulphur. A harbour, the moon glinting on the water, little boats bobbing on choppy waves.

It was a reprise of the first part of his dream. An identical chill of foreboding cloaked him, and for several seconds, he was blind and deaf to his surroundings.

Then Bryony was there. He felt her hand on his knee, and her face swam over his vision, blurred, as if he was looking through water.

"Cris, are you okay?" Her voice was muffled, distant.

His mouth declined to heed his brain. In the next instant, and with a kind of whoosh, everything cleared. The room came back into focus.

"Sorry, yes. I am fine. Merely a lapse in concentration." He could see Bryony wasn't convinced. He pressed his hand over hers in reassurance.

"Too much red wine will do that," Quentin lectured superciliously.

Certain he heard the man mutter 'typical Italian' under his breath, Cris inhaled a calming breath. Ignoring the jibe, he took a sip of his coffee, the robust flavour going some way to moderating his annoyance.

The images lingered, accompanied by a powerful sense of

recognition. Cautiously, and unwilling to suffer a repeat of his vision disturbance, Cris studied the ring on the screen. It was solid and looked heavy. A ring you would miss when not wearing it.

He surmised the man who once owned it could be, at least, equestrian status, possibly even senatorial. What *was* it about this artefact? While its inherent historical value was unquestioned, in all honesty, it seemed pretty innocuous. Just an old ring.

It is not ***just*** *an old ring,* an infuriated voice berated. *It is* ***our*** *ring.*

The voice belonged to Marcus.

Cris spun in his chair, half-expecting to see his ancient counterpart standing alongside him. The man's wrath seemed to pulse around the quiet room. Their connection was stronger, almost tangible, and Cris was out of his depth.

"Excuse me. I shall return momentarily," he apologised and before anyone could speak, left the office at a fast clip.

He hurried out of the building through the back door, into the warm sunshine. In front of him, nestled the ruins of Magnis.

Inexorably, Cris was drawn towards the meagre remains, coming to a halt in the centre of the grassy expanse. In antiquity this was likely the quadrangle.

Thankful the museum didn't open for another hour, Cris closed his eyes, emptied his mind of all the questions swirling around, and attempted to summon up the past. He needed answers and the only person who could provide them was Marcus.

"What is so special about this ring? Why are you so angry? What can I do?" he pleaded inwardly.

Nothing.

Cris waited.

It was one thing to meld with someone in your dreams, but deliberately invoking a shade, or entity, probably not the most sensible tactic, especially one so enraged.

Cris searched his brain for a way to describe the paradox. Marcus wasn't dead... well, strictly, he was... but not in this moment. In this moment, he was as alive as Cris, only two millennia ago... and thereby hung the enigma. A rift in time, perhaps? A breach in the space time continuum?

How is it here? In Britannia? In a glowing box? The staccato questions burst into his reverie.

"I do not know. It is to be auctioned."

A quizzical sensation trickled through Cris and he permitted himself a wry smile. "Like a slave auction, except this is for artefacts, not people," he clarified.

He was aware of a nod of comprehension.

"Did you lose this ring?" Cris asked.

No. It is my brother's. He died. The blunt response was filled with sorrow.

"Forgive me. I did not intend to remind you of his demise." Cris could hear the formality of his internal dialogue and pondered briefly whether he had forsaken English for Latin, or Greek.

It is over a decade since he vanished.

"Vanished?" Cris blurted out, before he could stop himself.

He perceived the man in his head was thinking, debating whether to divulge what was understandably, a painful episode.

"Please, such things are private and personal. My reaction was impolite."

If this ring has caused our strange association, the story behind it may be important.

"I would be privileged to hear it."

Another long pause, and Cris had the oddest impression, Marcus was discussing what to say with a third person.

Hannah?

Not the Hannah currently sitting in the office building, the Hannah of Roman Britain. The enormity of this hypothesis provoked a bout of mirth which, under the circumstances, he stifled.

Presuming Marcus had decided against disclosing the details surrounding the loss of his brother, Cris began to retrace his steps, scanning the perimeter of the site.

It was blessedly empty. The last thing he needed while in some weird trance-like state was a flock of inquisitive tourists.

CHAPTER 20

He was supposed to be away from the farm a month at most. He was meeting with some business associates to finalise a deal... my family was in the wool trade. He never returned.

Cris halted.

"Where was this gathering to take place?"

Herculaneum

One unassuming word. Yet it opened the floodgates.

The wharf. The smell of sulphur. The deafening roar. The screams. The claustrophobia.

Herculaneum. A place of fascination, mystery, and myth.

His childhood playground.

The port town destroyed, buried under metres of lava, to be unearthed centuries later. Decades of painstaking excavations, uncovering a multitude of priceless artefacts.

Frescoes, mosaics, food, crockery, cookware, amphorae, furniture, jewellery, human remains. Conservation, preservation, protection... and thefts... Cris' thoughts spiralled out.

Thefts.

Memories surfaced. A small boy listening to his father talk about a brazen break-in, the previous night, when thieves had snatched items of jewellery from one of the arcades.

Meeting Massimo Caravello, and his son, Gian — the former being the reason Cris joined the Art Squad. The obsession with solving that *one* crime committed against his beloved Herculaneum.

His determination to thwart the trade in stolen artefacts. Everything came back to a small — and, in the scheme of things, insignificant — ring.

An onyx intaglio ring.

He had come full circle.

The desecrated remains were those of Marcus' brother... they *had* to be. This could *not* be a coincidence. A wave of sadness washed over Cris. A baffling emotion. Why did he feel grief for someone he did not know, *could* not know? The man was barely even a footnote to history, one of thousands killed when Vesuvius erupted. He only rated a mention because of the ring... and yet...

Cris felt a nudge of impatience from the man in his head.

"Again, my apologies. I was reminiscing. Herculaneum constituted a major part of my childhood. My father investigated a theft from the site. One of the items taken was an onyx ring—"

How was this ring taken? Marcus quizzed.

"Many people died on the dockside. They were waiting for boats to carry them to safety when the lava flow engulfed the city and everything in it. During the excavations groups of skeletons were uncovered, huddled together, presumably in the hope the boatsheds offered protection. Regrettably, they became tombs.

"Coins and jewellery were found with some of the bodies. It is difficult to keep discoveries of this magnitude secret. Inevitably, there are those greedy or unscrupulous enough to swoop in and steal anything of value, the benefits outweighing the risks."

My brother's ring was stolen from these boatsheds? That was his place of death?

"I am afraid so."

To violate the dead is an odious crime.

"And perhaps explains our…" Cris hesitated, still not quite sure how to describe their relationship.

…link.

"You might be interested to know, the manner of the robbery prompted mention of a curse on the thief."

Manner? Please elaborate.

"It was posited the thieves were disturbed because, in their haste, they snapped the finger which bore the ring. Your brother was among hundreds in the arcades whose deaths were traumatic. Their bodies had lain at peace for millennia, only to have their rest shattered. The director of the excavations was heard to say he hoped the poor souls were forgiving."

If the burial ritual is not performed, the spirit of the deceased may not find repose.

"He said that too."

This man is respectful.

It was a rhetorical statement. Cris did not feel the need to agree; it was implicit.

Now my ring appears in a glowing box. How is this possible?

Cris frowned, how on earth could he describe a computer screen to a man who could not conceive of the concept, never mind visualise it. Then, something Hannah had said the previous weekend when they were discussing her special situation, popped into his mind. She was joking about the difficulties she had faced trying to describe television to Maxentius.

"Do you recollect Hannah talking about a box of fire? It was shortly after you arrived at Magnis."

There was a pause. Again, Cris discerned a hurried conversation.

The ring is in a box, similar to the box of fire? You cannot touch it?

"No, I cannot touch it but, hopefully, later tonight I shall be able to secure it.

This ring... it is all I have of my brother. To lose it again...

Cris heard the note of melancholy in Marcus' reply. It evoked the haunting cry of a curlew.

"I may not be successful. There are others bidding. I can only pray to Fortuna, that my bid is the highest. Upon my honour, I will do everything in my power to acquire the ring," Cris pledged, simultaneously cursing himself for so precipitous a promise.

There was a reasonable chance he would lose tonight. Now they knew Quentin was, if not the brains behind this trafficking ring, certainly in it up to his eyeballs, it was conceivable he already had someone prepared to pay an astronomical sum to guarantee him the artefact. A trusted member of his enterprise.

The budget Miles had arranged was substantial, but when the limit was reached, that was it. There was nothing extra on which to draw. Suddenly, to lose this heirloom, this ring which belonged to his ancestor, had become untenable. While the funds might not be enough, Cris had some savings. Using his own money to augment a bid had never been a consideration.

That changed today.

Relief swept over Cris, and he registered its source was Marcus.

Thank you. I too will make an offering to Fortuna, and pray our petition is rewarded.

"Marcus, even if I win the auction, the ring will not come back into my hands. It will be taken to a museum, probably Naples, where it will be either displayed for the public to view or held in their vaults."

Museum?

"A place which cares for and protects relics of signifi-cance." Was the easiest description Cris could come up with.

This is better than the alternative.

Closing his eyes, Cris sent up an entreaty to every god in the existence of the world, then bowed. An odd gesture, especially as Marcus was unlikely to see it, but it felt appropriate.

The connection faded, receding like the ebb of the tide.

He was alone.

A hand clasped his. Cris opened his eyes to see Bryony standing in front of him, her head canted in question.

"Marcus?"

"Yes. It is his ring. Well, his brother's, which means it is a family heirloom." Cris heard how absurd he sounded, but what else could he say? It was naught but the truth. "I cannot allow it to fall into the hands of Quentin or any of his cronies."

"Then, it is imperative we win." She smiled up at him. "Come on, the gates are open, and we don't need to be caught up in a horde of visitors. Another coffee is called for."

The pent-up emotions of the last hour coalesced, and before Bryony could take a step, Cris drew her close, stealing her lips with a fierce ardour. Bryony's arms slid around his waist, and she returned his kiss with avid interest.

He felt the drum of her heart beating against his chest, inhaled her intoxicating fragrance, and heard her breathing stutter. In that moment, everything else warring for his attention retreated. All that mattered was being with Bryony.

Magnis - AD 91

"Marcus, *Marcus*, **Marcus**."

Marcus felt an insistent pressure on his forearm, and heard his name being repeated in concerned tones. The daze which had enveloped him dissipated, and awareness returned.

He was surprised to find himself sitting on a bench at the edge of the quadrangle, with no recollection of how he came to be there.

He turned his head slightly, to see Hannah studying him, speculatively.

"Back with us?" she quizzed. Marcus had asked her to clarify one or two points during his conversation with Cris, but she knew the aftermath of the contact left a person feeling oddly detached. Losing focus was the least of it. Fortunately, it was short-lived.

He nodded, slowly. His brain and his mouth not yet in concert.

"Are you able to elaborate on what you discussed?"

He nodded again, offering a half-smile as the hubbub in his mind settled, and the ache of loss subsided.

"I know the reason for our connection," Marcus' voice

sounded stilted to his ears. He worked his jaw and rolled his tongue over his teeth.

Hannah handed him a goblet. "Drink this, it will help."

Marcus took a large gulp of the contents, tasting the sharp flavour of mint. He swilled it around his mouth before swallowing. She was correct, the drink did indeed refresh. His head cleared.

They sat without speaking.

It was a beautiful day. Not too hot. A light breeze rustled through the trees. The fort was relatively quiet, it's inhabitants attending to their duties. Birdsong and the hum of insects blended with an occasional call from a soldier or one of the local tribespeople, and the clang of tools. It was a tranquil vista. One the garrison had worked hard to achieve.

"I love it here," Hannah's remark penetrated Marcus' thoughts.

"As do I."

"I did not expect to. For many years, I wanted to return to Masada, where everything began. Then we came here, and it felt as though this was my home. I cannot explain why. Maxentius believes it is because the other Hannah is close in place, even though she is millennia away in time." Her accompanying shrug, tacit acceptance of her husband's suggestion.

Marcus was aware she was giving him time to collect himself.

"I share your sentiment. Cris is my descendent. His family may not be from this land, but I believe he is now tied to it through Sen… Bri-oh-nee. An awareness which leaves him irresolute. His homeland is my homeland, as Senna's homeland is Bri-oh-nee's, a curious coincidence, yet oddly apt. I digress…" Marcus gathered his wayward thoughts and gave Hannah a detailed account of his 'conversation' with Cris.

"A ring, hmmm… it is astonishing to me that seemingly

insignificant items of jewellery possess the power to conquer time," Hannah said when he concluded.

"Cris says this one may be cursed."

"I am ambivalent as to the veracity of curses. I believe evil lingers, and I have no doubt the manner of a person's death might leave them wandering on another plane, endlessly seeking their rest, but curses…"

She stared out over the dusty ground. "I think it is more likely guilt on the part of the perpetrator than the malediction of an individual long dead, which causes the apparent blight on their lives. That said, who can tell? We are bound to people two thousand years in the future, one of whom has found your brother's ring. Who am I to question the preternatural?"

"Perhaps," Marcus acceded, "but I admit to a grim delight knowing those who have no right to my family heirloom might suffer for their iniquitous behaviour."

"Marcus," Hannah chided, mildly. "That is most unlike you."

He chuckled. "Forgive me, I fear my affront at the knowledge I have just gained has superseded my reason." He got to his feet. "I promised to petition Fortuna. Maybe a moment of contemplation will assuage my outrage."

"Please try not to let your bitterness at the desecration of your brother's body darken your humanity, Marcus. His death was not at the hands of a murderer, but an unforeseen catastrophe. The defilement will not happen for centuries and, had this peculiar circumstance not arisen, you would have remained none the wiser."

Marcus stared at Hannah. Her words struck a chord, and he made a concerted effort to bank down his ire.

"I will do my best," was all he said, with which Hannah had to be satisfied. He patted her on the shoulder and headed off to his quarters.

. . .

Hannah watched him go, a faint frown marring her brow, their conversation replaying in her mind. Her sense of foreboding intensified. Entering the residence, she hurried along to her bedchamber.

There on the cupboard lay her broach.

She picked it up and walked over to the window. The ruby glinted in the sunlight; its blood-red centre shimmered.

Absently, Hannah rubbed her thumb over the intricate setting, tracing the shape. Leaning against the window frame, she sent out a request. The bond strengthened and her mind met that of her modern counterpart.

She asked the question uppermost in her head.

"Are you in danger?"

No, I do not think so.

"Cris?"

Potentially. The people who deal in stolen artefacts are corrupt, but Cris is familiar with their perfidy. He will be on his guard.

"Marcus is worried. No, he is aggravated." Understatement of the month, Hannah thought to herself. "I am concerned his emotions will filter through to Cris and affect his judgement."

Trust me, I will do my utmost to keep him from harm.

It was the best she could hope for. "Thank you. Be careful."

Always

Hannah allowed herself a grin.

Don't laugh, she heard at the edge of her consciousness as their connection dwindled.

Replacing the broach, Hannah set aside her anxiety for the time being and continued with her day.

CHAPTER 21

NORTHUMBERLAND - JULY 2015

Cris gave Bryony an abridged account of his conversation with Marcus, adjuring her to make no mention of it in Quentin's hearing.

Her "as if I would be that stupid," made him smile and the pressure radiating from the base of his skull out over his shoulders began to ease.

"Oh, and the email had an addendum, something along the lines of 'a smorgasbord of unique artefacts will precede the main auction.' Added incentive, methinks. Wonder what the other items will be," she mused as they returned to the office.

Their preparations kept them busy through coffee until lunchtime. They were mid-sandwich when Cris asked Quentin what time he wanted to set off.

His nose buried in his laptop, Quentin mumbled around his food, "I shall make my own way there."

"That's not what we agreed. You know it's one car per bidder." Cris could not prevent a scowl.

"Do not fret, Captain Rossi." Quentin raised his head. "As it happens, I have some private business to which I must attend on the way. I will meet you at six o'clock outside the Black Swan pub in Hardington Village. It's about ten minutes from the venue."

Concealing his indignation at this deviation by the Art Squad liaison, Cris wondered how best to react. He opted for indifferent. "Fine. Have it your way. You get delayed, that's on your head. I won't wait. If you're not there by six, you're out."

Quentin's expression darkened. *Who did this —* in his mind *— subordinate officer think he was calling the shots?* He strove to maintain his composure. His association with these numbskulls was almost over. *Patience Quentin, patience. You don't need to tip them off.* "I shall be there." With an effort he infused a placatory note into his reply. "This is not my first auction you know."

Cris didn't rise to the bait. Quentin might have more experience, but Cris was no novice. Disinclined to argue the point, it would be a waste of breath — he grunted an indistinct response, which could be construed as anything from 'agreed' to 'eff off' — in Italian, of course.

Quentin took it to mean the former and smiled, a trifle condescendingly. "That's settled then." This apparently signalled the end of the matter because Quentin turned his attention to his lunch and ignored the other three.

Presently, Quentin tidied the desk he had been using, and closed his laptop. "As I'm driving straight home after the auction, I need to collect my belongings from the hotel. These past few days have been... interesting. Thank you for your hospitality." Quentin directed his gratitude to Hannah, ignoring Bryony completely.

"My pleasure," Hannah lied with a sunny smile. She shook his hand, quashing the same shudder she had felt when they first crossed palms. No two ways about it, the man was a slime-ball. She was extremely glad this was the last time she would see him.

"Cheerio," Quentin addressed the room in general. With a casual, "See you later," to Cris, he was gone.

"Right, now he's buggered off, we need to get serious." Relief at Quentin's departure making Bryony slightly giddy. "Cris, please tell us what happened with Marcus. Ohhh... how exciting, talking to a long dead ancestor. I'd give anything to have that opportunity with Senna?" Her enthusiasm was contagious, and Hannah's glower, currently aimed at the departing guest, lightened in expectation.

"Spill," she implored.

Cris repeated his conversation with his ancient counterpart, verbatim.

"I knew there had to be more than just your presence here," Hannah said. "A remarkable coincidence don't you think? The ring you have been searching for, virtually your whole life, happens to be the one being traded tonight. Not only that, but also it turns out to be yours. Wonder where it's been all this time? I wish you could keep it, Cris. Can you imagine your father's face if you took it back to Herculaneum."

Cris grinned. "His and Tomas Durante's, both. Probably Massimo Caravello as well. They all worked tirelessly to find it. Papa said it was odd that it vanished without a trace. Almost without fail, following a theft or disappearance of relics there were, still are, elusive hints when anything was moved or traded.

"Thieves talk, they can't help themselves. The investigation was exhaustive but there was nothing, even though a few of the other pieces turned up within a year of the theft. To return it would be an unforgettable moment."

"Where will it end up?" interposed Bryony.

"The Naples museum probably. That, or it might be added to one of the ever-circulating Vesuvius exhibitions touring the world. A newly recovered item in such excellent condition would be a tremendous attraction."

"Don't suppose there's any chance they could extract viable DNA from the skeleton? Granted, the manner of his death makes it unlikely, but with all the technology they use today..." Hannah said, optimistically. "That would offer definitive proof Cris is descended from the victim."

"Doubtful to impossible," Cris shook his head. "Nice thought though. Okay, I need to get ready. I don't want to get caught up in traffic."

Showered and changed, Cris walked into the lounge, his strapping frame encased in a dark grey suit, crisp white shirt, and blood red tie. His expression was grave. Cris' genial persona had darkened, eclipsed by an aura of danger.

A thrill ran down Bryony's spine when he stepped into the kitchen, holding an unpretentious gunmetal-coloured case. It did not quite counteract her nerves. These auctions were fraught, and the attendees devious. It did not take a great leap of imagination to figure out what might occur if things went awry.

"You have everything?" she asked for want of anything better to say, knowing fine well he would have triple checked everything before he left his room.

"I do," he smiled at her obvious anxiety. He murmured in her ear, "I will be on my guard. Trust me."

She turned as he spoke, and their lips met. A gentle kiss becoming fierce.

Breathing hard, Cris rested his forehead on Bryony's. "Will you be here when I return?"

"As long as Hannah's okay with me staying... *again*... yes."

"No use sending her home, she'd only mope," Hannah drawled as she came into the room.

"Me, mope, as if..." Bryony feigned affront. "Yeah," she conceded, "you're probs right." She failed to muffle a giggle.

"Right, you know I won't be able to text until this affair is over. I'm not taking my phone. It's not worth chancing it being checked. I've got the pre-paid."

"Please take care," Bryony whispered, reality kicking in.

"Always."

Cris nodded at Hannah and Max who had appeared at his wife's shoulder. "See you soon."

"There'll be a whisky poured and waiting," Max grinned.

"I'll need it." Cris gave a brief wave.

Moments later they heard the purr of an engine and the crunch of gravel as he drove off.

The three left behind stood motionless, each lost in thought. Their collective introspection was broken by the chirp of childish voices, and the twins burst into the room.

For a while, the adults were distracted.

Cris arrived at the Black Swan with half an hour to spare. He parked up a lane opposite the pub and, while he waited, reviewed the evening ahead. From experience, corroborated by what Miles had told him, these auctions generally adhered to a strict format.

On entry, each participant was handed a marker, which resembled a small table tennis paddle, bearing their designated number. Latecomers were barred... no exceptions.

Ushered to a reception area, the attendees were encouraged to partake of drinks and hors d'oeuvres. The more alcohol consumed, the higher the bids.

At the prescribed time, the guests were led into the auction room. Save the auctioneer, this part of the evening was conducted in silence.

The artefact considered to be of least significance and worth, relatively speaking, was auctioned first. The value of each subsequent item increased incrementally, building up to the main draw card.

The winning bidder received a text affirming their success, along with details regarding remittance of funds. Payment was to be made within fifteen minutes. Failure to do so resulted in grave repercussions.

Cash was preferred... inevitably... but an electronic transfer was acceptable — as long as it was untraceable. Guards — whose duties included checking an individual's phone prior to their departure to ensure they were not cheating the organisers — were positioned at all entry points.

Throughout his career, Cris had been witness to the reprisals inflicted on those who believed they could circumvent the system. Retribution was swift and severe. To trade in stolen artefacts was not for the ingenuous.

After devising and discarding a range of ideas, in the end, their plan was simple. The hardest part would be to win.

Acting the recluse, Cris would allow his seemingly implacable façade to crumble under the influence of too much wine. Becoming voluble and expansive, charming his fellow bidders with promises of holidays on his private island.

This was a tactic designed to lower the guard of his competitors. Cris employed it routinely, with marked success. His mellifluous Italian accent made him sound a trifle naive, lulling those around him into a false sense of security.

Unbeknownst to Hannah, Bryony and, crucially, Quentin — once primed about latter's duplicity — Miles overrode the department's customary policy regarding black-market auctions. He had arranged for a detachment of trusted officers to surround Hardington Manor. They were men trained to be invisible, even to the most discerning and suspicious eye, they appeared as nothing more than shadows.

The sum paid, and the artefact in his possession, Cris would take his leave. Once he had exited the manor, Miles' officers would swoop in to detain those remaining.

Anyone leaving would be intercepted and removed, quietly.

It was not possible to predict the outcome. Operations of this magnitude were not without the element of danger, but Cris and Miles were confident they could break this smuggling ring. More so given Quentin's role.

Cris sent up a wordless prayer. There was a lot riding on tonight.

Bryony could not settle. The afternoon waned and, when Hannah took the twins upstairs for their bath, Bryony paced around the kitchen, until Max felt dizzy and suggested she take Aggie for a brisk walk.

Easily persuaded, Bryony headed out, Aggie bounding alongside with the exuberance of a spring lamb. The hazy, early evening sunlight and gentle sounds of nature did little to mitigate the young woman's agitation, but at least Aggie got to burn off her energy chasing down leaves and other unseen prey.

On her return to the cottage, Bryony was greeted with a large mug of coffee, which she sipped gratefully. The full-bodied aroma of the freshly ground beans fired along her synapses, sharpening her wits.

With renewed purpose, Bryony opened her laptop and resumed her dual searches. While she had no problem accepting Cris and Marcus were related, she yearned for tangible proof. Anything would do, however small.

She was equally keen to unearth incontrovertible proof, Quentin was involved in the illegal trade of historical artefacts.

To that end, she had breached any number of rules and hacked Quentin's computer to plant a tiny bit of code which acted like a location beacon. She figured, in his arrogance, Quentin would never suspect anyone would dare put a tracker in his laptop.

After an exhaustive set of searches on Timothy Lawton, she had uncovered the odd snippet relating to his, less than legal, youthful activities. It seemed he and a friend had fancied themselves as cat-burglars. They were just kids, not even sixteen. Although questioned once or twice, there was no concrete proof, and they were released without charge — another reason why it took so long to unearth the information.

Her persistence didn't end there. A couple of days previously, she had contacted Todd, Miles' cryptologist, to beg a huge favour. Todd, furious with Quentin, had agreed with relish. The result was the icing on the cake, but Bryony was not quite satisfied — she wanted the cherry on the top.

Tonight, being the auction, some of the covert trading sites might be busier, leaving tell-tale indicators. The bidders had to be there in person, but that didn't mean they weren't monitored. Slipping into the dark web, Bryony crept through the multitude of layers, undetected, homing in on the sites she sought.

A new thread caught her attention. A gossamer fine trail, imperceptible to anyone who wasn't cognisant with the way entry was camouflaged. Deaf to everything else going on around her, she tracked it to its origin.

Her mouth tilted in malevolent glee.

"Yes!" She executed an ecstatic air punch.

"Find something interesting?" Max quizzed, not altogether astutely.

"Did I ever." She beamed across the table.

Hannah and Max stopped what they were doing and gave her their full attention.

There was a loud ping.

"Ohhh... hang on, let me..." Bryony didn't finish her sentence. Her listeners, used to their friend's distracted ways, waited... almost patiently.

"Nice, very nice," she crooned to the screen. "Come on, baby, all of it."

"Good job we know she's not into porn," Hannah muttered in an aside to her husband, who bit down on a guffaw.

Moments ticked by.

"Perfect." A few clicks and Bryony looked over the lid of her laptop.

"Care to share?" Hannah asked, amused by her friend's expression. Bryony was the personification of the phrase 'the cat has got the cream'.

"I would luuuurve to."

She shuffled in her chair, getting comfortable.

"Firstly, I can prove Cris is descended from Marcus. I don't know whether he, Cris I mean, is bothered, but once I'd started down this particular rabbit hole, I wanted to hit the bottom." Bryony gave a rapturous sigh. "I love history."

Hannah and Max smirked.

"Okay, thanks to Vincente and the fact Cris' grandparents kept masses of papers going back donkey's years, I managed to trace Cris' family tree to the early eight hundreds AD. Then it got really sketchy. Well, to be honest, it was pretty sketchy before that, but the villagers near the Rossi farm seemed to be sticklers for record keeping. Those people are my heroes." Bryony clasped her hands together beatifically.

"I was starting to think I might have hit a roadblock, only to find out they have some markers and gravestones, or fragments thereof, dated centuries earlier. How cool is that?"

Without waiting for the affirmative she expected, Bryony went on, "That ping you heard was Vincente sending an email. I asked him to check their farmhouse, specifically the basement or outhouses, and to do the same with any of the other houses nearby."

Hannah started to speak, but Bryony, anticipating her question, carried on.

"It occurred to me, if the early inhabitants of the area around the Rossi's farm were anything like those living in the vicinity of Hadrian's Wall, any and all suitable construction materials are fair game. Most of the stone from the forts along here was commandeered by the locals, the instant, probably even before, the Romans left, including grave markers and inscriptions."

Latching onto Bryony's train of thought, Hannah said, "You think there might be evidence of early habitation in some of the houses, even after so many centuries?"

"I do and there is." Triumphantly, Bryony swivelled her computer so the other two could see the screen.

Vincente had done her proud. He had scoured the neighbourhood, pestering everyone to permit him to check their walls, both exterior and interior.

In a tiny outbuilding, adjacent to a crumbling farmhouse — which the three studying the picture had no difficulty believing dated to the Roman era if not millennia earlier — Vincente had come across a faint inscription on a lichen covered block of stone.

CHAPTER 22

Hannah peered at the photograph; it was tricky to distinguish the details. Again, Vincente, not the son of an archaeologist for nothing, had foreseen this hurdle. He sent a photograph of the inscription to his father who had offered a best guess translation, with modern punctuation.

Lucius Didius Aelianus (poss. Aelius or Aquilinus?) loving husband and father. Died, 832 ACU (AD 81), aged sixty-five years and seven months.

It was conceivable there was more, but the slab formed part of the foundations and the lower portion was buried. It was a miracle this had survived the ravages of time, weather, and careless treatment.

"There is no doubt then?" Max quizzed.

"I don't think so. Marcus told me his home was a farm in the hills outside Rome and they had lived there for generations. This substantiates it. If by chance this Didius is *not* Marcus' father, and that's simple enough to check, it would have to be a relative." It was Hannah who replied.

Nobody spoke while they contemplated the evidence.

Other than in the main centres of the Ancient Roman

world, what remained from the era was meagre, more so in isolated regions. The dismantling of structures, the loss of which would be mourned in the future, was of no concern to a populace desperate for building materials. Practicality beat sentimentality, and much was commandeered for other uses; the original purpose beyond recall.

"Want to hear... no, more like see... my other news?" Bryony's eager voice broke the quiet.

At that moment, her mobile rang. Not recognising the number, she declined it.

It rang again.

"Oh, for goodness' sake." Exasperated, she plucked it up and hit the green icon. "What? No, I do not want double glazing, or to do a survey, and I most definitely do not have a virus in my computer..."

"Bryony, it's me." Cris' startled voice cut into her diatribe.

She glanced at the clock on the wall. It was 6:15. "Cris, God, sorry. I don't take calls from unknown numbers after hours. What's wrong?"

"Nothing, well probably nothing. I wanted to let you know our esteemed colleague has failed to put in an appearance."

"You are kidding me?"

"I do not kid."

"Bloody hell. What's his game? Hang on, I'll put you on speaker." She pressed the icon and waved her hand at Max and Hannah. "Quentin's a no show."

Hannah gaped. "Well, that's bizarre, how's he going to get..."

"He doesn't need Cris in order to gain access to the venue..." Max began.

"...because he's the mastermind," Bryony finished. "The cheeky bugger."

"I'm not... a moment..." there was the sound of money being shoved into a slot.

"Are you in a public phone box?" Bryony asked.

"Yes, and I wish I wasn't, but I did not want to use my mobile."

"Brave man." Bryony stifled a giggle.

"I fear I will never be rid of the smell. It has, however, served its purpose. I am not waiting for him. He has played his hand but does not know we are wise to his duplicity."

"Can you give me two minutes Cris? What's the number on the keypad of the phone? I'll call you back."

"I don't have ti—"

"Trust me, for this you do."

Cris' reluctance was clear in his tones as he read out the number.

"I wouldn't ask if it wasn't vital." Bryony tsked and disconnected the call.

Her fingers flew over the keys as she traced Quentin's whereabouts. Their suspicions were correct. His laptop, at least, was in a large room at the rear of the old manor house, probably the ground floor, although she could not be certain.

"Bryon—" Hannah started.

"Don't ask. What you don't know, won't hurt you."

"Will it hurt you?"

"There's a good chance." She winked unrepentantly and punched in the number Cris had provided. He picked up on the first ring, and she explained about the laptop.

"Before you go, I have proof of your relationship to Marcus, as well as evidence Quentin is in this up to his neck. Evidence we can use, I mean," she amended slightly guiltily.

"That is good news, I must go."

"Take care..." Bryony's plea was met by the dial tone. She

fiddled with her phone, disquieted by the knowledge she held. She sensed danger but was powerless to intervene.

"Bryony, what is this evidence." Max looked troubled.

"Okay, this is a two-fer. First, one of my searches brought to light that when he was still Timothy Lawton, Quentin was involved in petty theft. He was under eighteen, and never convicted, but it proves he had a taste for dealing in stolen goods long before this trafficking network was set up."

"Also explains how he knows so many people in that world. Maybe that's why he joined the force. The whole thing is a cover to continue his illicit trade," Max posited. "How long's he been in the Art Squad?"

"Not sure. We'd have to check with Miles, but my guess would be at least fifteen to twenty years," Hannah supplied.

"Yeah, that sounds about right," Bryony agreed. "Right, so that's the first thing. The second thing is that I asked Todd whether he'd be prepared to run a test for me on the invitation.

"There's any amount of information attached to pictures, but identifying and interpreting that information requires really nifty software. I can do a lot, but peeling apart images is not my forte. Todd, as a cryptologist, has access to a wide variety of techniques, you know, like alternate light sources.

"Anyway, he worked his magic and identified what we refer to as a signature embedded within the image, similar to a watermark. That signature comes from the computer which generated the file. Even if it's deleted, it doesn't actually disappear, just gets fragmented and dispersed within the hard drive."

She paused for dramatic effect.

"Wanna take a shot at whose computer created that beey-ootiful invitation?"

"Quentin bloody Taylor," Hannah all but spat.

"The very same."

"So now what do we do?"

"I wish we hadn't let Cris go on his own. Quentin knows he is using a false identity. He might decide to expose him." Bryony fretted. "I have a bad feeling about this."

"Miles has it covered. Cris will be fine," Max said, peaceably.

"Maybe, but…" Bryony stopped. "I'm going. I can't tell you why, but I have to be there."

"You aren't going on your own." Hannah jumped off the couch.

"Oh, dear lord." Max heaved a long-suffering sigh. "You women will be the death of me."

He got to his feet. "Before you go rushing into the breach, please remember we have two small children who cannot be left. Hannah, how about you stay, and I'll go with Bryony?"

Hannah bit her lip, vacillating. The idea of an adventure, however hazardous, was so very tempting, but Max was right, the twins took priority. "Damn you and your reason," she grumbled.

Reading her mind, Max pulled his wife close and kissed her. "I think you've had enough adventures for ten lifetimes. Leave some for the rest of us," he murmured.

She blushed and smiled sheepishly. "Fair enough. Oh, take Aggie, she's great protection and won't utter a sound."

Max looked sceptical.

"She will, and I'd feel better if you had her with you." She didn't have to add how dicey this affair could become. Max was no fool.

Within ten minutes they were ready. Being the height of summer, it was well into the evening before dusk fell. This was both a help and a hindrance. A help because they weren't driving into a situation already challenging in the pitch black. A hindrance because they could not use the darkness for cover.

Once Aggie was safely strapped into her doggie harness in the back seat — her elation at being included, demonstrated by her lolling tongue and occasional yips — Max reversed down the drive. Hannah waved them off and traipsed into the house.

It would be a long night.

Half an hour earlier, Cris was tapping a tune on the steering wheel, his eyes fixed on the pub. The time ticked by with ever increasing slowness. Six o'clock came and went. No sign of Quentin.

While Cris was pretty sure he would meet up with the man later in the evening, the fact Quentin didn't see fit to advise him he was delayed, if for no other reason than to maintain appearances, irked the Italian. He checked his phone for the twentieth time.

No message, no missed calls.

Grinding his teeth, Cris climbed out of the car and stretched, loosening up his limbs. The afternoon was cooling. The sun was warm but not quite as scorching as it had been earlier, for which he was thankful. A hot night was the last thing he needed. Made a person fractious and clouded their brain.

He marched up and down the lane for a few minutes before spotting the phone box.

It stood on a little triangle of grass at the edge of the road, the red paint peeling from the metal frame. Most of the windows were damaged or missing. It smelt as though the whole neighbourhood and most of the local wildlife used it as a public toilet but, by some miracle, the phone was in working order.

Rummaging about in his pocket for change — a rarity — he fed a few coins into the machine and dialled Bryony's mobile. It went to voice mail.

He tried again, to be greeted by a string of disjointed sentences. Once he managed to interrupt, he explained Quentin's absence.

A conversation ensued between the three on the other end of the line, then Bryony asked for his number. Pressed for time, he was loath, but did as she bade. Less than two minutes later she called him back. Her words ought to have appalled him, but they didn't, merely corroborated what they already suspected.

He wanted all the details but could not afford to get caught up in another discussion. Saying goodbye, he hung up without hearing Bryony's 'take care'.

Escaping the rancid cubicle, Cris stood for a moment, breathing in clean air, ruminating over the latest snippet. Quentin Taylor had to be stopped… that was not in dispute, but first it was imperative he, Cris, won the ring.

Assuming, of course, Quentin allowed the auction to proceed at all. Cris half expected to arrive at the venue only to discover it had been postponed, and everyone, except him, had been informed.

The entrance to Hardington Manor was easily missed by the less vigilant. A five bar, rickety wooden gate wedged open by a thick tuft of weeds, a few feet up a well-worn gravel track, was the only indication visible from the main road.

Swinging off, Cris spotted the deteriorating sign announcing Hardington Manor, as the ancestral home of the

Finlayson family. A tattered banner bearing a council logo was pinned diagonally across the shabby blue and gold. It declared the manor closed to the public and under notice of demolition, with an advisory about the structure being unstable.

The notice saddened Cris. To a devotee of anything relating to the past, razing a stately home was synonymous with the scuttling of a ship, or the destruction of an ancient ruin. An architectural, horticultural, and historical legacy irretrievably lost.

He shook off the twinge of melancholy to concentrate on avoiding the overhanging and protruding beech trees lining the driveway. It wound through neglected gardens and opened out onto an expansive frontage.

Cris stared.

Despite its dilapidated façade, the manor was imposing. Built from local stone, darkened with age, and curtained in ivy, the four-storey central tower loomed in weary splendour over the wings flanking either side.

The multitude of mullioned windows, remarkably intact, reflected the changing hues in the sky, and effectively concealed anyone within. The tiled roof was adorned with a crown of finely sculpted parapets and chimneys.

Cris had researched the manor, wanting some idea of its layout, and knew it dated to the late Jacobean period. The blend of classical and Elizabethan architecture, even though crumbling under the weight of the centuries, lent the structure a timeless quality. *Oh, for the money to bring it back to life.*

After parking at the far end of a line of cars, he alighted, collected the case from the boot, and locked the vehicle. Heading towards the grand front entrance, Cris' relief that the auction was going ahead as planned was tempered by a twinge of unease that Quentin might have prepared a nasty shock.

. . .

The organisers had contrived to give the evening a theatrical flavour.

Strung around the sweeping stone balustrades bordering the broad flight of steps, as well as the arched doorway, were numerous fairy-lights. *How had they accessed power? A generator perhaps?*

The massive double wooden doors stood open; a guard on either side checking details on an electronic tablet and fingerprint reader. Only those invited were permitted to cross the threshold into a spacious entrance hall.

Beyond, gaudy coloured bunting criss-crossed what Cris presumed to be an internal courtyard. The scattering of freestanding torches, their flames guttering in the light breeze, added to the festive air.

Cris, his Enzo Sculleri identity approved, was shown to the reception area, which turned out to be a room of generous proportions. The cracked wooden floor had been freshly polished to a soft sheen. Remnants of rich, gilt-patterned paper clung to the walls which, along with the four chandeliers suspended from the frescoed ceiling, suggested that, once upon a time, this was the ballroom.

The historian in Cris cried out to photograph the exquisite interior, even in its shabby state. He longed to explore and pondered the possibility he might be granted the opportunity during the aftermath of this event. Given it was about to become a crime scene, there was a reasonable chance.

A slight smile tugged at his lips, at the thought of bringing Bryony here, picturing her reaction, and enthusiastic commentary.

Shoving such delights aside, he concentrated on the evening ahead. Surreptitiously, he studied his fellow bidders.

They looked like ordinary people. Nothing noteworthy, everything about them was nondescript. Deliberately cultivated to ensure they were quickly forgotten.

While apparently admiring the room, Cris counted his competition. Seventeen, markedly few for the size of the venue. Perhaps there was an odd straggler, yet to arrive.

Considering the inherent disadvantages and likely pitfalls associated with convening an event of this nature, Cris continued to question why this specific artefact had been deemed worthy of such a convoluted process instead of the typical online auction. Yes, there was this so-called smorgasbord of objects, but the draw card was the ring.

Had it been offered as a way to whet the appetite, to galvanise the bidders into taking the bait? Was there something else? Something which warranted a shroud of secrecy. Something of worldwide importance?

No doubt he would find out shortly.

CHAPTER 23

Max and Bryony whizzed past the Black Swan in Hardington Village with barely a glance. Battered she might be, but Romi had eaten up the miles with smooth, if occasionally hair-raising, speed.

During the journey — which should have taken an hour but ended up being almost twice that owing to tractors, and sheep, and a slow-moving removal truck — Bryony and Max had discussed various methods of entry. Both conceded it was futile to attempt admittance without the proper 'documentation.'

"Not far now." Bryony knew this stretch of road, aware the turn off for the manor was hard to spot, especially in the early evening light. "There." She pointed out the secluded driveway.

Slowing, Max drove on until they could see the roof line of the manor above the trees.

"How about here?" Bryony suggested as they approached a wider than normal verge. "I bet we could sneak through the woods without being seen."

"Might work." Max swung the car into the lay-by and

parked against the low stone wall. "Hang on, I'm calling Miles."

"For why?"

"He has men stationed around the venue, we don't want to spook or run afoul of them. They don't take kindly to people interfering in a live op."

"How do you know that? He never said anything to us." Miffed, Bryony twisted to glare at Max.

"He rang yesterday. Seems he knows you and my wife very well." Max took no notice of her disgruntlement.

"Ha bloody ha," Bryony retorted. "Oh, *that's* why you weren't bothered about Cris coming on his own. You already knew about the extra officers. You coulda told us," she groused, and subsided into her seat, stroking Aggie's inquisitive head which came to rest on her shoulder.

"Miles. Max. Wanted to give you a heads up. I'm at the venue with Bryony and Aggie. Can't go into details but some kind of intuition or second sight alerted Bryony our presence was essential." There was a lengthy pause.

Bryony could hear Miles expostulating but couldn't make out what he was saying. Sounded as though he was succumbing to that conniption Hannah had mentioned a few days ago.

"I know, mate, but remember what happened last time we ignored her instincts. We've got Aggie for protection." Another pause. "Hey, don't you mock. She might be a softie, but I guarantee she'd protect us with her life."

Registering that Max seemed to know more about Art Squad business than he ought, Bryony muttered to Aggie. "I bet you'd become a snarling monster if the need arose, wouldn't you, poppet?"

Aggie licked her cheek and gave what Bryony took to be a doggie grin of complicity.

Max listened intently for a few more moments, then

nodded. "Okay, you got it. Featherstone did you say? Can you send him my way? We're at the lay-by about five hundred yards east of the gate." Another pause. "Cheers. Yeah, yeah… next time you're up this way."

Max cut the call.

Almost immediately, a burly figure detached itself from the tree line and crossed the road. He sauntered over to the car, motioned for Max to wind down the window, and leant in.

"Featherstone, sir. Commander Hathaway asked me to introduce myself and offer any assistance, you and your… errr…" he skimmed a dubious gaze over Bryony and the scruffy mutt next to her, but was too well-disciplined to comment, "…companions might require."

"Much appreciated, Featherstone, now…" Max got out of the car and the two men fell into discussion about the layout of the grounds, and the location of the players.

"Your man was one of the last to arrive, I reckon he timed it so he has ease of departure. Not totally daft these Italians."

Bryony smothered her mirth, as Aggie woofed her agreement.

"Right, let's make tracks. The Commander assures me you can be trusted not to interfere or put yourselves in harm's way." He pinned the pair with a piercing blue gaze.

They nodded, respectfully.

"Please be careful and stay out of sight. I haven't time to be babysitting a couple of wanna-be detectives. You do anything to scotch this op and I'll lock you up myself. Am I understood?" His tone was measured but implacable.

Bryony gulped a little and vowed, in a voice not quite as perky as usual, she would be on her best behaviour. Max added his word. Aggie wagged her tail, and panted, straining a little on her leash, the delectable aromas filtering from the woodland teasing her nostrils.

Featherstone gave a curt nod, and led the way through a gap in the fence.

Bryony's unease intensified when they approached the gardens. She wished she knew where Cris was. She stared at the building, running her mind's eye over the layout. The sun was sinking toward the horizon, suffusing the façade in burnished bronze, camouflaging anyone or anything behind the windows.

Two men, whom Bryony presumed to be part of Quentin's security detail, stood guard at the front door. Scanning the length of the manor, she spotted two more halfway along each wing, and another patrolling the car park. She guessed there would be several more inside and possibly at the rear.

"He's not taking any chances," she muttered to Max.

"Would you?" he replied.

"How will we know friend from foe," she asked.

"My men won't shoot you," Featherstone spoke over the top of her head, a hint of humour in his remark.

"How do they know who *we* are?" she demanded in a heated whisper.

"Miles sent us your photos, well not the dog."

"Aggie," Bryony introduced sweetly.

"Beg pardon?"

"The dog... her name is Aggie," Bryony clarified.

"Ahhh. Nice to meet you, Aggie." Featherstone bowed and ruffled the dog's ears.

Aggie proclaimed her approval with a vigorous wag of her tail.

Featherstone took his leave and disappeared into the greying shadows.

Max and Bryony made themselves comfortable.

Smartly attired waiters moved among the guests. Some offered a selection of mouth-watering morsels. Others carried trays bearing glasses of wine, whisky, or fruit punch. It did the trick. The group started to relax, the oppressive quiet giving way to light chatter.

Cris threw himself into his act with formidable success. Glass of champagne in one hand, phone in the other, he circled the room, snapping pictures of everything. The wallpaper, the frescoed ceiling, the ornate chandeliers, even the window frames which had wooden shutters, carved with the family crest, on the inside.

His antics caught the attention of the other buyers, and he burst into a flood of voluble Italian when asked why he was taking photos. His audience looked blank, opening the way for conversation.

"Forgive me. I am enamoured of this old English mansion. She is very beautiful. Regal, like an ageing queen." He waved his hand at the walls. "See this wallpaper, so finely made. Yes, it is faded, but the craftsmanship is undeniable. The *lampadari*... hmm... chandeliers," he translated, seeing confused faces, "they are *magnifici*." He exaggerated his accent, waxing lyrical about the features of the manor.

"What on earth makes you want a reminder of a mouldy old English manor when you have the Colosseum and the Pantheon and Pompeii?" an older gentleman chimed in. "They cannot compare."

"Ahhh, yes, I agree, my country has many wonderful relics, but this building is equally compelling. See the..." Cris launched into an animated monologue about the significance of antiquated buildings such as Hardington Manor. From there, directing the discussion to more personal topics was smooth sailing.

He mentioned his island, and how he loved to entertain, and show off his collection. This created a stir, and by the time they were led into the auction room, Cris, in the guise of Enzo, had affirmed he would be delighted to host a house party at his villa. Without reservation, his fellow bidders provided names and contact information.

Cris was pretty sure most, if not all, were as false as his, but surmised, if warranted, a detailed investigation would uncover their genuine identities.

The room set aside for the auction was on the second floor. Mindful of the fragility of the building, Cris ascended the stairs, which swept in a lazy curve up the central tower from the atrium, with a healthy degree of caution. The uneven floors and creaking walls did little to allay his misgivings, sparked by the notice at the gate.

He dared pause to admire the arched stained-glass window which dominated the wall above the main doors. Two storeys high, it needed a good scrub but, even in its grimy state, was striking.

Escorted in, the buyers saw a podium in the centre, over which hung a huge spotlight, causing Cris, once again, to question the source of electricity. A house marked for demolition would be unlikely to have a working power supply.

Currently, the only illumination came from within a white-faced four-sided clock atop a box in the middle of the pedestal. The slender, black, second hand ticked inexorably towards the twelve, loud in the stillness.

Cris positioned himself at the far side, opposite the door, and slightly behind the bidders to his left and right. From this angle, he could see everyone.

Anticipation heightened, along with nervous mutterings. Listening, but not engaging, Cris fixed his gaze on the podium.

The clock struck seven.

The spotlight blazed into life, its glare dazzling those standing underneath.

A voice boomed out, although none could tell who spoke.

The room fell silent.

From their vantage point, Bryony and Max spotted the light in the room on the second floor.

Bryony glanced at her watch. It was after eight. "I wonder if that's the auction room. How long do you reckon it'll take?"

Max shrugged. "Not a clue. It probably depends on the bidding and how many items are being auctioned. I can't believe they've got power. Someone must have brought in a generator. I doubt there's any electricity or water connected to the property anymore. They've certainly thought of everything."

"It's to be hoped no one wants to use the loo," Bryony mused facetiously. "Wish we were close enough to hear proceedings."

"I bet you do," Max countered with a grin. "Be patient."

Aggie whined and shuffled restlessly. Max placed a calming hand on her ruff, and with a grunt, the dog sank onto the leaves, head on her paws.

All they could do was watch and wait.

The auctioneer was a portly and very dapper gentleman, attired in a charcoal grey suit. Crisp white shirt under a garish waistcoat — complete with a fob watch — and matching tie. His balding pate and thin-rimmed spectacles gleamed under the light. In his left hand he held a wooden gavel. Under his right arm, a black folder with gilt edging.

A guard followed him in and set down a solid-looking dais behind which the auctioneer stood.

The man's mincing gait reminded Cris of Toad from *The Wind in the Willows* — a story he had read as a child — an image he could not, for the life of him, expunge. If nothing else, it served to diffuse his internal disquiet.

With a dramatic flourish, 'Mr Toad' opened the folder.

The auction began.

The first few pieces were interesting. Behaving in the manner of a reclusive billionaire, Cris raised his paddle once or twice, wholly aware he would be outbid. In his opinion, none were worth squandering precious coin on, but it maintained his cover.

A sizeable painted tile, purportedly from Leptis Magna. A fragment of an inscription from Palmyra. A handful of rare coins, minted in the second century AD. Some brooches of decent quality. A cameo. Three scrolls of papyrus.

Cris nearly relented and bid on these last two. His hand was stayed by reasoning that if Miles' men were worth their salt, everyone would be intercepted on their departure, arrested for dealing in stolen goods, and the items confiscated. It offered a modicum of comfort.

Finally, the moment he had been waiting for.

The ring.

The bidders watched a guard convey the ancient object to the podium.

Nestled on a cushion of creamy velvet, the ring glittered dully.

The spotlight accentuated the patina of the onyx. For a split second Cris thought he saw a wisp of black mist hovering over the artefact, to dismiss it as a trick of the light, or the humidity in the atmosphere.

The auctioneer described the ring, implying — in a very roundabout fashion — that it had been 'found' during one of the excavations at Herculaneum. He started the bidding at an unexpectedly low, £5,000.

Initially, the bids came in thick and fast, the price escalating rapidly until it hit £11,000. The offers slowed. The auctioneer exhorted his audience, reminding them of its origins and the historical value of owning such a piece, once lost to the ravages of a volcanic eruption.

The price crawled up to £12,100, then stalled.

Cris held his breath. His was the high bid. He had a feeling the others in the room believed there might be one more item. Something making so clandestine an auction worth all this effort.

The auctioneer called. "Going once, twice." He raised his gavel. "Any more bids? For the final time at £12,100..." he held it for agonising seconds.

Nobody moved.

"Gone, sold to number 14." He banged his gavel on his wooden dais and pointed it at Cris.

. . .

Cris exhaled a pent-up breath, astounded to realise he was trembling. Acknowledging the smiles of approval from those in the room, he almost missed the auctioneer's announcement.

"I know you expected the ring to be the last artefact, but we received a late submission, which we decided must be included."

This elicited startled mutterings among the bidders, presumably concerned they had already blown their budgets.

The relic turned out to be a badly corroded broad sword; purportedly the one used to decapitate Maxentius after the Battle of the Milvian Bridge in AD312. Cris scrutinised the object, grateful the gloom hid his amusement at the gullibility of treasure hunters.

The cursory details provided, regarding the sword's provenance, did nothing to persuade Cris of its authenticity. The design appeared to be period correct, but that it was the genuine article was highly improbable.

It was a clever strategy. To introduce an item of such apparent significance to an, essentially, captive audience was like dangling the proverbial carrot in front of the donkey. Attested to when, as the bidding began at £10,000, paddles shot up all around the room, and the price sky-rocketed, doubling, then tripling in a matter of minutes.

Cris stepped out of the glow cast by the spotlight and observed proceedings. The bidding was frantic and climbed to an astronomical sum. He shook his head in disbelief. Gullible wasn't the half of it. He envisaged the organiser rubbing his hands together with relish at the profit he was about to make.

That brought his mind around to Quentin. Was he here? If so, where? Cris speculated as to whether he could evade the guards and search the premises, only to discount it. He didn't want to jeopardise the ring. He checked his phone. No message about payment. Presumably, it would come at the conclusion of the auction.

"Gone. Sold to number 7 for £45,000."

CHAPTER 24

The auctioneers' voice jolted Cris back to his surroundings. *£45,000? Merda. Some people had more money than sense.*

"Thank you for your attendance. Winning bidders, adjourn to the reception room and await your instructions. The rest may leave at your leisure. I look forward to our next meeting."

'Mr Toad' smiled genially, his expression guileless, prompting Cris to question whether the man had any clue as to the origin of the artefacts he had been party to selling. Then again, not a single item was accompanied by the requisite documentation substantiating their validity. An explicit indication they were acquired by less than honest methods.

Cris' tinge of regret that an innocent man had been fooled by Quentin and his cronies, evaporated.

The last to descend the stairs, Cris took his time. He noted where the members of Quentin's security detail were positioned, and where other possible exits might be located. The sun had set and, although relatively light outside, it was difficult to distinguish anything in the gloom of the sparsely illuminated interior.

He caught movement out of the corner of his eye as he reached the old ballroom and, turning his head, spotted two figures talking in a doorway at the far side of the courtyard. Cris eyes narrowed as he watched. A gust of wind caused the torches to gutter, shedding light on the pair, and he recognised the one on the right.

It was Quentin.

To deny the man's involvement was pointless but seeing him here at the venue in a, blatantly, supervisory capacity was, to Cris at least, a far more damming indictment than the proof Bryony had unearthed… however irrefutable.

He steadied himself. With one word, Quentin could blow his cover. Best to let Miles' men do their stuff and intercede only if necessitated by circumstance.

Cris stepped into the ballroom where he was greeted by the other winning bidders with victorious exclamations and excited chit chat. He acknowledged their congratulations, and returned the favour, affirming his invitations stood despite being outbid on one or two artefacts.

He felt his phone vibrate. Withdrawing it from his pocket, he read the expected message. £12,100 to be paid within fifteen minutes. As he scanned the text, Cris was distracted by a shuffling sound coming from the direction of the door. He glanced over.

Two desks and two lamps were positioned just inside the room, manned by more dark-suited staff, who sported the sallow complexions of office bound paper-pushers. Instinctively, Cris knew he could overpower both in seconds, should the need arise.

Acting the ever-so polite Italian, he waved the others forward, watching each transaction. The majority paid with cash; neat stacks of bound notes placed in a steel-grey safe-like receptacle between the cashiers.

In exchange, the individual received their prize or prizes. Bags of varying sizes were distributed to their rightful owner, the bidder asked to confirm receipt by adding their squiggle to something on an electronic pad.

Cris thought it apt that they were signing on a modern-day wax tablet.

His turn came. He lifted the case onto the table, keyed in the code, opened the lid, and counted out £12,100.

The cashier flicked through each bundle before dropping it into the safe. It never ceased to amaze Cris how carelessly these people handled substantial amounts of money. He accepted the bag handed to him, stepped to one side, and checked the contents. A small box in which sat the ring. Masking his elation, he scrawled his moniker on the tablet.

Almost done. He headed for the front door, chatting with a fellow winner. It happened to be the elderly gentleman who had questioned why he wanted to take photographs. They discussed the events of the evening before parting ways at the top of the steps.

"I wish to photograph this architecture. Soon it will be demolished, lost forever." Cris flapped his free hand at the tower, his tone one of regret.

"Ahhh..." the gentleman breezed, patting his arm in an avuncular manner. "Enjoy, enjoy."

Cris watched him totter down the steps, praying he was stopped before driving out of the grounds. His over-indulgence of alcohol, indisputable.

In the guise of taking a few more photographs of the exterior, Cris captured the faces of those guards loitering along the front of the manor. His sharp ears picked up a rustling in the trees. *Nocturnal animals in search of dinner, or Miles' officers?* It was probably the former, the latter's squad would be less visible than phantoms.

He checked his watch. Almost ten o'clock. Goodness the evening had flown by. It didn't feel like three hours since the auction began. One last look and, avoiding one of the dead rose bushes scattered at random intervals along what was once probably a tidily trimmed grassy bank, he strode down to the weed-infested lawn, the other side of which stood his car.

His was the only vehicle left. Cris presumed the organisers, staff, and security had parked around the back. The low purr of an engine floated towards him on the breeze then stopped. Had the driver been 'waylaid'?

It was eerily quiet.

He pressed the remote, hearing the vehicle unlock with a satisfying thunk. He lifted the boot lid, slid the case inside, and bent to tuck the bag in the convenient side pocket.

Cold metal nudged his left ear.

"Turn around very slowly, *Enzo*. Do not think of reaching for your phone or trying any sudden moves." The animosity in the order was unmistakeable.

Cris did as instructed. Leaving the bag where it was, he straightened up. Pivoting on his heel, he came face to face with the mastermind behind the trafficking ring. Strangely, now the moment had arrived, Cris felt no alarm, no acrimony. More, he was flooded with the abject relief he no longer had to persist with this farce.

In the twilight, Quentin's face was contorted, hostile. He believed himself in control.

"Such a shame," he sneered. "You should have stayed in Rome. Now they'll find your body in a car wreck. Tut, tut... driving at high speed on country roads under the influence of too much champagne. Typical Italian. Everyone knows they are idiots behind the wheel. Your death won't even be particularly newsworthy, nothing more than a statistic, another stupid tourist."

"And how do you propose to make me drive my car off the road?" While genuinely interested, it was also a way for Cris to stall for time.

"A simple matter of rendering you insensible, driving your car to the crest of one of the steep inclines, strapping you in and shoving you off."

"Do you not think they will investigate?"

"And find what? A man well over the limit of both alcohol and speed. What is there to investigate? The chloroform will have worn off by the time you're found. These back roads are very quiet overnight. I doubt anyone will come across the accident until first light, at the earliest."

"Ahhh, but I have not been drinking. My blood alcohol will be zero." Cris smiled affably. "I am more intrigued to know why?"

Quentin studied the tall, outwardly unconcerned, Cara-biniere. "You are not surprised?"

"Not in the slightest. We've known you are involved, if not the orchestrator, almost since your arrival here. Kill me if you must, but you will be hunted down, arrested and charged." Cris folded his arms and propped himself against the back of the car; his stance relaxed.

"Rubbish," Quentin derided. "Not possible."

"Although a trifle complex, if the person doing the tracking possesses the right skill set, the dedication and the time, it is eminently possible." Cris spoke without inflection.

He knew Quentin had no chance of carrying out his ultimate threat, but the man was as unstable as the building behind him and patently trigger happy.

"Give me the ring."

"No."

Quentin aimed the gun, the barrel inches from Cris' forehead. "Give. Me. The. Ring."

"Why should I? I was the highest bidder and paid more than its value anyway. It belongs in a museum, not in some private collection."

"I have a buyer willing to pay double. I *will* have it."

"I don't think so."

Quentin was losing his composure, while Cris remained coolly detached.

"I am not going to discuss this. Either way you look at it, I *will* have the ring and you *will* die. Rudi," he shouted, motioning with the gun to one of his henchmen who was loitering out of earshot.

A giant of a man ambled over.

"Sir." He raised a brow.

"You know what to do."

Rudi flexed his arms and cracked his knuckles. His intentions halted when Cris barked, "Now you are going to add *murder* to your growing catalogue of offences?"

"Huh?" The man hesitated, confused.

"Not you. Well, yes you too, but mostly him," Cris nodded at Quentin.

"Rudi, get on with it," Quentin huffed.

Rudi did not move.

"This man expects you to murder me. Not something an intelligent gentleman, such as yourself, ought to take lightly." Cris' tone was bland, almost solicitous. "Are you willing to gamble your liberty, on the off-chance you'll get away with it, just to follow his orders? It is a big leap from hired thug to killer."

The authority in Cris' voice, gave Rudi pause. The amount his boss paid might be ample, and he wasn't averse to using physical methods to subdue a nuisance, but he wasn't going to jail for anyone. To dispense a thorough beating was a bit of fun and usually gave him an adequate workout, but murder…

"Errr, Boss, you didn't mention no murder. What do you take me for?" Rudi whined.

"Oh, come on, it's not like I'm asking you to shoot him. All you have to do is let his car roll down a hill. No one will be able to pin it on you," Quentin sniped.

The two men argued the merits of aggravated battery over homicide, as though they were discussing a football match over a pint at the local pub.

Listening to the duo discuss his demise, it dawned on Cris that Quentin preferred not to get his hands dirty. *This* was why he had never been caught. He was always at least five steps away from the mess.

While that meant Quentin was less likely to use the gun — in fact, he might never have fired one outside his training — Cris wasn't out of danger. An agitated adversary waving a newly acquired weapon was a recipe for disaster.

"Quite prepared to give him a good thumping, but killin'? No way," Rudi objected.

"Coward," Quentin fumed, his temper fraying.

Rudi's gaze swung between Quentin and Cris. Perhaps not the sharpest tool in the box, neither was Rudi stupid. He shook his head, lifted his hands, and stepped back.

"Your crew, staff and cashiers are being rounded up, and taken in for questioning," Cris continued. "As has everyone leaving the manor. Whether you kill me or not, your organisation is finished. I have specialists working on obliterating the sites in the dark web and ensuring they cannot be revived."

"Bullshit." For the first time Quentin's veneer of formality slipped, and the gun wavered.

"Face it, Quentin. It's over."

"You lie," Quentin spat. He jabbed the gun in Cris' face, making his eyes smart.

"Actually, he doesn't," A voice to Quentin's right spoke up.

Spinning on his heel, Quentin saw a police officer wearing a uniform, which Cris identified as that of Armed Response, strolling towards them, his gun levelled.

"You!" Quentin's expression became one of resentful dismay, when stark realisation struck. His empire, the one he had created at no small cost was crumbling. *Oh hell, no, this was not in his plans.*

"One more step, Featherstone, and I'll blow his head off." There was a loud click as Quentin released the safety on his government issue weapon.

Cris closed his eyes. He really didn't want to die. He had too much to live for. An image of Bryony drifted into his mind. Her cheeky smile, her elfin face, her kisses which turned his knees to water.

"Stay back," Cris cautioned the officer needlessly. The man had come to a standstill a few feet away but did not lower his gun.

"Mr Taylor, you would do well to stop this malarky and come with me." Featherstone sounded like he was coaxing a recalcitrant schoolboy to climb down from a tree, not persuading a madman to surrender.

"Not a chance." Before anyone could blink, Quentin was

behind Cris, gun pressed to the side of his head. Quentin allowed himself a small smile; those hours at the gym had been worth the exorbitant monthly rate. "You will *not* be arresting me. If you are lucky, I will allow this fop to live, but only if you do *exactly* what I say.

Featherstone started forward.

Quentin's finger was on the trigger. "Don't be foolish, man. I have nothing to lose."

Cris appeared unruffled. "It's okay... Featherstone, is it?" He met the gaze of the officer, who bobbed his head. "If we all stay calm, we ought to get out of this unscathed. Isn't that right Quentin?"

"I'm not making any promises," Quentin snapped.

"So, what now?"

"I want you to reach into the car and get that bag. Slowly, slowly... no sudden moves," while Cris did as instructed. "Now remove the ring from the box and slip it into my pocket." That done, Quentin edged backwards, the gun grazing Cris' head. "Behave yourselves and you don't die today."

"We have you bang to rights, Taylor. The place is surrounded. You can't escape. Why make things worse for yourself?" Featherstone reasoned.

"I think you have me mixed up with someone who gives a shit." Quentin jibed humourlessly. "Do *not* move." The gun slewed towards Featherstone who had taken a step, then back to Cris.

"Why add murder to your crimes?" Cris asked. "Stealing a few artefacts is one thing, and I don't condone it, but the punishment is trifling compared with murder. You might get away with a couple of years in jail, possibly be expected to make restitution, but you'd still have the chance of a life afterwards."

Quentin snorted. "You really are a stupid, stupid man. I'm astonished Miles judged you competent to handle so complex an operation. It would be hilarious if it wasn't so pathetic. Now walk." He thwacked Cris' ear with the gun.

The impact stung, but Cris didn't react. In fact, he hardly felt it, feverishly scouring his brain for a way to thwart Quentin and retrieve the ring.

From their hiding place under the trees, Bryony and Max had watched the ruthless efficiency with which Commander Featherstone's men apprehended the participants.

Every car was stopped, the driver extracted, placed in handcuffs, and escorted to an unmarked van. An officer drove the car through the gate and parked it out of sight. A process repeated until all the attendees were in custody.

The winning bidders had their treasures confiscated, to loud complaints and demands for lawyers, it must be admitted. One by one they were read their rights, the few who claimed they had been duped, ignored.

Quentin's 'employees' had been subject to the same treatment. Most were eager to spill their guts regarding their boss' enterprise. Apparently, among these thieves there was not a single shred of honour.

All seemed to be going smoothly until Quentin slunk up to Cris and pointed a gun at his head.

Bryony clapped her hand over her mouth to muffle a terrified scream. "Crap, Max this is getting out of hand, we can't..."

"Stay right there, Miss," Superintendent Featherstone instructed quickly. "No one dies on my watch, but that's only if they do as they're told."

Bryony's cheeks took on a rosy hue.

"It's okay, sir, I'll keep an eye on her," Max appeased.

Featherstone grumbled under his breath about civilians, then strode out of the wood and into a stand-off.

The two remaining couldn't hear what was being said, but they didn't need to. The drama unfolding in front of them required no subtitles.

CHAPTER 25

Marcus was rocking Aelia to sleep when he felt his bond with Cris strengthen. Puzzled, he tried to comprehend the garbled emotions and pictures rushing into his head. His plea to slow down went unanswered... *something was badly wrong*. Placing a drowsy Aelia into her cradle, he left the room, in search of Senna.

He found his wife with Hannah in the triclinium. The two women were chatting about their day, while watching Cassia, Turi, and Luc playing some riotous game.

All five glanced up at him when he entered, but the three children carried on with their game. His habitual, 'Hey where's my hug,' went unsaid, which impelled Senna to study her husband more closely.

"Marcus?" she asked. "What is it?"

"Cris is in danger. He needs me."

"You cannot help him, Marcus, he is beyond our reach," Hannah said. "The people of his time will protect him."

"The man who threatens him has my ring. Although Cris won the ring, this man took it using dire threats and now holds him hostage with something called a gun. I have seen this man through Cris' eyes. He was once trusted, but has been consumed by greed, and deals in stolen treasures. He sets up buyers, only to trick them. I cannot let him keep my family's heirloom. To him it is worth only the coin he can make. To me it is all I have left of my brother."

"Marcus, please listen to yourself. I know you are linked to this man through your subconscious, but you cannot breach time. Even *if* that were possible, what could you do? You would be naught but a voice." Hannah tried to reason.

"I must do something." He sank onto the couch and concentrated.

The scene came into focus. It was almost dark, twilight giving way to night, throwing everything into shadow. A tall figure in black garb, with a military bearing stood to his left. To his right, a behemoth of a man wore a similar outfit, but something about it suggested he belonged to a different unit. Marcus felt the pressure of a metallic object on his neck and divined the fear Cris kept at bay.

The man holding Cris against his will was spouting a list of demands, most of which Marcus could not fathom. What he *could* fathom was the poison oozing from the individual. It reminded him of Gratius; a soldier consumed by madness who had attempted to usurp control of the garrison with fatal consequences. Not again.

"I am here." He sent the thought to Cris.

I take strength from your presence, came the faint reply.

"This man, he stole the ring?"

Not originally, but yes, tonight he has stolen the ring.

Marcus heard sorrow in Cris' tones. He perceived his counterpart's grief that his life might be snatched at the hands of a lunatic, leaving his family crushed. That he would lose a love he had only just found. That his death would sever this precious connection. All overlaid by a simmering anger in the knowledge the man had no compunction about killing him and, despite all his training, he could not prevent it.

Incandescent with rage that such evil was about to be inflicted on his descendent, Marcus absorbed Cris' emotions, feeling an inexplicable power begin to surge along his veins.

"Marcus."

The sweet voice scarcely registered. He saw Senna's hand on his arm and turned to face her. Her mouth was forming words, but he could not make them out. All he could hear was a whooshing sound, deafening him to all else.

"Hold my hand," he managed, and the triclinium vanished, to be replaced by something resembling an untended garden surrounded by woodland. In front of him, a building akin to an emperor's palace, fallen into disrepair.

His vision cleared.

Hardington Manor
Northumberland - July 2015

Clutching Aggie's lead, Bryony was edging towards open ground. The last of the light was fading and the moon had yet to rise. From this distance she couldn't make out what was happening, and it was driving her to distraction.

"Where do you think you're going?" Max grabbed her arm.

"Come on, Max," she appealed. "No one will see us."

"Bryony, use your brain," Max remonstrated in under-tones. "This could go pear-shaped in a heartbeat."

"If you think I'm going to sit here and do nothing while that tosser hurts Cris you've got another thing coming," Bryony retaliated in a fierce whisper. "It's too dark for Quentin to see us, so if he did happen to fire, I'm pretty sure he'd miss."

"Pretty sure, isn't very comforting," Max sighed but, because he knew she would go anyway, capitulated.

Keeping downwind of the little group, they crept forward. Aggie padded alongside, her hackles up, an occasional growl rumbling low in her throat. Every now and again, she stopped and sniffed the air, one paw raised. Bryony swore the creature had extra-sensory perception.

Reaching the lawn, using the odd bush as cover, they got within ten feet of the protagonists. It was evident the situation was becoming increasingly volatile. Quentin's behaviour was unpredictable, his demands ridiculous in the extreme.

If it was not for the gun aimed at Cris' head, Bryony might have burst out laughing when she heard him request a helicopter. The man was off with the fairies.

Marcus took stock. He could not see the man, because he was behind him, but he felt the weight of the strange weapon. He frowned. *How did this weapon work?* An image appeared in his mind, depicting what Cris had referred to as a gun, and he observed the mechanics of it firing something called a bullet.

A series of pictures demonstrated its effectiveness, causing Marcus' stomach to roil. While the terms used were foreign to the Roman, the damage it could inflict was not. He was both repelled and fascinated. A modest force wielding so compact a weapon could annihilate an army many times larger. Most advantageous in a conflict.

Be thankful it is not invented for centuries, Cris remarked drily. *For once it is, it will bring mankind to its knees.*

With an internal grin, Marcus wrested his thoughts back to the current battle. "We must retrieve the ring and remove this pestilence."

Any and all ideas welcome.

Marcus noticed a slight movement out of the corner of his, Cris', left eye. Peering into the darkness, he made out three shapes. One was rather squat. There was a familiarity about them, but their identity eluded him. Ignoring the trio for now, he ruminated on how a spectral voice might be received.

"Do people in your world believe in spirits?"

Some do, why?

"I am thinking a dead man whose finger was broken might decide to pay a visit."

Marcus felt a ripple of amusement.

I thought you could only observe, not participate.

"I am uncertain, but believe I am, temporarily, inhabiting your body."

Cris' shock jarred Marcus and he felt his connection to this world begin to detach. Summoning up his ire, he fought to hang on. It was vital he stayed.

If you can intimidate this excuse for humanity into lowering his gun, I would be most obliged.

Marcus/Cris writhed against the hand restricting his movement.

"Stop wriggling," a nasal twang insisted.

"You **dare** to take my ring?" The voice coming out of Cris' mouth prompted badly stifled gasps and a few expletives. It sounded nothing like the Italian.

"*Your* ring? Oh, get over yourself. You had it in your

possession for less than half an hour. If Miles had let me run this op, you would not have seen it let alone won it," Quentin jeered, exasperated.

Cris knew the man was losing patience, this could get messy.

"It was stolen from my place of rest, many years ago." The voice thundered, echoing off the nearby building. "I have been searching for the thief ever since. The robber violated the dead, desecrated my remains. I cannot cross the Styx until I have recovered what is mine."

There was a kind of keening wail, drawn out before dwindling to a moan. "To roam the world forever, search-ing... searching... is a curse I wish on no one. Save the one who refuses to restore my heirloom. I pray he suffers the savagery of Tartarus."

"T-T-Tartarus?" Quentin stammered, slack-jawed. Without relinquishing his grip or dropping the weapon, he turned Cris, in order to look into his face. The man was unrecognisable.

Ice coasted down Quentin's spine. *This was bizarre. Was it some kind of trick?* Memories of another night long ago reared up. With sheer force of will, he pushed them aside. He did *not* believe in ghosts.

"The place to where the most iniquitous are dispatched." The voice almost purred with malevolence.

With supreme effort, Quentin tried to counter the terror beginning to claw at his mind. "Stop play-acting, Captain Rossi." His manner was abrupt, unyielding. "Do you think I can be frightened off?"

Without waiting for a reply, he pulled the trigger.

The flare from the muzzle lit the tableau for a split-second.

His ears ringing, Cris was stunned to realise he was still alive.

Featherstone gave the signal.

With a shriek worthy of a banshee, Bryony propelled herself across the gravel, Aggie on her heels. *No bloody way was this dickhead going to kill Cris.*

Max tried to stop her, but she was too quick. He sprinted after her, thinking the only good thing about this was that his wife remained safely at home.

Marcus exploded with a fury rivalling Vesuvius. Spinning around, he grabbed for Quentin's arm. The gun fired again. The bullet went wide.

A flurry of fur, a guttural snarl and Aggie hurled herself at the man, teeth snapping. Quentin kicked out, catching Aggie in the ribs, making her yelp.

A piercing scream and Bryony entered the tussle, dodging around the two men, desperately trying to seize the gun, which Quentin was waving erratically. Trying to evade her grasping hands, he swung his arm down and the barrel of the weapon smashed into Bryony's jaw.

She slumped to the floor.

That did it. His action was doubly heinous.

To Marcus it was as though Quentin had hit Senna.

Cris' heart stopped. *Bryony. What the hell was she doing here?* He fell to his knees, checking her over, reassured that, although unconscious, she seemed otherwise unharmed.

Max appeared.

"Protect her." The voice issuing the order was two merged together, giving the words a peculiar resonance.

. . .

The detachment of officers hovered on the periphery, prepared to intervene at Featherstone's signal. In the limited light, it was too difficult to determine who was who.

Although imperative their quarry did not get away, use of firearms was generally frowned upon unless they had no alternative.

Moreover, Miles had been unequivocal in his orders. Quentin Taylor didn't rate a quick death. He merited a long confinement at her Majesty's pleasure.

All they could do was watch.

The souls of the two men, ancestor and descendent combined.

"You would hurt a defenceless woman?" they roared. "You are the very scum of the earth. I pray birds peck out your entrails while you still breathe. Crucifixion is too good for you. Perhaps if your blood is spilled in the arena..."

Quentin was gibbering, gawking at the distorted face of the man leering over him. To his disbelief it kept changing. One second it was Cris, the next an unknown foe. The language was stilted...formal... suggesting the speaker had learnt English from a phrase book, but the content was no less horrifying.

"Give me my ring." Marcus held out his hand, palm up.

"*Never*. I lost it once I have n—"

"*What* did you say?" Cris demanded.

Quentin stared at the mercurial countenance of the Italian. *This had to be a bad dream. Nobody's face could do that.*

"Quentin," Cris snapped.

"I said I lost it once, I'm not losing it a second time."

"When did you lose it?" For a moment it was Cris speaking. Marcus retreated briefly.

"Never you mind."

"There was no 'other' buyer was there? It was you all along. Why did you include the ring in the auction if you wanted it?" Cris was confused.

"Unless I am the supplier, I see the items at the same time as the bidders. There are strict protocols to which traders must adhere, across all sites. A way to keep privacy and distance intact. A middle-man assumes charge of the artefacts." His tone inferring this somehow made his dealings legitimate.

"And why you needed to see the description on the email?"

"So irritating."

"Why didn't you install your own 'bidder'?"

"I was on the verge of doing so when Miles contacted me to ask whether I would act as liaison." He grinned, his teeth gleaming white in the gloom. "The timing proved… fortuitous."

"One more question. Why didn't you denounce me as a fake?"

"Too hard. Your Bryony is highly skilled. I knew Miles wanted the item, and the budget would be enough to secure it. Better to let you all think I was a bumbling geek, than the brains behind the enterprise. Once you won, all I had to do was remove you." Quentin spoke in all seriousness, seemingly unaware of the absurdity of his words.

"When did you lose it the first time?"

The gun, which had been pressed into his ribs came back up, but this time Cris was ready. He grappled for the weapon, managing to get hold of the barrel, trying to wrench it from Quentin's fingers. The latter refused to yield. His strength, unexpected.

"Tell me," Cris rapped.

"Bugger off. I *will* shoot. Don't think I won't." Quentin's voice was shrill in the darkness.

"No, you won't. You don't do the shooting. You employ others to do that," Cris scoffed.

They struggled. Cris gained the advantage and twisted the gun until it was under Quentin's throat. "I, on the other hand, have no qualms about blowing your brains out." He felt Marcus' strength aiding him. It was *the* freakiest sensation, but he welcomed it. "Tell me."

Quentin sagged, then straightened up. He tried to jerk his head away from the barrel with minimal success. "Why do you care?"

"Your comment intrigues me. You believe this trinket is yours... prove it."

CHAPTER 26

An eerie hush descended.

Even the breeze had dropped, but the air prickled with anticipation and something else. Something indefinable, causing the hairs to rise on the napes of those watching, and their skin to break out in goosebumps.

Her jaw throbbing, Bryony sat on the grass, resting against the trunk of a gnarly old oak tree, Aggie's head on her lap. Absently she stroked the dog's head. Max had assured her although perhaps bruised, Aggie was uninjured, which did little to douse Bryony's indignation.

She strained to see what was going on. She had no doubt Quentin would be apprehended, the man had nowhere to run. It was what he might do in the meantime which bothered her.

"Stay," Bryony commanded Aggie, and scrambled to her feet. Aggie blew a huff, but didn't move, her velvety brown eyes following Bryony who snuck up behind the group of policemen, to Cris' car.

"I came into possession of the ring twenty years ago." Quentin spoke quietly, but his words reached even the furthest among them. "Foolishly, I trusted my partner, only to find out he was using me and my knowledge to obtain the highest quality artefacts."

"Came into possession? Obtain? Please elaborate," Cris urged, his patience wearing thin.

"Do I need to spell it out?" Quentin hedged peevishly.

"Oh yes, I think you do."

"Only if you take the gun out of my throat."

Reluctantly, Cris lowered it, slightly. His need to know the truth warred with his desire to give Quentin the beating he so richly deserved.

Neither man loosened their hold on the weapon.

"When I was a kid, I was always on the lookout for things I could sell for a decent profit. Then I joined the force. Best decision I ever made, especially when I got promoted to the Art Squad, because now I knew what to look for, their training is second to none," he boasted.

"It started out as a bit of a lark, acquiring items the public didn't know existed or had forgotten about, careful not to take anything large or hard to sell on. Des, my partner, had read an article about the docks at Herculaneum. I thought all the valuables had been removed. It was too good an opportunity." Quentin's voice assumed a far-away note, he even smiled.

Marcus wanted to wring his neck.

"I had some holiday due, so Des and I decided it was worth the trip to Italy. It took meticulous planning and even back then, the site was hard to access, but we were successful. Even so, we were damn nearly caught. That's when I broke the finger of the skeleton. Tried to hurry. Rookie mistake." He grimaced.

"How did you lose the ring?" Cris sounded no more than moderately interested, but Marcus, itching to dispense some rough justice, prowled in his head like a panther about to pounce.

Using the car as cover, Bryony inched closer.

"About three weeks later, after the furore had died down, we decided it would be best to pass on most of the stuff to a fence we knew. He was reliable and invariably got us a good price. The morning we were supposed to deliver it, I woke up to find Des had upped and offed.

"Thieving toe-rag took the lot. He was my best mate and we'd been partners since we were teenagers. Who does that? Mind, if I ever catch up with him…" Quentin didn't finish that thought. His friend's betrayal continued to rankle, two decades later.

"Was that what got you into smuggling?" Cris asked, trying to quell the outrage he could feel emanating from Marcus, while marvelling at how glibly Quentin described his life of crime.

"Eventually. It was so easy. Working for the Art Squad, I get to travel the world, to ancient ruins, museums, art galleries, private collectors. I have customers lining up, willing to pay ludicrous sums for the most insignificant artefact.

"It started off as a way to make a bit of extra money, little bits here and there, but before long it became a game. Neither do I consider it to be smuggling, rather it's a… re-appropriation." Quentin smiled benignly.

Cris could hardly believe his ears. The man thought he

was doing the world a *favour*? Floored, he steadied himself, Quentin was still speaking.

"Initially, I infiltrated a few illegal trading networks as part of my job to track down stolen items, but when I dug deeper, I figured out it would be far more lucrative for me to start my own. So, I did."

"*That's* why you want the ring? You think it's yours because of some fictitious criminal code?" Cris quizzed. "I admit to being impressed, and appreciate your explanation, but the game is over. Your enterprise is being dismantled, and you are going to jail."

The futility of his situation wasn't enough to prevent Quentin trying to wriggle free. The hand clamped around his arm tightened.

His hold never slackening, Cris, wanting to keep Quentin rattled, tried another tactic. "Why did you decide to assume another identity?"

"What?"

"You were born Timothy Bryce Lawton. Why did you steal Quentin Taylor's identity?"

Dumbfounded, Quentin gaped at Cris. His eyes slit and his face reddened. "That interfering bitch couldn't keep her God damned nose out, could she? Wish I'd bloody well shot her when I had the chance. Can't trust anyone anymore."

"If you hadn't been such a pompous ass, we wouldn't have asked her to investigate you. That's on your head," Cris retorted, hearing a smothered chortle from Featherstone's direction. "Suffice it to say, your behaviour made us suspicious, and here we are. Now, hand over the ring and I'll leave you in Superintendent Featherstone's gentle custody."

Hearing this, Featherstone, preparing to arrest Quentin, barked an order. Beams of light appeared as the officers switched on their torches.

.   .   .

Galled at his spectacular lack of success, and in spite of the insurmountable odds stacked against him, Quentin clung to the belief he could evade capture and disappear. He would lay low for a while, then reappear with a new identity.

"Taylor."

God was that bloody Italian still griping about the ring. Wearied of the charade, Quentin called upon his training. So, Cris was a Carabiniere, and there might be a few lowly cops stationed around the grounds, but Quentin had been trained by Interpol. Featherstone would only approve deadly force as a last resort.

Since he, Quentin, had not caused any significant injuries, they would give chase, but would prefer to let him go than chance harming civilians.

His smile was sly. "Fine, but for God's sake stop begging, it doesn't become you."

Cris glowered at the insult but kept his peace. All that mattered was getting the ring. Warily, he relaxed his iron-grip, but with a cacophony of alarms going off in his mind, Cris didn't release Quentin. The man was as unpredictable as a cut snake.

That was his first mistake.

The instant Quentin felt the pressure on his arm decrease and the gun move away from his chest, he executed a swift shimmy, leaving Cris holding a jacket with no one inside it. In a millisecond he had control of the weapon and released the safety.

In an attempt to recapture Quentin, Cris moved, and his gaze met the glare of a flashlight, blinding him.

That was Cris' second mistake.

He wouldn't make a third.

. . .

Quentin's objective was the manor and, using the shadows to his advantage, he started to run.

Spots dancing before his eyes, Cris gave an infuriated bellow, and set off in hot pursuit. Already fit, the presence of an enraged ancestor boosted his speed, and he closed the gap quickly.

Bryony, without thought for her own safety, hared after them.

Max, flabbergasted by her recklessness and hearing Hannah's voice in his head, followed Bryony, Aggie at his heels.

Beams of light bounced as Featherstone's men brought up the rear.

It was late evening. Night was subsuming the last remnants of daylight and the manor was cloaked in darkness. It was *not* the best place to be chasing a tenacious thief.

As luck would have it, Aggie had Quentin's scent and, her rumbling growl unceasing, she streaked past Bryony to fall into step alongside Cris.

"Careful, girl," Cris muttered when he felt her wet nose nuzzle his hand. "Our quarry is dangerous." He heard Aggie whine and took that to mean she understood, blithely ignoring the fact he was carrying on a conversation with a dog. Bearing in mind he was currently sharing his body with a man who lived centuries ago, chatting with Aggie sounded eminently plausible.

The two trailed Quentin to the manor. Cris could hear him stampeding down the maze of corridors. Unerringly Aggie followed, her canine eyes adjusting to the lack of light.

The pounding of boot clad feet heralded the arrival of a handful of officers, the remainder fanning out to skirt the perimeter.

"Quentin," Cris bawled.

His shout reverberated around the manor. He heard a faint cackle and sped in its general direction, but his target was fleet of foot and had, apparently, vanished.

Bryony, whose childhood had been spent exploring historical monuments of every ilk, was well acquainted with the intricacies of old buildings. She slipped silently along, pausing every few steps to listen. The creak of the floors, a reliable indicator as to the various locations of those within.

Glad she had thought, once they knew the auction venue, to delve into the local council's website for any blueprints pertaining to Hardington Manor, Bryony recalled a private set of passageways. These led from what had been the domestic quarters to invisible doorways in each of the main rooms on the ground floor.

Originally constructed to allow the staff to go about their duties virtually unseen, they became convenient escape routes whenever the need arose. *Did Quentin know of them?* It was feasible, and a crafty way to avoid detection.

Getting her bearings, Bryony turned right and entered a large room, the shelf-lined walls with a handful of battered-looking books indicative of a library. Her eyes had become accustomed to the obscurity and she scanned the room for the bellpull or call button.

Finding the button, she knocked gently on the surrounding panels, until one sounded hollow. Pressing the edges, she grinned when it swung open.

It was blacker than pitch inside and she shuddered at the brush of cobwebs across her face. Pulling out her phone, she risked switching on the inbuilt torch, dimming it with her hand... in case she was not alone. There was no sign Quentin was ahead of her, but she was cautious in her footsteps.

Wishing she had Aggie for company, Bryony continued her solitary path, checking each secret panel. At some point she detected a faint lessening of the darkness and followed it, coming to an arched opening. Peeping out, she found herself in an alcove jutting off another passage.

Pocketing her phone, she stole into the first room which happened to be the kitchen. Nothing. She padded noiselessly along the corridor leading to the old baize door, pleased to note it stood ajar, the desiccated green material crumbling under her fingers when she touched it.

Pondering which way to go, she heard the scrape of something behind her, like a chair being dragged across tiles.

Whipping around, she flattened herself against the wall.

A figure loomed up. *She would be seen.* It was all she could do not to scream, unaware whether it was friend or foe. At the last minute, instead of going into the main house, the person took a sharp left and headed the other way, towards the back door.

A whiff of cologne tickled her nose. She recognised the headache-inducing scent as the one Quentin doused himself in and pinched her nose to stop a sneeze. He was mumbling to himself, and his body looked hunched. Bryony questioned whether the man was injured until she realised, he was toting a backpack.

She gave him four strides' head start, then followed, keeping close enough to monitor which direction he took, but far enough back that he ought not hear her.

. . .

Cris, Marcus circling his consciousness, and Aggie had searched the first floor. There was no sign of Quentin and nothing to suggest he might return to this level. They were descending the rickety stairs when Cris spotted his prey vanishing through the door leading to the domestic sphere.

Ensuring his phone was on silent mode, he sent a quick text to Max and Featherstone apprising them and hurried after Quentin. The scenario had all the hallmarks of a slapstick television skit, and Cris gave a grim smile. This would probably not be quite as funny.

He edged around the baize door, without opening it any wider — Aggie, his silent shadow — to see two people disappearing towards the rear exit. Cris frowned. *Two? Who was the second individual? Did Quentin have an accomplice?* He hadn't seen anyone tailing the liaison. A litany of oaths on the tip of his tongue, Cris tightened his hold on Aggie's leash.

Carabiniere and canine caught up, as Quentin shoved at the back door. He had to put his shoulder to it, the heavy wood yielding with a grudging rasp. The bottom of the door had swelled with damp and age, no longer fitting its frame, the wood splintering on the stone flags.

Quentin swore. He stopped, his head swung from side to side, and Cris saw his face — pallid in the gloom. When nothing happened, Quentin stepped out into the night. His shoes crunching on the gravelled courtyard.

Dropping Aggie's leash, Cris closed the small gap to grab Quentin's pursuer, clapping his hand around the person's mouth to prevent them drawing attention.

The figure squawked and wriggled frantically. An elbow jarred his ribs, and a booted foot came down hard on his polished shoe. *Figlio di puttana!* He spun his attacker around and was about to slam him up against the wall when a shaft of light from the doorway caught a glimmer of spikey auburn hair.

Cazzo, it was Bryony.

CHAPTER 27

"*B*ryony?" Despite his shock, Cris managed to keep his voice low. "What the hell are you doing in here? I thought you were safe with Max."

"He kicked Aggie. He hit you. He was going to kill you. Do you think I'm going to stand around and do nothing?" she hissed.

"He also hit *you*. The man has no scruples." Cris scrutinised Bryony's face, the bruising on her jaw distinct even in such paltry light. "*Dio*, woman, *I* nearly hit you..." He gathered her against him, kissing the top of her head.

"Sorry, didn't mean to get in the way. I was just so mad." Her reply muffled in his shirt.

Her arms slid around his waist, and she heard the erratic tattoo of his heart. An oddly comforting sensation.

They stood for a moment, until Aggie inched between them, desperate for a pat.

"Come on, we haven't time for this now." Bryony said. "Let's get the bastard, then..." she let that dangle.

Cris smiled down at her and snuck a quick kiss. "Deal."

. . .

The moon was rising, bathing the landscape in soft luminescence. Shapes which had been indistinct, now took form.

In single file, the trio left the house, and crossed the rear courtyard towards the outbuildings, at the far side of which was a semicircle of tarmac. A modern addition no doubt, and Cris guessed this was where the staff had parked. A lone vehicle remained, but no sign of Quentin.

Beyond, he spied what appeared to be a terrace leading to a large pond, glimmering in the moonlight, not a ripple marring the obsidian surface. To their left, trees encroached, slowly reclaiming the land.

Surely the man hadn't fled through the woods.

"Where else could he go?" Cris questioned out loud. "The outbuildings?" There was no answer. "Bryony?"

He turned, expecting to see Bryony right behind him, but she was several feet away.

Aggie growled.

"It appears the tables have turned... again..." Quentin sneered. He had one hand under Bryony's throat, his elbow pinning her, the other hand brandishing the gun.

Heedless of the weapon, Bryony fought like a wild cat. Her struggles proved ineffective against her captor's superior strength and larger physique.

Cris closed his eyes. He had never wanted to take another's life, but right at this moment it would give him extraordinary satisfaction.

"Let her go, Quentin. This has gone on long enough. Seriously man, is it worth it?"

"I'll release her, *after* I have been allowed to leave unhindered," Quentin stipulated.

Baring her teeth, Aggie pulled at her leash.

Marcus surged to the forefront of Cris' mind. *I am wearied of this man's lunacy. It is time to finish him.*

"While I agree, we cannot take his life. It is against our laws," Cris replied inwardly, wondering where the other officers were.

"Get off me," Bryony snapped, squirming.

"Quit your yammering." Quentin's fingers tightened, Bryony's protests becoming a choked squeak.

A red haze swam over Cris' vision, but he managed to control his temper. Losing it would get them nowhere.

Marcus loitered, his ire a kaleidoscope of jagged sparks.

Believing himself invincible, Quentin taunted the irate Italian. Swapping the gun to the hand under Bryony's chin, he retrieved the ring from his pocket, and held it aloft between his finger and thumb.

Bryony clawed at him, trying to snag the artefact to no avail. She *was* able to kick him in the shin.

Quentin cursed and, closing his fist around the heirloom, retaliated with a brutal blow to her face.

Blood trickling into her mouth from a split lip, Bryony saw stars, and nausea threatened but she refused to gratify Quentin with a reaction. Instead, she concentrated on how delightful it would be to fillet him, slowly with a blunt knife. It helped.

"To paraphrase a well-known trilogy... it is interesting how so small a thing can cause such angst." Quentin smirked. "One last look." He displayed it on the palm of his hand.

A moonbeam winked off the onyx.

A wisp of the finest black vapour appeared to coil above the stone.

The watchers stared, mesmerised.

Aggie whined and paced restlessly.

Cris recollected that curious moment during the auction... *was it his imagination...?*

The vapour floated upwards and hovered.

Then, impossibly, seemed to inflate.

The mist took form. A cadaverous apparition emerged, and a noxious aroma began to permeate the air.

Cris felt Marcus give a peculiar jolt and recognised his ancestor was aghast.

"What is it?" he sent the thought.

Remember what I told you about violating the departed?

"Yes." He drew out his reply, not wanting to hear the answer.

May I introduce my brother? Titus Salvius Aelianus.

Cris' jaw dropped, *definitely imagining things*. He shook his head to dispel the apparition. Nothing changed.

*It is **not** your imagination.*

You would steal from the dead not once but twice? A strident voice railed. Titus Salvius Aelianus was very definitely vexed.

Quentin babbled something unintelligible but did not relax his hold on Bryony... or the ring.

To violate a corpse, even one who perished long ago is a profanity we cannot excuse. Restore the ring to its rightful owner unless you wish to languish in Tartarus. Salvius howled, and Cris was certain he could distinguish the wails of a legion of troubled spirits amplifying the command.

"Th-there is no r-rightful owner," Quentin stuttered, his eyes wild.

"That's where you are mistaken." Cris stepped forward, Marcus coming into ascendency.

Once more, Quentin was witness to the merging of their

faces, the features fluctuating like quicksilver. He stumbled backwards, towing Bryony with him.

The two tumbled to the ground. The impact caused Quentin's grip to loosen, and Bryony, terrified the gun would go off, rolled free.

She was on her feet and out of Quentin's reach before he blinked.

Quentin didn't notice, his petrified gaze fixed on Cris and the black miasma, now ballooned to epic proportions, above him.

"If there *is* a rightful owner of an artefact buried for two millennia, rediscovered, stolen, then passed through innumerable hands to be sold at an illegal auction, it is I," Cris divulged, with remarkable calm.

Quentin spluttered a repudiation. "Preposterous. You are delusional."

"Let me elaborate. The ring belonged to one of my ancestors, who was killed during the eruption of Vesuvius. He lay buried under tons of ash for centuries. Once unearthed, his remains were left relatively undisturbed until the night you decided to break into Herculaneum.

"Instead of respecting the deceased, you defiled them by stealing their treasures, the last thing they touched in the moment their life was so cruelly extinguished. An insult repeated tonight." The aberrant duet resounded off the dilapidated outbuildings.

Return the ring or suffer the repercussions. Reiterating its demand, the grotesque face leered close to Quentin. Malevolence pulsed, and more than one pair of eyes watered as the group was enveloped by the stench of sulphur.

Quentin's teeth chattered as he shuffled backwards, waving his hand in an ineffectual attempt to bat away the cloud. *This had to be a nightmare. This wasn't real, couldn't be real.*

. . .

Bryony scanned the ground for anything suitable with which she could wallop Quentin. A good wallop might distract him long enough for Cris to grab the gun. Getting the ring would be child's play once the weapon was no longer a threat.

She spotted a bundle of wooden boards stacked against the outbuilding closest to her. They were warped and cracked but ought to do the trick. She edged backwards, careful not to draw attention to herself, and hoisted the plank closest to her. It was rotten and disintegrated in her hands.

Swearing under her breath, she tried the next one, same thing. By the fourth slat, she was beginning to think someone was having a lend. *Why keep a pile of crumbling timber?* The sixth piece was much better. Thin, but solid.

She hefted it in her hands, getting used to its proportions, making sure she wasn't going to get a palm-full of splinters. A wicked grin curved her lips and, mimicking a soldier with a broad sword, Bryony slashed the air.

Quentin was sitting on the dirt — his legs outstretched, the gun on his lap — snivelling about artefacts and ownership. His whole focus on the macabre illusion suspended above him.

Bryony thought it was the coolest thing she had ever seen, not in the slightest afraid. She wasn't its prey. This gave her pause. She considered her nonchalance at being within ten feet of a huge, scary, ancient phantom currently threatening to drag a human to Tartarus, that Cris had spoken to his ancestor, and Hannah's bombshell about her past.

She had embraced each mind-blowing element, never questioning their veracity. Hannah was right, it was a gift this knowledge.

Keeping an eye on Quentin, she sidled out of his eye-line, catching Cris' gaze as she did so. She smiled sweetly when he shook his head. Yes, she trusted he had this... more or less... under control, but she didn't trust Quentin one jot. The man was slippery as an eel. He had already slithered out of their clutches once.

Now, all she needed was the opportune moment.

With as much dignity as he could muster, Quentin got to his feet and drew himself up to his not inconsiderable height. With reckless disregard, he aimed the gun and pulled the trigger. The report was deafening in the tranquil night, the bullet zinging harmlessly though the nebula.

"Begone," he yelled, waving one arm as if he was invoking some kind of banishing spell.

Hollow laughter erupted, disconcerting to those within hearing range, which included Featherstone and his men who were closing in, stealthily. They exchanged startled glances, wondering what on earth was funny about this saga.

The pall of murk seemed to lift and gather itself, the seething mass becoming impenetrable. Bryony watched spellbound as it lunged, towering over Quentin.

In a voice wintry enough to transform the hottest lava flow into a glacier, the wraith of Salvius vowed, *Return the heirloom or I will ensure the judges hear of your treachery.* A refrain the tormented souls, coveting their rest, parroted in ghastly chorus.

Paralysed by dread, Quentin could not shift his gaze. "J-judges?" he stammered.

Aecus, Rhadamanthys, and Minos, Salvius enlightened, his

sardonic tone indicating his quarry should be acutely aware of to whom he referred.

Bryony tiptoed closer, flexing her shoulders in readiness. Glancing around, she picked out Featherstone and his men advancing, cautiously, confounded gazes tilting sporadically heavenwards.

Off to her right, Max had materialised. Aggie abandoned Cris, to wind around the legs of her master, with muffled whimpers of delight. Max, his eyes never leaving the scene in front of him, looped Aggie's leash securely around his wrist, and slipped her a bite-sized doggie biscuit, his hand coming to rest on her head.

Cris faced Quentin, who was gawking upwards.

It was now or never.

Darting forward, Bryony yelled — for no reason she could think of, "This is for Senna," and swung the plank with all her strength at the back of Quentin's knees.

His legs buckled; his body arched then lurched forwards. He flung out his arms, pitching the gun and the ring into the air. They soared in dual arcs, to bounce in opposite directions across the compacted earth.

Cris saw the ring land in a clump of grass. He pounced on it.

Quentin, realising his error, gave vent to an eldritch screech and chased after him, only to find his way barred by a dense blackness.

I warned you, Salvius whispered in his ear, coating the sensitive skin in ice crystals. *If you ravage the dead, you pay the price.*

Transfixed, Quentin moaned his terror.

Ensuring the ring was safely buttoned into the inside pocket of his jacket, Cris grabbed the collar of the erstwhile mastermind, firmly.

"If you would be so benevolent as to permit a brother's intercession." Cris faced Salvius but it was Marcus who spoke.

Marcus? The shade that was once Salvius sounded thunderstruck.

"Yes, beloved brother, it is I. By an inexplicable twist of fate and the grace of Fortuna, I, who lost you in our time, found you here, millennia hence."

Yet your appearance is unfamiliar to me.

"My... hmmm... host is our descendent, Cristiano Rossi, whose family continue to farm in our stead. Our mysterious bond was unexpected, precipitated by a spate of incidents which culminated in this evening's... errr... event."

How did my ring come to be here, far from our homeland?

Cris took over and supplied Salvius with a concise account of how the heirloom ended up in the wilds of Northumberland. Much would be alien to a man born prior to the technologies and inventions of the modern era, but Salvius seemed to grasp the gist. He nodded in vague understanding — as best he could, given his lack of bodily structure.

All that remains is to punish this odious excuse of a human. Perhaps he could be fed to the lions at the next games? Salvius grinned evilly.

"Alas, such practices have been prohibited for an eon," Cris felt the need to apologise.

Regrettable. Salvius belched what could only be described as an aggrieved humph.

"Perhaps you might consent to me assuming responsibility for meting out retribution? I give you my word the penalty will be harsh and protracted." Cris bowed.

The black fog swirled, emitting a sound akin to the thrum of a highly tuned engine.

"His word is to be trusted, my brother," Marcus asserted.

Then it shall be done. Once the injustice is redressed, perchance I may be afforded a ride with the ferryman. The words were followed by a sigh which seemed to echo down the ages. Salvius reached out, the dark mist formed fingers which curled over Cris' hand.

An unforeseen boon, Marcus. You are fulfilled?

"My life is blessed. I have a beautiful wife and three children who lighten my heart every day. Be at peace, Salvius."

The mass began to shrink, only to swell to monstrous proportions.

Beneath it, the watchers most of whom were rendered mute by this… phenomenon, could not avert their eyes however much they wanted to.

With a hideous scowl, the spectre enveloped Quentin. Although somehow liberated from Cris' custody, he could not move. He was lost to sight, and all noise ceased.

Silence reigned.

CHAPTER 28

A wise man does not provoke the wrath of the Gods, the time has come for you to make amends. Heed my advice. Salvius exhorted in a tone guaranteed to cow even the most foolhardy.

Ashen-faced, Quentin — who was far from foolhardy — nodded, not trusting himself to speak. His composure might be hanging by the slenderest of threads, but his brain was working furiously. Agree to whatever this thing wants and you're home free, his internal voice insisted.

Then let this be done. I renounce my claim on your soul and surrender you to the man Cris.

Salvius retreated, the dense cloud retracting from around its hapless victim.

The mass seemed to bow at Cris, who did the same.

Thank you.

The long-craved release was repeated by the unearthly throng, voices fading in a discordant requiem.

Delivered from his purgatory, Salvius exhaled a euphoric sigh.

As though being sucked into a vortex, the black mist

began to evaporate, leaving naught but a withering wail in its wake.

Then it was gone.

The players stood motionless, each trying to assimilate what they had witnessed.

Quentin sucked in clean air, certain he would never be rid of the stink of sulphur. Livid at being caught unawares, of being bested by a subordinate officer, and an Italian to boot, not to mention threatened by whatever pestilence *that* was, he did *precisely* what he had been cautioned against.

The gun lay in the dirt. In the chaos, no one had thought to retrieve it. Quentin's lip curled and he made a grab for it.

Cris swore, viciously.

Backing towards his car, Quentin sniggered. "I don't know who taught you that trick, but if you expect me to believe some dead guy from Herculaneum can manifest in a car park in Northumberland, you are more asinine than you look."

Unlocking his vehicle, Quentin was about to open the door when Bryony dashed across the tarmac like a berserker of old.

"Don't you bloody dare, you worm," she yelled.

So close to freedom he could smell it, Quentin cast caution to the winds, pointed the gun in Bryony's general direction, and fired.

Cris, who didn't trust Quentin as far as he could toss him — and he *really* wanted to toss him — had already signalled to Featherstone and was pounding towards the car. He barrelled into Quentin at the same instant as the latter pulled the trigger.

The next few seconds unfolded in slow motion… or so it seemed.

The muzzle flashed in the darkness.

The bullet grazed Cris' arm. Intent on his quarry, he barely registered the searing burn as it ripped through his jacket, nor did he hear a stricken squawk. His momentum catapulted the two men away from the car and they tumbled over the ground brawling like a couple of wrestlers.

Cris had the upper hand. Quentin, taken by surprise, was unable to fend off the incensed Italian. They rolled through mud, grass and onto cold unforgiving slabs of stone, Cris administering a well-earned thrashing.

A loud splash, and the torrent of invective accompanied by the thunk of fists against flesh came to an unceremonious halt.

Featherstone and his men dashed to the edge of pond, curbing their laughter when the pair reared out of the water, still cursing, and throwing punches. Wading in, Featherstone hauled Quentin away and cuffed him, while one of his colleagues helped out Cris.

Drenched, their suits ruined, and sporting a generous amount of smelly pond weed, the two glared at each other, gulping lungs full of air.

"I think this time, you are done," Featherstone intervened, calmly, and read Quentin his rights.

Cris looked around. *Where was Bryony?*

"Bryony?"

"She's here, mate," Max shouted from in front of the car.

Cris saw him, Aggie at his side, crouching over a figure prone on the tarmac. *Bryony.*

"Bryony." He sprinted over, to fall on his knees next to Max and Aggie. "We need more light," he shouted, checking her vitals. Although waxen, Bryony's pulse was strong, if a little fast, and her breathing — although coming in sharp spurts — didn't sound unnatural.

Cris took her hand. "Bryony, sweetheart."

"Buggeration, it hurts," Bryony groaned through clenched teeth. She stared up at the worried faces of the two men and giggled, weakly. "You look funny, kind of swimmy."

"Where does it hurt?" Cris kissed her knuckles.

"Chest."

While Aggie emitted sad little whines, Max shone the torch on his phone, the feeble beam picking out a red stain colouring the front of her summer-weight jacket.

With great care, Cris lifted the material by the lapel. Bryony's turquoise T-shirt was soaked in blood. The gravity of her injury unknown, Cris didn't want to make things worse by attempting to remove her coat.

"First aid kit? Towel? Cloth of any kind?" he called, astonished by how cool he sounded.

A blanket appeared followed by a substantial first aid kit. Cris sent up a silent prayer of thanks that Miles had the foresight to assign Featherstone and his unit to the manor.

"If you might stand aside, sir, Craddock here is our medic," Featherstone urged.

Unwilling to leave Bryony, Cris shuffled around, and gently raised her head to rest it on his calf. He watched as Craddock cut off her jacket, then sliced the scissors along the body of her long-sleeved T to reveal a, mercifully, small wound in the fleshy underarm region of her upper left chest.

"Sorry I've had to ruin your top, ma'am," Craddock apologised.

"I'm not a ma'am, please call me Bryony," that young woman insisted, with a tight smile.

"Conclusion?" Cris didn't want to ask how severe it was, aware Bryony was listening.

"Not bad at all, sir," Craddock consoled with typical British understatement, as he inspected it, palpating the flesh around the injury, gingerly.

Bryony sucked in an agonised breath.

"Sorry, ma... Bryony. By some miracle, I reckon the bullet has missed lung and bone, but it's left a bit of a mess. She'll need scans to rule out anything major. I'm afraid you'll be sore for a week or so," he addressed this last to Bryony. "Hospital's the best place for you."

"Don't want to go to hospital," Bryony grouched.

"You need a proper check-up in more sanitary surrounds." Craddock beamed comfortingly and patted her uninjured shoulder.

"We should hurry." Cris strove to suppress his alarm.

"Right you are, sir, but let me clean and pad it before we go." Craddock's placid manner soothed Cris. "Pop this blanket under her head and give me a bit o' space, there's a lad." Blithely ignoring the fact, the 'lad' was his senior in both age and rank.

Grudgingly, Cris did as he was bidden and got to his feet.

"This might tickle a bit. Feel free to swear." He heard Craddock explain, a grin twitching at his lips when this was quickly followed by a "bloody bugger and sod," and an, "I did warn you."

"I'll update Hannah," Max said and moved a few feet away from the group to call his wife.

Cris nodded abstractedly; he had spotted two other officers leading Quentin away.

"Wait." He hurried after the trio. "Might I have a moment," he requested politely.

The two men glanced at each other, uncertainly. They

had orders not to let go of their suspect. Even cuffed, he was judged a major flight risk.

"I do not wish you to release him. The fact you are holding him, makes this a whole lot more satisfying." Bunching his hand, Cris unleashed a powerful blow to Quentin's solar plexus and, as the man groaned and bent forward, followed it up with a sharp uppercut to his chin.

"*Li mortacci tua!*" Cris rebuked, employing an infrequently used but extremely offensive Italian insult. Nodding at the officers, he stalked away, leaving two looking flummoxed and one bleating querulously about his fate.

As he approached the cluster of people tending to Bryony, Cris paused. His link with Marcus was fading, it was perceptible, but tenuous. Time to let go... for now.

"A connection such as ours, even though forged under unexpected and abhorrent circumstances is, nonetheless, a privilege and an honour. One I cherish and pray will endure. Thank you for aiding my quest. While I have breath within me, I promise the ring will be treated with the utmost respect." As he had with Salvius, Cris bowed, uncaring who saw his silent soliloquy.

He sensed Marcus reciprocating.

I return your appreciation one hundred- fold, and I too relish this fusion of our spirits which, although ephemeral, warms my heart. Your perseverance in recovering our heirloom, reunited me with my brother, whose demise in so gruesome a manner devastated my family and, I believe, hastened the deaths of my parents.

Cris felt Marcus heave a ponderous sigh.

I beheld the aftermath of Vesuvius. For a time, Maxentius and I feared Hannah had perished in the catastrophe, with no inkling Salvius was also a casualty.

The path which brought us together was convoluted, but

perhaps it was foreseen long ago, in a tiny town under an angry mountain, and who are we to question the Gods?

A farewell never uttered has been spoken. A felicitous bond cemented. A legacy, born of flame and ash, restored. A debt I can never repay.

The thread was weakening.

"Gnaeus Marcus Aelianus, son, father, brother, and friend, there is not, nor has there ever been, any debt," Cris adjured. "I trust this is not an end, but a beginning. We have been granted an exceptional gift. It would be a travesty to waste it." His lips quirked as he felt Marcus chuckle.

Go, take care of your Bri-oh-nee. I will be here when you need me.

The connection severed.

Cris heard what sounded like the dying notes of a harp in the far recesses of his mind, then nothing.

Aggie flung back her head and howled. An ululating lament which sent shivers down more than one spine.

Cris drew a long, fortifying breath and focused on the present.

A van appeared and willing hands lifted Bryony into the back, where she was covered with a warm blanket. Craddock turned to say something to Cris, only to tsk in exasperation.

"Why didn't you say you'd been injured?" He pointed at the gaping rip in Cris' sleeve.

"It's nothing."

"Let me be the judge of that." Waving for more light, Craddock helped Cris shrug out of his jacket. Centimetres above his elbow, a jagged hole and a dark red blob marred the pristine white of his shirt.

"Aye, but you were lucky, it's a nasty little nick. More blood than, I'd expect, but that's probably because you've been giving that arm a bit of a workout," Craddock chastised, peering over his glasses at Cris who flushed.

"To be honest, I scarcely noticed it. I was too busy beating the living daylights out of him." He inclined his head in the general direction of Quentin.

"That's as maybe, but it'll be better for a proper clean, 'specially as you ended up in yon pond, and doubtless you'll need a stitch or two, along with your lovely lady." Craddock rinsed the wound with saline, patted it dry, and bound a gauze patch in place.

"As it appears I am to be bullied into attending the hospital, I'll travel with Bryony, if that is permitted." Cris made it a statement not a question.

"No problem, Rossi," Featherstone agreed from behind Craddock. "Vallier…" he waited for Max to join them. "You coming or heading home?"

"I'll go home, Hannah is beside herself, and I think I'd be better off there than loitering around here getting in your way. You've enough to contend with. You know where I am when you want to interview me?"

"Yes, sir, thank you. Miles was right." Featherstone didn't elaborate, but his approving nod spoke volumes.

Max acknowledged the tacit accolade with a grin and said his goodbyes to Cris. "We'll arrange to get your car back tomorrow, don't stress about that. Is there anything in it you need?"

"Nothing. Oh, hang on, Max you'll need the keys." He handed them over. "Wait…" he fished the ring out of his jacket pocket, "…please take this home with you. One less thing for me to worry about tonight."

"You got it. Take care, message us once you know when they'll discharge you, and one of us will come pick you up."

"Cheers, Max, that'd be great. I confess, I am inordinately relieved tonight is over." As Cris spoke, a chime of a distant church bell floated on the breeze. "Yet it's just struck midnight. Amazing what you can pack into an evening." He gave a wry grin and trudged over to the van.

Max shook his head and, the faithful Aggie at his side, went to beg a lift from one of the officers to where Romi was parked in the lay-by.

While they were transported to the local hospital in Carlisle, Cris meditated on the past few hours. Although Marcus had retreated, Cris was aware of a sadness in his ancient counterpart. Memories of his lost brother haunting him.

The rest of the night disappeared in a blur. They were passed between a variety of medical personnel, sent for x-rays and scans, had their wounds examined... again and again... before they were cleaned and dressed.

Bryony was informed, in no uncertain terms, she would be admitted for observation. Her unmitigated and vocal disgust only slightly mollified when the doctor agreed Cris could stay in the room with her.

"I'm perfectly fine."

"Of course, you are, but it wouldn't do any harm to be perfectly fine here overnight with a doctor close by," Cris appealed.

Bryony grumbled her acquiescence. In truth, her chest hurt, her head ached and, even knowing Quentin was safely in custody, she felt vulnerable. The warmth of the brightly lit, modern hospital was far removed from abandoned buildings, ill-tempered ghosts, and psychotic thieves.

Propped up on numerous pillows, Bryony snuggled under the covers, her eyes drifting closed. Exhaustion, accompanied by an injection of painkillers, lulled her into slumber.

Cris watched as her breathing evened out. They were holding hands, but when he tried to untangle their fingers, Bryony's clasp tightened, pulling a hint of a smile. Even in sleep she wanted to boss him around. He had to admit, he was not averse.

Making himself comfortable in the chair, he stared at the woman who had stolen his heart, his soul and, had she but known it, his body. Bryony looked unnervingly fragile. Inky lashes, dusky fans above wan cheeks. Her bruised face, which already sported a black eye, her lips sore and swollen. Fury stalked, leaving Cris both thankful and frustrated that Quentin Taylor was beyond his reach.

He turned his mind to more positive thoughts. He would be going home soon. Home. He wasn't even sure where home was anymore. Never could he have envisaged a life anywhere outside Italy. Yet to be apart from Bryony was inconceivable. *Would she be prepared to uproot her world to be with him?* He couldn't see how else they could be together. His career tied him to Rome.

Worried about Bryony and despite being wearied beyond reason, after so harrowing a day, Cris did not expect sleep to come easily. The unfamiliar comings and goings of a hospital settling down for the night proved an oddly restful backdrop and, before he knew it, oblivion had claimed him.

CHAPTER 29

MAGNIS - AD 91

Warily, Marcus opened his eyes onto a room shrouded in darkness, save a dull glimmer opposite. He was reclining on something very comfortable, but it didn't feel like his bed. Squinting, he tried to pinpoint his whereabouts.

Slowly, his surrounds took shape.

An immense hearth, its embers responsible for the faint glow. Across the low table — on which sat a neat pile of papyrus, a goblet, a pitcher, and a few children's toys — he could see two ample sofas. He was on the third.

Home.

He wasn't alone.

Alongside him, fitted to his burly frame, lay Senna.

She was holding his hand.

How long had she been lying there?

A tear pricked in the corner of his eye. He tried to blink it back, but it trickled down his cheek.

Very carefully, he shuffled until Senna was on top of him.

She mumbled something but did not wake, burrowing into his embrace with a contented sigh. He kissed the top of her head and whispered his love for her.

He thought about the scenario he had been a part of. His mind whirled with the enormity of his encounter. Now, he understood why Hannah was... well... Hannah; sincerely grateful he did not have to bear the burden of his new-found knowledge alone. How she had handled it and not been taken by madness, he could not fathom.

Yes, there were questions to be asked, answers to be provided, and explanations to be made, but they could wait. At this moment, all Marcus cared about was being where he should be. As his eyelids drooped, he sent up a heartfelt prayer of thanks to Fortuna, drew Senna close, and slept.

Senna stirred, becoming aware she was enfolded in her husband's arms... *bliss*. She stretched and yawned, glancing around, expecting to see their bedroom, to realise they were in the triclinium. She levered herself up. Marcus was fast asleep, snoring softly.

Unable to help herself, she curved a gentle hand around his jaw, tracing the outline of his bottom lip with her thumb. Ten years they had been together, and she loved him as fiercely today as when she had first registered the depth of her affection.

Recent revelations, while mind-numbing in the extreme had served to strengthen rather than shatter their bond. When Marcus begged her to hold his hand, she had clung on, watching her husband withdraw into himself. Unintelligible mutterings and incomprehensible phrases tumbled over his lips, his expression displaying a gamut of emotions.

In an instant, Hannah, discerning what had happened, gathered up the children. Distracting them with games and fun, she had kept an eye on them, allowing Senna to stay with Marcus.

Food appeared, was eaten one-handed, and the platters removed — their fingers interwoven.

In spite of Hannah's assurance that Marcus' lack of response to his surrounds was normal, a knot had formed in Senna's stomach. *What if he couldn't come back to her? What if he was lost forever out of time, between worlds?* She had caught herself. *Panicking won't help or change anything. Just be here to guide him home.*

Letting her thoughts stray, Senna ruminated about the woman, Bri-oh-nee. Their connection seemed fleeting, more fluke than design, yet while she waited for Marcus to do whatever he had to do, she thought she had heard her cry, 'This is for Senna'.

Pushing her agitation to the back of her mind, Senna prepared for a long night. The hours ticked by. At some point Marcus relaxed, his countenance no longer distorted. A serenity settled over him and, he slouched against the cushions on the sofa.

Inwardly rejoicing that her husband had returned, Senna exhaled a weary sigh and curled into him, never relinquishing her grasp. As slumber reclaimed her, she smiled. The outlandish knowledge she had accepted as truth, almost without question, might test her mettle, not to mention her sanity, but she wouldn't change it for the world.

Northumberland - July 2015

Bryony developed a low-grade fever, resulting in her hospital stay being extended. Although disgruntled, she owned up to feeling wretched and succumbed to the inevitable.

By Monday afternoon, the consultant was satisfied she was on the mend and was prepared to discharge her, on the proviso she agreed to rest.

Promise given, Bryony was sent home armed with a list of instructions, a letter for her doctor, and all manner of medical supplies.

Hannah insisted Bryony stay with them, at least until she no longer required help dressing the wound. An invitation Bryony, who ached like the dickens, accepted, readily.

Max drove to Carlisle to collect the couple and, on the return journey as they approached Hardington Manor, their lively chatter dwindled. Some instinct moved Max to pull into the quiet lay-by where he had parked two nights previously. *Was it only two nights ago?* To the three in the car, it felt much longer.

The engine idling, they stared at the weathered roof with its crown of chimneys peeking over the trees, each lost in thought.

"Don't really know why I stopped, it seemed appropriate. Do you want me to drive in?" Max said.

"Not 'specially," Bryony replied with a slight shudder. "Cris?"

"No. I am, as you say, all good, but it's nice to see calm has been restored. No policemen chasing through the woods, no madman wielding a gun, and no very large ghoul." Cris gave a lopsided grin.

Max chuckled. "When we picked up your car yesterday there was a contingent of police swarming all over the place. Crime tape and everything. Hannah, as you can imagine, wanted to help with the investigation. The twins thought the whole thing was some great game and were thrilled when one of the cops offered to let them turn on his siren. I am *very* pleased they are too young to understand any of it."

"Will they be there again today?" Bryony asked.

"Changed your mind about going in?"

"I don't know…" she hesitated. "I wonder whether I ought to, you know to see that it's back to normal.

"Okay, how about I drive up and see how you feel," Max suggested. "I think it might be a good idea for your own peace of mind, even if you can't cross the taped area."

Bryony nodded. "Yeah, let's do that. Are you sure you don't mind?"

"'Course not." Max drove the few hundred yards to the secluded gateway, of which Bryony had only caught a passing glimpse, the night of the auction.

She felt a twinge of sorrow when she saw the rotting board advertising Hardington Manor, hating that so many of these beautiful old mansions were falling into rack and ruin.

Sensitive to the subtlest change in Bryony's demeanour, Cris twisted in his seat.

She met his gaze. Their shared smile declaring they were in complete accord.

The car came to a halt on the gravel where the chain of events had started. There was no sign of the police, but the crime scene tape fluttered in the breeze.

"Do you reckon…" Bryony began.

"Don't see why not. They can only turn us away, plus

we're eyewitnesses, so..." Max replied reasonably, and switched off the engine.

They climbed out of the car and, ducking under the tape walked towards the front door, which was standing open. The faint sound of voices wafted through the stillness.

Stepping into the atrium, Bryony looked up. Dust motes danced in the rays of sunlight filtering through the grubby stained-glass window above the door.

"That was the reception area, and up there was where the auction was held." Cris pointed out the ballroom and the room on the first floor.

There was nothing to indicate anything had happened here for decades, let alone a party of sorts and a chaotic chase.

"This house was loved, I think," Bryony said as they strolled through the building. "Even after what happened on Saturday night, it feels benign. I wish someone would rescue it."

"It would be a costly exercise," Max, the engineer, interjected. "I reckon the whole place requires a complete overhaul of the electrics and the plumbing to bring it up to code. To say nothing of the damp proofing, structural issues and total interior refurbishment."

"I know, when I win the lottery," Bryony grinned and, shaking off her pensiveness, soaked in the gentle ambience.

They came out into the rear courtyard to find Featherstone overseeing his men.

"Ah, Vallier, Rossi, and the lovely Miss Emerson. Checking up on me?" Featherstone grinned a greeting. He joined them. "Nearly done, making sure we've not missed anything. You'll be pleased to know we got the bullet, Miss Emerson..."

"Please call me Bryony. Miss Emerson is worse than Ma'am. It sounds like I'm an elderly librarian," Bryony implored.

"Right you are, Miss... Bryony," Featherstone acceded. "Anyhow, they got the bullet which, of course, ballistics is matching to the gun. We know he fired it, but we don't want him to find any loopholes," he added at Bryony's indignant splutter.

"How are you both?" He swung his gaze between Bryony and Cris, who affirmed they were fine, all things considered.

They chatted for a little longer then, as Featherstone returned to his tasks, Bryony, Cris and Max traipsed back through the empty manor.

"Thanks Max, you were right, that helped, oddly." Bryony smiled.

Cris had been quiet, his mind swirling with a motley array of images. In the sunshine, the auction and its aftermath might be discounted as a nightmare, or a bad movie. If not for the ring and their injuries.

He glanced across at Bryony, taking in the contusions marring her lovely face and the hint of bandage under the collar of her shirt.

He met her gaze.

Her eyes sparkled as she broke into a dazzling smile.

His heart lifted.

Bryony took his hand. Raising herself on tiptoe, she bestowed on him a kiss laden with promise. "It's done, and we had a deal."

Cris spluttered with mirth at the wicked gleam in her eyes. "Really? With a bullet wound?"

274

"I'm sure there are ways..." she waggled her eyebrows, comically.

"Bryony Emerson, I love you." Cris burst out laughing.

"Cristiano Rossi, the feeling is entirely mutual."

Almost the instant the lengthy interviews had been completed, Cris was recalled to Rome. It seemed sudden but, as he explained, all things remaining equal he would have departed immediately after the auction. The extra week, its reason notwithstanding, was an unforeseen bonus.

He and Bryony had spent every available moment together, planning their future. A future, but for the execrable aim of a maniac, might have been eliminated before ever it began.

Although acknowledging it would be a challenge, if the last month had taught them nothing else, it was that they were more than capable of meeting challenges head on and surmounting them.

They had revisited some of Cris' favourite haunts along Hadrian's Wall. Even going as far as Kielder Water where Cris, Max, and Aggie hiked one of the shorter trails, while Bryony — who tired easily, to her chagrin — and Hannah entertained the twins. Balmy days and mild evenings lent the week a holiday feel.

If not for these jaunts, the mood among the four adults might have fallen flat.

The episode at the manor was discussed in detail, dissected, recorded, then, much like the artefacts they so loved, archived. It was over and no amount of rehashing it could alter the outcome.

It might be months before the case came to court, given the plethora of evidence being accumulated and the protracted nature of the investigation.

Cleared to return to work, providing she didn't overdo it, Bryony was asked to assist in the search for the sites on the dark web linked to Quentin's enterprise.

Already on the hunt for the second and third artefacts, initially listed with the ring, it was a request to which she agreed with fiendish relish.

Now it was the evening before Cris was due to leave. While indebted to Hannah and Max for their hospitality, the pair had chosen to stay the night at Bryony's cottage, privacy trumping company.

Takeaway eaten and a bottle of wine half-drunk, they were stretched out on the sofa, loosely wrapped together. Hands explored, not necessarily to induce passion — although that was a delightful consequence — more possessed by a compulsion to imprint the other into their minds.

Since the auction, they had shared a bed; the excuse that Bryony was suffering from nightmares, in no way fooling their erstwhile hosts.

That said, apart from appeasing their mutual appetite with some seriously scorching kisses, the couple had not taken their intimacy to the next level. Bullet wounds had a tendency to dampen even the most ardent desire.

"I'm going to miss you," Cris murmured into Bryony's hair, breathing in the heady fragrance of her coconut and lime shampoo.

"I should hope so," she parried, prompting a quiet laugh.

"I'm already counting the days until I get to see you again, and I haven't left yet." He twisted one of her short auburn locks around his finger.

"Perhaps we ought to create a memory, something to sustain us." Bryony slid inquisitive fingers under his shirt, tiptoeing over heated skin.

Cris groaned and caught her wandering hands. "While I cannot fault your suggestion, I'm not sure you are healed enough to risk it." He kissed each of her fingers, swirling his tongue around the tips.

"Well, that's not the way to cool my jets," Bryony husked.

"Cool your jets?" Cris arched a brow, grinning when she clarified.

"We had a deal. We vanquished the dragon, metaphorically speaking, and I do believe I told you once we got this sonofabitch, you could seduce me until I screamed your name." Her words harking back to their dawn tryst.

"Are you a man of your word, Cristiano Rossi?"

A true gentleman, Cris provided a *very* thorough demonstration of his honour.

CHAPTER 30

From her sneaky vantage point on the verge of the entrance road to one of the airport hotels' car parks, Bryony watched the Airbus 320 rise into the early morning sky before banking and heading to London.

She waved, even though she knew Cris couldn't see her, and stood until the plane was nothing more than a tiny speck in the cloudless blue.

Glad it was a weekday, Bryony pointed the car towards the office. Once there, she immersed herself in her work and tried not to dwell on the miles which would soon separate them.

She was an adult. She could do this. She had no intention of being one of those women who couldn't function without a man, however swoon-worthy — okay... staggeringly, heart-poundingly, intoxicatingly gorgeous, and sexy, and charming — that man might be.

Hannah didn't allow her to brood. There was plenty to keep them occupied and, although the office seemed somehow smaller without Cris, the day flew by, aided and abetted by copious cups of coffee.

Magnis - AD 91

The daily routine at Magnis afforded Marcus the perfect distraction. Life in the remote north of Britannia was harsh and unforgiving. Stability was a luxury none took for granted, and maintaining a pacified outpost of Empire took dedication, patience, and a healthy dash of common sense. It did *not* allow for hours wasted on introspection.

A practical man, Marcus seldom squandered his energy on things he could not change. As Hannah had said, one of Marcus' finest traits was that he listened, accepted, and moved on. This time, however, in quiet moments, he struggled. He mentioned his dilemma to Hannah one evening when the four adults were relaxing at the end of a busy day.

"I think it is because you were directly involved. This was not something you could have predicted. Previously, any connections to the future were through me. Yes, you were supportive and protective, but I know you preferred not to discuss it. On this occasion, you had no choice. It was thrust upon you without warning, and without context," Hannah speculated.

"Perhaps." Marcus shrugged. "I am at a loss as to why it continues to circle my mind. My brother is at rest, Cris and his Bri-oh-nee are safe, and the thief has been apprehended. Why do unsettling thoughts torment me."

"Do you think there is more? Is Cris disquieted?"

"I have no perception of anything ominous. More that something remains unresolved."

"Here or there?" Senna interposed.

"There, I think."

"Then, you can do naught. Cris knows you are a mere thought away. If he needs you, the thread will tighten."

His wife's guileless acceptance of so radical a concept, steadied Marcus, and he took her hand. It was hard enough for *him* to understand its complexities and he considered himself quite worldly.

While familiar with folklore and superstitions, that Senna — whose whole life had been spent within a ten-mile radius of where they sat — not only believed Hannah's claims, but embraced them, was humbling.

"When did you become so wise?" he teased, feeling lighter of heart.

"I have always been wise, but discretion is the better part of valour." She sent him a cheeky grin, her flippant riposte sparking a round of lighthearted banter.

Maxentius steered the conversation to less weighty topics but made a mental note to keep an eye on his second. Hopefully, between them, Hannah and Senna had assuaged his anxiety, but it wouldn't do to be complacent.

Rome - August 2015

Cris stared at the screen in front of him, his mind miles

away from the report he was supposed to be typing. He had been home for a fortnight, yet he was restless. His spacious and comfortable apartment, a place Bryony hadn't seen a photo of never mind visited, felt empty, cheerless.

It used to be his haven. Now, he avoided it, working late into the night, coming home long enough to shower and sleep. He was worse than a moonstruck teenager, but he missed Bryony so much, it was a physical ache.

Perhaps a long weekend at his parents' might help? He hadn't seen them for months and he was due a holiday. His father would be excited to hear the full story of the heirloom.

Mind, he might not tell him every detail. Much as Alessandro Rossi was devoted to history in all its guises, he was a pragmatist. Tales of ancient spectres would be categorically rejected. Cris felt the beginnings of a dry smile, *Tomas Durante, now he was a different story.*

The more he deliberated, the more attractive the idea became, and he rang his mother before he talked himself out of it.

Plan in place, he called Bryony.

"Buon pomeriggio." Her sunny greeting floated down their connection.

"Good afternoon to you too, smarty pants," he replied.

"I'm learning ten new words a day. At this rate, I'll have mastered Italian by…oh say… 2025."

Cris chuckled at her self-deprecating tone. "Knowing you, you'll be fluent in three months," he countered. "Wanted to let you know I'm going to my parents for a long weekend. I'll drive over on Friday morning and come back Monday afternoon. Papa is desperate to hear about my time in England, and I can pop into Herculaneum while I'm there."

"At least three times," Bryony chimed in.

"Quite probably," he conceded.

They chatted, catching up on each other's day. Their

conversation was lighthearted and ended with loving good-byes but, as ever when he disconnected, Cris felt faintly dissatisfied. Phone calls, whether they be voice or video were not nearly enough.

While addressing his pile of work, he began to mull over his options. Until recently, a career outside the Carabinieri Command for the Protection of Cultural Heritage was inconceivable, but one he was seriously contemplating.

Quite *what* else he was qualified for was another matter. What *did* matter was how a change of profession might bring him closer to Bryony.

Northumberland - August 2015

Bryony stroked the screen of her phone, seeing the photo she had taken of Cris at Housesteads smiling back at her. This was rubbish. The whole, I *am adult and can handle a long-distance relationship* sounded all well and good when they discussed it in bed, limbs entangled, when they could make-believe their parting was not imminent.

In the cold light of day, it had lost all attraction… if it ever really had any in the first place.

"You okay?" Hannah's question broke into her reverie.

"Yeah," Bryony's half-hearted response belied her smile.

"Could've fooled me."

"Sorry, don't mean to be a mope."

"You're not, but I get it. You two fell hard for each other.

You've been together almost 24/7 for the last month or so, then suddenly he's gone, and you feel alone, abandoned almost."

"That's it exactly. I don't want to be the clingy girlfriend, unable to function without my guy. I don't *think* I'm that pathetic, but his absence has left such a big hole, it's like I'm missing a part of me."

"Have you told him?"

"You're kidding, right? What guy wants to hear his girl bellyaching about them being apart. It's only been two weeks," Bryony replied, adding in a high-pitched whine. "Oh, Cris, I can't live without you?"

Hannah rolled her eyes. "Get a grip, you wally. Try looking at it this way. You *are* functioning perfectly well without him, it's the not wanting to that's the issue. "

Elbows on the desk, Bryony twiddled with her pen. "Yeah, I know, but how do I fix that?"

"Go get him."

"Say what?" The pen flew over the table.

"Go get him."

"Hannah, seriously? I can't just up and off to Italy. I wouldn't have a clue how to find him. Anyway, he's going to his parents' this weekend." Bryony retrieved her pen and resumed her seat.

"So what?"

"This argument could go on all day. I'll be fine."

"Sure you will." Hannah tilted her chair and, tapping her lips meditatively, studied her friend.

"Nothing to see here," Bryony chirped, flapping her hand. She avoided Hannah's penetrating gaze but could not prevent the faint colour burning her cheeks. She knew what was stopping her, but to articulate it, gave it power.

· · ·

Middle of the afternoon, Hannah gave a whoop. "Bryony Emerson, get your butt around here."

With conspicuous reluctance, Bryony wheeled her chair to Hannah's side of the desk.

"What?"

Hannah swivelled her screen. "There you go, flights and accommodation booked."

Bryony gaped and shook her head. *No.* "What did you do?" she whispered, fingers skewering through her hair, making the spikey strands stick out at crazy angles.

"Emailed Vincente, to beg the address and telephone number of his parents in Ercolano. He replied so fast I swear he was hanging out for my message.

"Besides supplying me with the info, he wrote this, and I quote, 'Cris is loco about her. I have spoken to my brother twice since he got home and do I hear about Hadrian's Wall, or the case, or the reason I was hunting for inscriptions? Oh nooooo. All I hear is Bryony this and Bryony that. Please, she will be doing everyone a favour if she comes here. I shall personally pick her up at Fiumicino and drive her to my parents.'

"I expect there were assorted gesticulations attributed to that email, but he didn't include emojis..." Hannah shrugged her shoulders, beaming with triumph. "Come on, whaddya say?"

Bryony blushed. She believed a gentle camaraderie had developed with Vincente, who was so eager to assist in her search. The sincerity and speed of his response to Hannah's latest scheme bolstered her opinion... but...

"I don't know," she vacillated.

"Can't back out, it's all paid for."

"Hannah..." Bryony stopped, overwhelmed.

"What are you afraid of? That Cris didn't mean what he said? That he's some kind of Casanova? Seducing gullible women 'til they fall for him, only to waltz away, leaving them broken-hearted?"

Bryony's fiery cheeks were answer enough.

"Give him some credit," Hannah chastised. "He never once gave you, or us for that matter, the impression he was using you for a quick fling. He's an honourable man, Bryony. Want to hear the rest of the email?"

Not entirely sure she did, nevertheless, Bryony nodded slowly.

"Vincente says he's never seen Cris like this. Apparently, even though he's had a couple of girlfriends, no one in the family ever knew their names. Since the day he arrived here, his texts and emails have been all about you. On top of that, do you not see? This romance was ordained millennia ago."

"See that bothers me too."

"Explain," Hannah demanded, folding her arms, and trying to look severe.

"This whole thing with him and me being connected down the ages. It's a bit twee isn't it? That somehow, I am descended from Senna and Cris from Marcus. It smacks of a fairy tale. Is he buying into the premise because he feels he ought to, because of what you told him, or is it genuine?"

"You think he's that shallow?" Hannah asked curiously.

"No, not really... but..." Bryony opened her palms.

"Yeah, it's scary, but sometimes you have to seize the moment. Don't let your insecurities overrule your intuition. Okay... how about this? If you don't take the chance, you'll never know. If he's a tosser, better to find out now than when it's too late... although I guess for you, it's already too late." Hannah's smile was warm with sympathy.

"Bryony, he adores you. We can all see it. Trust your heart. What does it tell you?" Dramatically, Hannah patted her chest and spoke in time with the rhythm. "True love. True love. True love."

Shaking her head and, with a resigned smile, Bryony gave up. "Okay okay, I'll go."

"Yes!" Hannah gave a jubilant air punch.

Ercolano - August 2015

Dawn had scarcely broken. The Gulf of Naples, a vast expanse of indigo under a sky morphing from soft pink to the dazzling cerulean, typical of Mediterranean summers. To the left, Capri; to the right, Ischia — shadowy shapes, like sleeping giants awaiting the life-giving touch of the sun. Far out over the sea, the horizon was hazy, heralding a hot day.

Awake with the birds, Cris — coffee and cornetti in hand — strolled down to the great iron gates beyond which lay the ruins of Herculaneum. It was hours before the official opening time but that was no obstacle. Alessandro had already alerted security to the probability his son would be at the site early and had entrusted Cris with his keys and pass.

Waving his father's pass at the sentry, who wished him a good morning and opened the gate, Cris entered, hearing the lock click into place behind him.

Leaning on the railing overlooking the ruins, he sipped the aromatic brew and ate the pastry, without really tasting either. Even at this time of day, there was a hum of traffic in the background.

Bryony would love this.

. . .

He had called her last night, hating that she sounded so far away. *No, this had to stop.* He pushed aside what he could not alter and reflected on his father's reaction to the tale of dastardly deeds.

Leaving out any reference to a disgruntled shade and a bond with an ancient ancestor, Cris had regaled his parents with a detailed account of his escapades in Northumberland, long into the night.

Alessandro was flabbergasted when informed of his personal connection to the artefact. He had also taken gleeful delight in reminding his son about a certain conversation on the day of the theft, two decades previously. His 'I told you so,' making Cris grin sheepishly.

As expected, his father was eager to view the ring, and Cris could see a day trip to the Naples museum in his not-too-distant future. It would be a bitter-sweet reunion of sorts. Technically, he could lay claim to the ring, he had proof aplenty and had no doubt Massimo Caravello could pull all the right strings if asked.

While part of him yearned for that privilege, the historian in Cris wanted the millions of visitors to this fascinating corner of the word to be afforded the opportunity to admire and learn the story behind that which had been hidden for so many centuries.

Grimacing at his fanciful thoughts, he dropped the empty coffee cup and serviette into a bin. About to head down the long ramp to the site, the creak of the gate made him spin around.

Presuming his presence had been reported and a different security guard was coming to check his credentials, he pulled out the pass. There was a guard, but it wasn't he who grabbed Cris' attention.

He froze in stunned disbelief. *Bryony?*
He blinked, certain she was a mirage.
Then she was next to him, her hand slipping into his.

"I heard that witnessing the sun bleed light into the ruins at Herculaneum was spectacular. An experience I deemed essential to see for myself. Know anyone who could show me around?"

Cris whisked her into his arms and kissed her with unbridled passion.

Bryony revelled in the tumult of sensations his touch ignited. There was no need for words, their kiss said it all — a claim, a vow and a lifetime.

As the sun rose over the ruins warming the stones, Cris and Bryony sealed their fate.

Magnis - AD 91

Thousands of miles in distance and millennia away in time, Marcus Aelianus felt his heart settle. The strange ache which had plagued him for days diminished, and his spirit lifted.

He smiled down at Senna walking alongside him.

"My love, it is done." He had no need to clarify.

Their eyes met.

Suffused by the sense that harmony had been restored, Senna stretched up to kiss her husband's cheek. "How wonderful. Perhaps we can get back to normal.... whatever that is." She teased and felt a laugh rumble through him when he gathered her close.

"Normal is overrated." Marcus grinned, as they turned for home.

EPILOGUE

THREE YEARS LATER NORTHUMBERLAND - DECEMBER

Midwinter in Northumberland. Not for the faint hearted. Snow lay thickly on the ground. Hoar frost clung to the leafless branches of the trees, dry stone walls, and the scattering of scrubby bushes.

The blinding white was alleviated by patches of evergreen, and all sound was muffled. Emerging through the wispy clouds, a feeble sun strove to thaw the frigid air with marginal success.

In the centre of an almost imperceptible square, alone save the occasional inquisitive bird, stood a couple — motionless.

"*Felice anniversario, amore mia,*" Cris broke the silence.

"Happy Anniversary, my love." Bryony tilted her face for her husband's kiss, which he bestowed with devastating efficiency, sending ribbons of heat all the way to her toes. "Mmmmm, *delizioso.*" She leaned back in anticipation of his reaction.

Cris didn't disappoint, dissolving into laughter. "I think you might need to resume your classes."

"Didn't I say your kisses are yummy?"

"Yes," he drew out the word, "but I'm not sure one lesson every few months is enough. Three years, Bryony Rossi, three years. You ought to be fluent by now."

"Say that again," she entreated.

"What?"

"My name."

"Bryony Rossi."

"I love hearing the way you say it. It rolls off your tongue in the most sensuous manner. Quite thrilling." She wafted her gloved hand in front of her face, parodying a lady from a period drama.

He bent close to her ear and repeated the words, slowly, seductively. Bryony melted in his arms.

Three years previously, six months after they met, the couple was married in this same spot. Almost by accident, it had become a tradition to spend a few moments at the unassuming remains of a once bustling fort, on their anniversary.

Family and friends had declared them crazy for choosing to marry here at all, never mind in December, but to Cris and Bryony it was perfect. Their connection to this place was profound, an association only Hannah and Max appreciated.

Bryony's unexpected visit to Herculaneum proved a catalyst for the next chapter of their lives. Regardless of the brevity and somewhat fraught circumstances of their acquaintance, to be apart was untenable.

If it turned out to be a happily for now, not forever, this burgeoning romance deserved their undivided attention, explored to its fullest.

To enjoy an official 'first date', to indulge in long walks or rushed meals or quiet evenings. To learn how to be together as a couple. To talk, really talk. To luxuriate in the pleasure of getting to know each other at a more personal level; their likes, dislikes, hopes, dreams, and aspirations.

All the things they had skipped in the heat of the moment... well, to be fair... several moments.

Content with their lives, neither Cris nor Bryony were looking for love, still less a fleeting affair, especially bearing in mind they lived at opposite ends of the continent. Nevertheless, if the two Hannah's were to be believed, their meeting *was* destined, and the couple had admitted to a flicker of recognition on the day Cris arrived at the museum.

Serendipity or Fate?

Did it matter?

They *had* met and they *had* fallen in love. Now they needed to determine whether it was for a season or a lifetime.

Subsequent developments had Bryony siding with Fate.

Shortly after their impromptu holiday, Cris was approached by his superiors, offering him a secondment to the British division of the Art Squad. His dogged diligence, particularly during this latest operation had been duly noted, inspiring the powers that be to request his inclusion in the joint task-force they were in the process of forming.

Although tastes and therefore demand varied — one week it was illuminated manuscripts, the next 17th century table automatons or medieval religious icons — the popularity of artefacts from the ancient sites scattered around Italy and Greece never abated. Instead of concentrating his efforts domestically, Cris' expertise could be put to better use on an international platform.

Apparently, negotiations for a dedicated unit, staffed with personnel from around the globe, to be located in the UK were already underway prior to the recent auction. The results merely reinforced its necessity and accelerated its establishment.

The Italian government approved the transfer on the proviso that, if Cris agreed, he also spent some portion of each year in the Rome bureau.

Miles Hathaway sweetened the deal confirming it was Cris' choice whether he was based in the London headquarters or elsewhere. This meant — museum administrators and the two ladies in question permitting — he could work out of the office he had used there, or Bryony's cottage.

For Cris, to be afforded the opportunity to live with and work alongside Bryony required no incentive. His acceptance, a foregone conclusion. Their discussion revolved around how quickly he might relocate, not whether he ought to.

By October, Cris was back in Northumberland, slotting into the generally sedate environment of the museum, seamlessly.

In November, he proposed.

Typical of the season, the weather was grim. A week of dense fog was followed by days of torrential rain and biting winds, triggering flood warnings. On the last Sunday of the month, the sun broke through the grey and patches of blue could be seen.

"If there's enough to make a sailor a pair of trousers, it'll fine up," Bryony predicated while they ate breakfast. "Shall we take a chance and go somewhere?"

"Where do you fancy?" Cris asked, sipping his coffee, grinning at the old-fashioned phrase. Proverbs and folk-wisdom Bryony had learnt from her grandmother and recited with amusing regularity.

"Hmmm… how about one of the forts? We haven't been to any since you got back."

"Okay by me… Housesteads? I think it will be the quietest given the hike across to it. Or will it be too muddy?"

"I think it will be disgusting, but only at the bottom of the dip. Yes, let's do it."

Wrapped up against the weather, and picnic packed, they arrived at the fort. The man who took their entrance fee mentioned that the path to the fort was a mite slippery.

Bryony lifted her boot clad foot. "Hoping these'll have enough grip." She beamed.

They set off, taking care on the slope. Engrossed in conversation, they were almost at the bottom when Bryony's concentration lapsed. In that split second, she mis-stepped, gave a loud squawk, fell backwards, and slithered the rest of the way on her butt.

Guffawing at her appalled expression, Cris followed her, cautiously.

"Great, just great," she grumbled. "Now what am I supposed to do."

"Give me your hand."

She clutched his outstretched fingers, scrabbling to get a foothold. The mud making everything twice as difficult.

"Hang on, I need a rock or something for leverage," she

puffed. She swivelled around onto her knees, adding to the liberal coating of mud. "So much for a day out."

By the time she was upright, Bryony resembled the creature from the black lagoon. Nothing, and that included her hair, had escaped a splattering. She tried to brush it off, but that made it worse.

"Perhaps we should go home, get you cleaned up and come back later. I'll ask the office to endorse our tickets, that way we don't have to pay again," Cris suggested.

"Nah, it's only mud. If you don't mind being seen with the swamp thing, it's all good. I don't want to waste the day."

"I *do* find swamp things very cute," he confided with a wicked twinkle. "Sure?"

"Absolutely." Bryony, putting her words to action, took his hand and they began the tramp up the incline.

Feeling mud squeeze between their fingers, Cris stifled his hilarity. She looked a wreck, but didn't seem to care, chatting airily as they walked.

They reached the fort and made their way to the highest point. Save a handful of sheep, they were alone. The air was fresh, with enough warmth from the sun to dispel the crisp edge. From their vantage point the view, barely changed by time and virtually unspoilt, flowed out in every direction.

Bryony spread her arms and gave a contented sigh. "Would you look at that. It's so beautiful," she breathed.

Cris stared at her. She was utterly filthy. His lips twitched and he desperately tried to curb his mirth.

Bryony caught his glance and made a creditable attempt at being affronted, failing dismally, aware of how comical she must look. She bit her lip, but the giggles bubbling up refused to be contained, and her merriment rang out over the stillness. Cris gave up trying to stem his laughter and joined in.

As the couple regained their composure, Cris helped Bryony try to remove some of the dirt.

"Never mind, it's well and truly stuck." Bryony straightened up and smiled, disarmingly.

His heart thudded and something deep in his psyche clicked.

Uncaring he was going to get muddy, Cris pulled her close and kissed the tip of her grubby nose.

"You're the one who's beautiful," he contended.

"Awww, whispering sweet nothings when I'm covered in dirt. It must be love." She pretended to swoon, her glorious amber eyes glistening in her smeared face.

"I do love you, Bryony Emerson." He stroked a gentle finger along her jaw.

"I'm not sure when it happened. I was already intrigued when I read your file on the plane. An awareness heightened when we shook hands in your office. All I know is, when we kissed at Hexham, I was irrevocably lost, and the strength of my feelings has only increased since then.

"This isn't, has never been, an affair or a fleeting romance. This is our forever, and even though we are living together, it is not enough."

Bryony studied him. Hearing the formality of his phrasing, the solemn note in his voice, a frisson of joy began to spiral through her, and her slow smile was nothing short of rapturous.

He grazed his thumb over her bottom lip. "Just because we might be connected by our ancestors, didn't mean we would fall in love. The sentiment you stir in me is not influenced by an ancient union.

"We were strangers, thrown together by events, I suspect can be attributed to Fate but, even though the scene was set, emotions are capricious, they cannot be forced. Imagine my surprise when, in a mere handspan of time, and entirely unexpectedly, my soul recognised it's mate.

"I love your wit, your intelligence, and the passion you have for your work. I love your smile, your fragrance, your sublime body, and your eclectic style. Your exuberance, your temper, your courage, and your bewitching kisses.

"Bryony, we met less than six months ago, but my heart knows you are my other half. Will you grant me the greatest honour and consent to becoming my wife?"

Bryony was frozen to the spot, her mouth slightly open, her eyes wide. She managed a strangled croak, but the frisson had reached her throat and she remained, uncharacteristically, tongue-tied.

She gulped, willing her brain to follow instructions.

She expelled a breath and gave a loud whoop, scattering a nearby flock of starlings, who rose into the air flapping furiously, their vexation loud in the stillness.

"I love you too, Cristiano Rossi, and *yes* I will marry you. Nothing would make me happier than becoming your wife. I'd stopped believing there was someone out there who would love me as I am, without demanding I change or conform to some outdated ideal.

"Then we met, and I knew there was something different about you, aside from the obvious Greek god thing."

She waved her hand.

"The first time we touched, I felt as though everything in my life had led me to that precise moment but dismissed it as nonsense. How was that possible? As you so rightly said, we were strangers. Regardless, I do not trust insta-love, and wondered whether what we shared was insta-lust.

"The day we kissed at Hexham, everything changed. Without knowing anything about you, I wanted you to take care of me, cosset me, protect me, possess me. I confess to a few speed wobbles, which started after you left. It was Hannah who persuaded me to listen to my heart."

"What did your heart say?"

Theatrically, Bryony tapped her chest. "True love. True love. True love."

Now, here they were three years later and their love, kindled in such extraordinary circumstances had flourished and strengthened.

Bryony, worried working in close proximity might kill the magic, the romance, discovered the opposite was true. Their complementary skills meant they avoided stepping on each other's toes.

That's not to say they never squabbled. Both possessed fiery personalities, but Bryony usually won any argument by dint of kissing Cris into submission.

Whether he might be goading her deliberately to elicit such a reaction, *did* cross her mind, but she chose to ignore it — why spoil the fun.

"Three years." Bryony removed her glove to admire her rings gleaming on the third finger of her left hand. Her engagement ring was an oval onyx in an aged gold setting, the gemstone etched with an entwined C and B, echoed the

Aelianus family heirloom. Her wedding band curved slightly so the two nestled together, neatly.

"I love you, *Signor* Captain Rossi."

"I love you, *Signora* Rossi."

Slowly, they became aware of a subtle shift in the frigid air.

Two figures, hazy in the weak sunlight seemed to take shape, the snowy landscape visible through their transparent forms.

Bryony's hand flew to her mouth to stop the rush of exclamations threatening to spill over.

"Don't panic," Cris exhorted in undertones, presuming the manifestation had frightened his wife.

"I'm not panicking. This is sooooo cool," Bryony hissed, hearing a low chuckle from her husband.

Marcus and Senna approached.

Cris and Bryony bowed. A gesture their ancient counterparts mirrored.

Bryony held her breath afraid, if she exhaled, she would blow them away.

Across time, the two women studied each other, trying to spot similarities. They were there — minor but unequivocal, and Bryony had to quell an almost irresistible urge to rush forward and hug her ancestor.

Senna smiled, and inclined her head in unspoken complicity, warming Bryony's heart as she realised this bond — while it might wax and wane like the moon — was theirs for life.

. . .

"The thread tightened." Marcus' voice seemed to come from a great distance... which, perhaps it did. "Does peril stalk you?"

"No, we are safe. Today is a celebration," Cris replied.

"Our legacy continues?"

"It is the annual observance of our union," Cris elaborated.

Bryony stepped forward. "Your legacy is safe. What began in flame and ash, was sealed in the same ruins, and now endures."

Perplexed, Cris twisted to face his wife.

Bryony interlaced their fingers and placed their conjoined hands on her stomach, a gentle smile lighting her face.

Cris arched an incredulous brow and she nodded.

"I found out late yesterday and was going to do a big reveal this evening over dinner. An anniversary gift of sorts." She blushed. "But I don't think I could ask for a more perfect moment than this to tell you."

Rendered speechless, Cris stared, but words were unnecessary. His love radiating off him, tangible as an embrace, he kissed Bryony's forehead.

"You are blessed." Marcus and Senna beamed, and faded into history as the future beckoned.

I hope you enjoyed this book.

An excerpt from Etched in Starlight, the prequel to my Hannah's Heirloom Sequence, follows - the story in which Marcus is introduced.

EXCERPT FROM ETCHED IN STARLIGHT

HANNAH'S HEIRLOOM SEQUENCE - PREQUEL

Prologue
Masada AD 66

The pain was unbearable, Lucius Maxentius Valerius could hardly breathe and his head was pounding. He tried to move but his limbs refused to respond. Where was he?

As he lay on the cold floor, memories flooded into his mind. An ambush. The sound of clashing weapons. The screams of his men. The smell of blood. He recalled being set upon by several bandits who, intent on cutting him down, had backed him along a corridor.

He thought they would kill him, for he had no chance of escape. How on earth had they come upon this citadel unawares? What had happened to the men on the watch-towers? How had they missed this horde of unruly insurgents?

Accepting he would die in this savage wilderness, Maxentius had experienced a fleeting moment of sadness knowing he would never see his mother and sister again. All they would have to remember him by would be a formal missive stating he died defending Masada.

Then relief when a familiar voice, bawling curses, distracted the bandits. Screaming they had better get off his commander or they'd be sorry, the voice belonged to Quintus Sergius Crispus; a young man who had only been on the outpost for a few months. Yet even in so short a time Sergius had proven himself a loyal and competent soldier. Far more so than many of the other men under Maxentius' charge, most of whom were insubordinate and fractious. Disillusioned with the army and fed up with guarding an outpost in the middle of a desert, miles from what they considered to be civilisation.

Sergius was slashing at everyone who moved and slowly, very slowly, was beating them back. Metal against metal, metal against flesh, these sounds would haunt the exhausted man for days.

As a soldier, of a little more than twenty and six years, Maxentius had already seen countless battles. He felt he was too young to be in charge of a garrison, but his actions in Armenia and Parthia had been commended, and his superiors deemed him a solid and reliable leader.

Now his soldiers were under attack, he was unable to defend himself, never mind the garrison and he had no clue how many had been injured or worse.

This brief respite had given Maxentius and his second in command, Gnaeus Marcus Aelianus — who had followed Sergius into the corridor — the break required to beat back their assailants. Sergius, despite his berserker strike, was wounded and leaning against a wall, a vicious gash across his abdomen.

He dropped his gladius, the sword clattering onto the tiles and blood from the blade splattering dark red across the pristine floor. While Marcus ensured the last of their attackers would not be ambushing anyone ever again, Maxentius rushed over to Sergius, catching his subordinate as he slithered down the wall.

All around them an eerie silence descended. It was as though they were the only three left alive on this citadel. Marcus came to help his commander with Sergius, the two of them virtually carrying their injured comrade along the corridor, into the first room they came upon. It was sparsely furnished — one of the rooms they had rarely used.

A rug lay over the geometric black and white tiles. A large wooden cupboard stood against one wall with an empty shelf above it, and against the opposite wall stood two ornately designed chairs. A few large baskets were stacked near the doorway, but that was all.

The room was airy and quite spacious; it was also quiet and away from the main entrance to the palace. Maxentius hoped if they managed to remain undiscovered, they might have a slim chance of escape, once Sergius had rested.

He heard an odd sound and glanced towards the doorway. A strange woman stood in the shadows, half-hidden against the frame. She was wearing the most peculiar attire, nothing he'd seen before. Absently, he wondered whether it was a new fashion for Hebrew women.

He held her gaze — she had the most startlingly green eyes — and tried to convey his desperation without words. He fancied she nodded and then she was gone. It happened so quickly, he wasn't sure whether he'd really seen her, or she was a figment of his fevered imagination.

Shaking his head to dismiss such nonsense, Maxentius' attention reverted to Sergius. The soldier was failing rapidly, his breathing coming in sharp bursts, his jaw clenched in agony. Maxentius muttered they had to try to stem the bleeding.

Wrenching open the doors of the cupboard, he noticed a

pile of what appeared to be clean cloths stored inside. Grabbing a handful, he pressed them against the gash, holding them firmly in place.

Gently lying Sergius on one of the rugs, he motioned Marcus to fetch some more cloths, which he bundled together to form a pillow of sorts, keeping Sergius' head slightly raised.

Maxentius was capable of no more. He collapsed against the wall, gasping for breath. His own injuries sapping what little strength he had left. Marcus had not fared much better, bleeding from several wounds all over his upper torso.

Unless their attackers had taken whatever they had come for and fled or, by some miracle, Marcus and he could carry Sergius unnoticed to the side gate in the western wall just beyond the administration building, they were doomed.

The two men chatted desultorily for a little while, listening for the footfalls, which would herald an approach, but all remained quiet. The only sounds were their own breathing and Sergius' occasional moans. Their comrade was deeply unconscious and neither man had enough knowledge of healing to help him. Maxentius had never felt so impotent — so much for being capable enough to command a garrison.

The next little while was a blur, all three men slipped in and out of varying degrees of consciousness, and Maxentius was astonished, Sergius had survived that first night. On a shelf in the adjacent room, he found a flagon of water and a few small bowls but knew any food was stored in the kitchens across the courtyard and did not dare risk trying to get there and back unobserved.

Occasionally they heard footsteps and muted chatter from distant voices, but for some reason, no one came into the room where they lay. The days merged into one, Maxentius did what he could to keep Sergius' wound clean. Rinsing a piece of cloth in the small amount of water they had left, he wiped away any pus or blood which had congealed and then covered the gash with a fresh piece of material. Beyond that, he could do nothing.

Eventually, owing to loss of blood, lack of any decent sustenance, and utter exhaustion, all three fell into a stupor.

Unbeknownst to them, a young woman had decided she would quite like to use a couple of the rooms off the court-yard as her own quarters. They were away from those the rebels had commandeered yet conveniently close to the laundry and kitchens. She thought one could serve as place to store all her medicines, and the other as a bedchamber.

She was busy caring for a large number of Zealots, wounded when they attacked the garrison. Appalled at how many had died before she could help them and frustrated at such a shocking waste of life for the sake of a few Roman swords, the young woman was determined, none of those she was treating would succumb to their wounds.

She had spent hours mixing salves, balms and ointments, which she applied to a whole host of injuries. She hoped her remedies would prevent any poison, concealed deep within, from all the dust and dirt kicked up in the melee, from becoming entrenched.

While checking the rooms surrounding the courtyard, she noticed a large pool of what she immediately recognised to be dried blood marring the tiled walkway, as well as a sword propped haphazardly against the wall.

Wary now, for she was certain all the Zealots were accounted for and had been assured no Roman remained on the plateau, she continued her search. Unsure who or what had bled so profusely, she was startled to come across the room where the three men lay.

Stifling a scream and with complete disregard for her own safety, she fell on her knees and began to examine the one closest to the door. After a hasty check of all three, she flew along to the makeshift office where her brother was ensconced.

"Aharon, please come, there are three badly wounded men. I need you to help me get them into proper cots."

Her brother gaped at her in shock. "Who are they?"

"I have no idea, just three soldiers." She shrugged. To her it did not matter who they were, she just knew they needed her skills, or they would die. Although dubious as to whether any of them had a chance, she wasn't letting them go without a fight.

"If they are Romans, sister, I will call Simeon and Malachi and we will finish them."

"No!" Her reply was sharper than she intended, and she softened her tone, pleading, "Aharon, it is three days since our men ambushed this rock. I know what damage the Romans inflicted upon our people. I have spent hours trying to heal them, yet I refuse to stand aside and let you kill three unarmed men in cold blood. It would be murder and is against our laws." She took a breath "You cannot."

Her brother stared at her for long moments, debating whether it was worth arguing. She would never forgive him if he followed through with his threat and he really wasn't up to dealing with her ire.

His sister watched his face; desperately hoping her brother would acquiesce to her demand. She knew the second he'd decided and flung her arms around him.

"Thank you, Aharon. Thank you so much."

"Do not make me regret this. Even wounded, these men are dangerous."

"Trust me, my brother, this is one of the best decisions you have ever made." She kissed him on the cheek and shot off in the direction from which she had come, yelling out for help to move three pallets into the room.

Although perturbed, Aharon grinned to himself. His sister was utterly irrepressible. Persuading Hannah to accompany them to Masada was a responsibility he had not taken lightly, but there was no one left in Jerusalem to watch over her. The unrest within the city was enough of a threat he could not countenance leaving Hannah there on her own. Shaking his head, he followed slowly after her, wanting to see these men for himself.

Entering the room, Aharon could tell, without any medical experience, all three were seriously ill and one was much worse than the other two. He bit his lip, uncertain whether he should share his opinion with Hannah. Before he had a chance to enunciate his concerns, she spun around to inform him, in undertones, one of them was unlikely to survive.

"That said, I intend to do everything possible for him, for all three of them. If nothing else, Aharon, I can ease his pain. If we do lose him, his death will be less agonising." Hannah's riotous chestnut curls were falling out of her tidy plait and her elfin face — usually so bright — was marred by a frown as she concentrated on what she needed to do.

Simeon and Malachi had carried in three cots. Hannah was covering them with soft blankets and double folding a sheet over a lump of straw, she had fashioned into a pillow.

"Just have a care, my sister. Please have a care." Aharon pressed her arm, and she nodded abstractedly, her mind focused on the task in front of her. Aharon left her to it, making a mental note to tell his wife what her friend was doing.

· · ·

Hannah bustled about, tucking clean, fresh sheets over the blankets. Then, carefully, her two assistants lifted each man onto a cot. Covering all three with yet another sheet and one more blanket, she began to prepare her remedies. Salt dissolved in a bowl of water, a few drops of myrrh and frankincense added, to help fight the poison.

A batch of the ointment she had been using on the other injured men would be suitable also. Then she poured a small measure of poppy juice into a flagon of diluted wine and honey, to help dull their pain.

Trembling a little, she lifted the tunic of the man closest to the door and nearly vomited. The gash was horrendous. She could not understand how he still lived. The stinking wound oozed with a greenish-yellow pus and dark blood. She gritted her teeth, swallowed and, taking short shallow breaths, began to clean it.

It took some time, for it was long and deep and some of the skin had to be cut away because it was too shredded ever to heal. The man never stirred, he was barely breathing, his heartbeat little more than the fluttering of a bird's wing.

Eventually, satisfied she had cleaned the wound thoroughly, she pressed as much embrocation into the wound as possible before covering it with a piece of cloth soaked in the same mixture. Spying several other injuries, she rinsed them all, adding more of the same balm, and making sure the bindings were not too tight, just enough to stop the salve-soaked cloths from slipping off.

Washing her hands, Hannah moved onto the next man, repeating her actions, checking every cut, nick and slash. The young man was riddled with them, some deep, some superficial. Hannah coated all with salve, bandaging everything neatly. Finally, only one man remained. He looked to be older than the other two, although not by much.

His tunic was smeared with blood, but Hannah surmised

some of it might well be that of his comrade. He had received a considerable number of nasty lacerations, but it was his chest which bothered her. His breathing seemed laboured and the colour of his skin wasn't normal.

Uncertain exactly what was going on, she cleaned his cuts, bandaging those which required it and decided to try massaging some arnica into his chest. It could do no harm and if there was bruising, this particular ointment ought to reduce it somewhat.

As she completed her ministrations, he regained consciousness, his eyes locking with hers. For a moment their dark emerald depths mesmerised her. His face registered confusion and fear and he made to sit up, but she pushed him back with a gentle hand.

The pain was unbearable, Maxentius could hardly breathe and his head was pounding. He tried to move but his limbs refused to respond. He stared at the woman, who took his hand and spoke in gentle tones.

"I do not know whether you can understand me, but I am here to help you."

He looked at her steadily and inclined his head slightly.

She smiled and pointed to herself. "My name is Hannah."

ABOUT THE AUTHOR

Rosie Chapel lives in Perth, Australia with her hubby and three furkids. When not writing, she loves catching up with friends, burying herself in a book (or three), discovering the wonders of Western Australia, or — and the best — a quiet evening at home with her husband, enjoying a glass of wine and a movie.

Website: www.rosiechapel.com

OTHER BOOKS BY ROSIE CHAPEL

Historical Fiction

The Hannah's Heirloom Sequence

The Pomegranate Tree - Book One

Echoes of Stone and Fire - Book Two

Embers of Destiny - Book Three

Etched in Starlight - Prequel

Hannah's Heirloom Trilogy - Compilation — e-book only

Prelude to Fate

Regency Romances

The Linen and Lace Series

Once Upon An Earl - Book One

To Unlock Her Heart - Book Two

Love on a Winter's Tide - Book Three

A Love Unquenchable - Book Four

A Hidden Rose — Book Five

The Daffodil Garden

The Unconventional Duchess

Rescuing Her Knight

His Fiery Hoyden

A Regency Duet

A Regency Christmas Double

Fate is Curious

A Christmas Prayer *with Ashlee Shades*

The Lady's Wager

Winning Emma

A Love Impossible

Unravelling Roana

Love Kindled

Fairy Tale Romance

Chasing Bluebells

Contemporary Romances

Of Ruins and Romance

All At Once It's You

Cobweb Dreams

Just One Step

His Heart's Second Sigh

HISTORICAL FICTION

The Pomegranate Tree
Hannah's Heirloom - Book One

Hoping to trace the origins of an ancient ruby clasp, a gift from her long dead grandmother, Hannah Wilson travels to the fortress of Masada with her best friend, Max. Strange dreams concerning a rebel ambush begin to haunt Hannah and following a tragic accident, she slips into the world of Ancient Masada.

A woman out of time, Hannah must rely on her instincts and her knowledge of what will befall this citadel to survive. Will she escape, or is she doomed to die along with hundreds of others as Masada falls — and what does any of this have to do with an ancient ruby clasp?

Echoes of Stone and Fire
Hannah's Heirloom - Book Two

Pompeii - a vibrant city lost in time following the AD79 eruption of Vesuvius. Now rediscovered, archaeologists

317

yearn for an opportunity to uncover the town's past. Some things, however, are best left alone - revealing the secrets hidden beneath the stones could prove perilous. Hannah and Max are brought to Pompeii by a surprise invitation to join an excavation team who are trying to uncover the city's long history.

After entering an excavated house that bears a Hebrew inscription, Hannah's two worlds collide, and she falls back through time to ancient Pompeii. A place where her ancestor is a physician to gladiators engaged in mortal combat, where riotous mobs run amok and where a ghost from the past returns to haunt her.

Will Hannah and her loved ones manage to escape the devastation she knows is coming, before the town is engulfed in volcanic ash? Will she ever find her way back to Max the love of her life, waiting not so patiently millennia away? Or will echoes be all that remain?

Embers of Destiny
Hannah's Heirloom - Book Three

AD80 - Hannah and Maxentius must embark on a new journey to Northern Britannia. This harsh frontier is far from the comforts of Rome and danger lurks where least expected; a garrison of soldiers, some unhappy with their isolated posting; local tribes, outwardly accepting of their Roman occupier, but who may still resent the seizure of their lands.

Millennia away, Hannah Vallier finds a familiar item while working in a museum near Hadrian's Wall. It is the pomegranate; carved by Maxentius on Masada. Before Hannah can discuss it with Max, disaster strikes! Believing her husband has been killed, Hannah retreats into the past, her soul melding with that of her ancestor, but with little idea of what they could face. Is the risk from the conquered tribes, or much closer to home?

As rebellion threatens to shatter a fragile peace, Hannah's heart whispers that just maybe Max isn't dead and that he is calling her home. Can she trust her heart, or will she remain caught out of time, her destiny floating away like embers on a breeze?

Etched in Starlight
Hannah's Heirloom - Prequel

Maxentius - a Roman soldier fresh from the battlefields of Armenia, arrives to take command of the military outpost of Masada, Herod's isolated citadel in the Judaean desert. A seemingly mundane posting after years of warfare, Maxentius finds it more challenging to maintain a focused garrison than to face the wrath of the Parthians across a disputed frontier.

Hannah - a young Hebrew physician spends her days dealing with injuries from street brawls, deprivation, disease and loss. As her beloved Jerusalem plunges into chaos, her brother — who belongs to a band of rebels determined to drive out their Roman occupiers — tells her of their plans to storm a desert fortress and steal the weapons stored there, persuading his reluctant sister to go with him.

Masada - following the ambush, Hannah finds and treats three badly wounded Roman soldiers. In the aftermath and against impossible odds, Hannah and Maxentius realise that they are more than healer and captive, their fate already etched in starlight.

Prelude to Fate

For Lucia, staring into the jaws of an horrific death, escape seems impossible.

Rufius Atellus, a veteran Roman soldier, is appalled when he recognises one of the victims about to be executed. Surely this is a ghastly mistake?

A ferocious she-wolf, anticipating a tasty meal, suddenly finds herself under a human's control.

In an unexpected twist, and as danger threatens, the lives of all three become inextricably entwined.

Was it chance brought them together in that theatre of bloodshed, or simply a prelude to fate?

REGENCY ROMANCES

Once Upon An Earl
Linen and Lace - Book One

When Fate saw fit to intervene in the life of Giles Trevallier, the very respectable Earl of Winchester, by dropping a female — soaked to the skin and with no memory of who she is or how she came to be there — literally at his feet, no one could have predicted the outcome.

While uncovering her identity, Giles realises he is falling hopelessly in love with his mystery guest, who unbeknownst to him, is succumbing to similar emotions; but, when the heart is involved, a thoughtless word or gesture can thwart even Fate's best-laid plans.

Faced with misunderstandings, whispers of scandal, secret documents and foreign agents, their chance at a happy ever after seems elusive, but fairy tales often happen when least expected, and love — however inconvenient — usually finds a way to conquer all.

To Unlock Her Heart

Linen and Lace - Book Two

Abused by a duke, and shunned by Society, relief seems at hand when Grace Aldeburgh is bequeathed a house in a small village, far from malicious gossips.

Once there, a tentative friendship blooms between Grace and Theo Elliott, the local doctor, who has already resolved to be the man to unlock her heart.

Just when happiness appears to be within her grasp, her erstwhile tormentor once again stalks Grace. After a failed kidnap attempt, the duke's quest culminates in an acrimonious confrontation, and the reason for his venal pursuit becomes agonisingly clear.

NB: This book contains adult themes and situations which, although minimal might be a trigger for some.

Love on a Winter's Tide
Linen and Lace - Book Three

Every day, Helena disappears into a world few acknowledge, helping the poor, downtrodden, and abused. A husband is the last thing she can be bothered with.

Busy managing his shipping line, Hugh Drummond sees no need for a wife, whose only joy is dancing and frivolity. If — and it was a huge if — he ever married, it would be to a woman as capable as he, not some giddy society Miss.

Then, Hugh meets Helena and despite their resolve, fate, it seems, has other ideas. As their attraction deepens however, treachery threatens to tear them apart. Will they uncover the perpetrator in time, or will their love be swept away, lost forever on a winter's tide?

A Love Unquenchable

Linen and Lace - Book Four

Jessica Drummond, a bright and cheerful young woman, rarely gives romance, let alone love, a thought. Long hours working in her brother's shipping office affords little chance of her ever meeting an eligible bachelor.

Duncan Barrington, veteran of the Napoleonic Wars, believes himself wounded in both body and soul. He has no intention of inflicting his demons on anyone, certainly not a beautiful and, in his opinion, irresponsible city lady.

One cold and snowy morning, the plight of a bedraggled puppy throws Jessica and Duncan together and, as a spark of something indefinable yet wholly unquenchable begins to burn, it is unclear who rescued whom.

A Hidden Rose
Linen and Lace - Book Five

After witnessing his mother's grief at the loss of his father, Nick Drummond resolved never to cause someone he loved such distress. Even the happiness of his siblings would not sway him — until he met Rose.

Rose Archer was almost content assisting her doctor father in a tiny fishing village in the north of Yorkshire. To experience the world beyond, a tantalising dream — until she met Nick.

Unexpectedly, the impossible becomes possible, and the renounced — desired above all things, but the shipwreck that brought them together, may yet tear them apart. Will Nick learn to trust his heart, or will his love for Rose remain forever hidden

The Daffodil Garden

Horrifically scarred during the war, William Harcourt - Marquis of Blackthorne - prefers to spend his days in the quiet of his daffodil garden; plants do not pity, turn away, or judge.

Lucy Truscott, whose life is far removed from that of the *ton*, has no idea that by saving the life of a young woman, to whom she bears an uncanny resemblance, her own will be placed in mortal danger.

A chance encounter leads to something more. William begins to trust that Lucy sees the man beneath the scars, while Lucy is persuaded that love might actually transcend status.

Unfortunately, before their courtship has really begun, someone has every intention of ending it - permanently.

The Unconventional Duchess

Refusing to suffer the humiliation of her husband flaunting his mistress at Society events, the newly married Duchess of Wallingstead, Ella Lennox, takes control of her life. She leaves London for the family's country seat in remote Yorkshire.

A woman alone, Ella spends the next four years turning a cold, grim house into a home, and transforming the fortunes of the estate. Not afraid of hard work, she soon earns the respect of those around her with her determination and unconventional attitude.

Out of the blue, the duke arrives. Resigned to another arduous visit, Ella is stunned when it seems he is attempting to court her.

Impossible!

Could her dream of a happy marriage be about to come true?

Everything hangs on a snowstorm, a herd of cows and an uninvited guest!

Rescuing Her Knight
The *de Wiltons* — Book One

A story, invented to keep a little girl distracted, marks the beginning of another tale. One destined to remain unfinished for twenty years.

At thirteen, Adam Marchmain became Kitty de Wilton's 'Knight of the Garden' — a title bestowed following an accident which resulted in six-year-old Kitty having her knee sutured. Kitty never forgot his gallantry, but pledges made as children rarely survive into adulthood.

Their paths separated until Fate decreed, they meet again.

Widowed, badly disfigured and his sight ruined, Adam returns to his family home, a shadow of his former self.

Similarly afflicted, although her scars are invisible, Kitty — against her better judgement — is persuaded to help Adam banish his demons. This requires a subterfuge which, if discovered, might shatter more than the bonds of friendship forged two decades previously.

To Kitty, determined to break through the shield Adam has erected, the risk is worth it.

To see his smile and hear his laughter.

To rescue the knight of her childhood.

Just when a fairy tale ending is within her grasp, Kitty is threatened by the man who murdered her husband. In a cruel twist the tables are turned, and Kitty is the one who needs rescuing.

His Fiery Hoyden
A Novella

Livvy has no respect for the nobility; they let her down when she most needed them. Why should she accede to their demands now?

Philip, Lord Harrington, is stunned to discover the young heir to the dukedom lives a stone's throw away in a ramshackle cottage, and resolves to restore the child to his birthright.

They meet in a clash of wills, but just when it seems Livvy might surrender, the victory Philip desires, may not taste all that sweet.

A Regency Duet
Luck be a Pirate

Luck wasn't something retired pirate Kennet Alexson believed in — good or bad. However, even he had to concede that landing a job at Trentams shipyard, and meeting Lynette Collins, was more than coincidence.

Fortune it seemed, was smiling on him for once.

As Kennet adjusts to life on dry land, his friendship with Lynette deepens into something far more enduring, and what once seemed elusive now becomes possible.

Unfortunately, fate has other plans, and Kennet's good luck is about to run out.

The Highwayman's Kiss
Surrendered Hearts — Book One

Nothing exciting had ever happened to Juliette St Clair. Her days were spent assisting her father or calling on friends, wandering art galleries, taking constitutionals or, and more preferably, escaping into her books. Her evenings her evenings — an endless round of balls, where she preferred to remain invisible.

Until the day she was robbed by a highwayman.

A Regency Christmas Double
Heart Rescued

Four years since Jasper lost the woman he was hoping to marry. Four years since he closed his heart and withdrew from Society. He has no idea his reclusive existence is about to be shattered.

Enter his sister's best friend, Harriet, a flame haired beauty, who needs his help.

Reluctantly he agrees and as they spend time together, it is clear their feelings run deep. Although Harriet affects Jasper in a way no woman ever has, he believes her to be out of his league ~ but it's Christmas and she might just be the one to melt his frozen heart

Catch a Snowflake

Romance often blossoms in the most unlikely of places - but in a ward full of wounded soldiers - surely not?

When Lucas Withers comes face to face with Jemima Parsons - a young woman who blames him for her brother's injury - falling in love is the last thing on their minds. What neither of them anticipated, was the magic of snowflakes.

Fate is Curious
A Novella

Happily, ever after? No such thing! Bereft, following her beloved husband's sudden death, Lady Charlotte Sherbrooke has lost her belief in romantic nonsense.

Successful shipping merchant, Zacharie Romain, is no stranger to loss; his business can be hazardous. Moreover, his wife died in childbirth and even though it happened a decade ago, he has no mind to expose himself to such sorrow again.

They meet in less than joyful circumstances but, as the year turns and grief diminishes, the woes of a small boy become the catalyst for something wholly unexpected. Can Charlotte and Zacharie trust what Fate has in store or will past heartbreak prevent them from taking a chance on love?

A Christmas Prayer
with Ashlee Shades
A Short Story

An entreaty from a frightened child.

Orphaned and only nine, Caroline Thorne has to grow up

before her time. She is doing everything she can to keep what is left of her family together and out of the workhouse but is terrified her prayers are not being heard. Or maybe they are...

A petition from a woman desperate for a family.

A chance meeting with three orphaned siblings, tugs at Elizabeth Barrington's heart strings. Thus far, she and her husband have not been blessed with children and, as Christmas approaches, a plan begins to form - one which might just be the answer to her prayers.

Two Christmas prayers, as different as they are the same.

Will they hear and, more importantly, heed the answer?

The Lady's Wager
Surrendered Hearts- Book Two
A Novelette

Ged Mowbray will do anything to avoid being married off to the suitable prospects his parents insist on parading in front of him.

Melissa Bouchard is under no illusion her sizeable dowry is the attraction to suitors, not her.

An overheard conversation leads to an offer too good to refuse, but what happens when a lady's wager, becomes a gamble on the happily ever after, you did not even realise you wanted?

Winning Emma
Surrendered Hearts - Book Three
A Novelette

Randolph Craythorpe — earl, covert operative, and occasional highwayman — believed his dalliance with Lady Felicity Hartwich would lead to marriage. It did, but not to him! The arrival of an unwelcome guest, however, provides the perfect opportunity to indulge in a little retaliation.

Emma Newbury accompanies her cousin, Lady Charity Anscombe, to London for the Christmas season. Once there, she comes face to face with the three men who witnessed the humiliating aftermath of her father's disgrace — one of whom, to her irritation, has taken up residence in her dreams.

Their infrequent encounters only serve to confuse but, while winter tightens its grip on the city, what was inconceivable becomes the one thing for which they both yearn, yet bound by Society's rules, cannot admit.

As the snow falls, Randolph begins to understand that to win Emma, he will have to surrender.

A Love Impossible
A Regency M/M Novelette

Tasked with investigating a heinous crime, Edward Lindsay travels from London to Dublin — a city which holds too many memories — in the guise of guardian to his sister. He knew it could be hazardous, and relished the challenge, but that wasn't what caused his stomach to tighten as they approached landfall.

Dublin held more than just a murderer.

There was also Aidan.

While attending a party, Aidan Griffen is astonished when he comes face to face with a man who fled Dublin two years previously. A man he has desperately tried to forget.

As Edward closes in on his quarry, a fire, deliberately extinguished, is rekindled. But what of it? Edward and Aidan share a love impossible, and to acknowledge their feelings — more dangerous than confronting a killer.

Is there any hope of a happily ever after?

Unravelling Roana
A Regency Novelette

Tired of being ignored by her husband, Roana Dumont, Countess of Brooketon does the one thing guaranteed to get his attention. She runs away… to Venice, leaving behind a set of riddles for him to solve… *if* he feels their marriage is worth saving.

Gideon Dumont, 6th Earl of Brooketon is flabbergasted when he discovers his wife has apparently vanished off the face of the earth. A series of puzzles, the only clue as to her whereabouts.

The question is… will he unravel them?

Love Kindled
A Regency Novelette

Recently widowed, Amelia Ingram - Countess of Gresham, decides to shake off the fetters from her arranged and loveless marriage. Exploiting her new-found independence, Amelia indulges her yearning to explore - incognito.

Her ploy works so well, she receives an offer of employment from the dangerously handsome, Rupert Latimer - Earl of Badlesmere. On impulse, she accepts and finds herself governess to Cate, a delightful scamp of a child. What began as a bit of a game on Amelia's part, evolves into something far more profound, and a flame she presumed impossible to ignite, is kindled.

An unexpected turn of events leads to yet another offer. This time there is far more at stake and, determined history not repeat itself, Amelia confesses her ruse.

Rupert has been burnt once. Will he douse the spark, or take a risk and trust his heart?

FAIRY TALE ROMANCE

Chasing Bluebells
A Fairy Tale Novella

Once upon a time, somewhere in France, there was a man whose reckless obsession led him down a dark path — one which, ultimately, cost him his life. That ought to have been the end of it. Regrettably, as is so often the case, those who least deserve it, suffer for the actions of others.

A decade after being sent away, Sebastien Daviau returns to the little village where everything began. Hoping to lay the ghosts of his childhood to rest, he studiously ignores the possibility, he might run into Charlotte de Montbeliard.

As luck would have it, Charlotte is the one who runs into him… well, his horse… and although the brief encounter leaves a lasting impression, neither recognises the other.

A name revealed causes a freak accident, catapulting Sebastien's past into his present, and bringing him face to face with a man whose reputation would intimidate the most ardent of suitors.

Can whatever is blossoming between Charlotte and Sebastien survive the challenge imposed, or is their happily ever after about to fade as quickly as the bluebells they loved to chase?

CONTEMPORARY ROMANCES

Of Ruins and Romance

Kassandra Winters has intrigued Gabriel St Germain since he accidentally knocked her flying outside her university professor's office. Her face haunts his dreams, yet he never expected to see her again. So, he is surprised when she appears, as though destined to do so, in the middle of a ruin, and he concocts a plan to win her heart.

Gabriel's old-fashioned courtship touches something deep inside Kassie and, although struggling to believe someone as handsome as Gabriel could possibly be interested in her, she soon realises she has fallen irrevocably in love with him. However, just as Kassie shares everything of herself with Gabriel, her world comes crashing down.

Can their romance survive, or will it fall in ruins, like the relics of antiquity that brought them together?

All At Once It's You

When Alex arrives in the small village of Rosedale Abbey, to take up a position as a research assistant for a renowned archaeologist, the last thing she is looking for, or expects to find, is love.

Jake was perfectly happy with the status quo. When it came to relationships, he didn't do committed or long term. He called the shots, and if his current flame didn't like it, she knew what to do. A philosophy, which served him well - until he met Alex.

Romance blooms, but even as the untamed wilderness of the North Yorkshire moors weaves its spell, a long-buried secret might yet jeopardise their happily ever after.

Cobweb Dreams
A Novella

A holiday on the Scottish isle of Mull was just the break Chloe Shepherd needed, an escape from her boring office job and her complete lack of anything resembling a social life. Romance, it seems, isn't on the cards and, although Chloe dreams of finding her soulmate she is beginning to believe love is like cobwebs — spun overnight, only to vanish in the early morning breeze.

Under sufferance, Dominic Winters makes a flying visit to Mull to check on a rental property owned by his family. He hasn't got time for this — so indulging in a holiday fling is the last thing on his mind.

A lamb stuck in a bog proves a most unexpected match-maker and, while Mull weaves its magic, Chloe wonders whether those fragile cobwebs might be far more stubborn than she thought.

Just One Step
A Short Story

In the aftermath of an horrific car accident, Daisy Forrester travels to Italy - hoping, so far from her memories, she might begin to heal.

Archaeologist, and single father, Adam Willoughby is too busy looking after his young daughter to give romance let alone love, a thought.

Neither expects a chance encounter in an ancient ruin to be anything more, but sometimes, that's all it takes.

His Heart's Second Sigh
A Novella

Reuben Faulkner and Paige Latimer are two happily single people, who have no desire to upset the status quo.

Unexpectedly, they are thrown together, only to discover both want far more than a casual friendship.

Just when things take an interesting turn, Reuben's past catches up with them, and threatens to derail their blossoming romance before it has chance to start.

CPSIA information can be obtained
at www.ICGtesting.com
Printed in the USA
BVHW090716150621
609530BV00009B/1709

9 780645 198515